THE DELUSION SERIES

THE DECEPTION

LAURA GALLIER

wander
An imprint of
Tyndale House
Publishers, Inc.

Visit Tyndale online at www.tyndale.com.

Visit Laura Gallier online at www.lauragallier.com/delusion.

TYNDALE and Tyndale's quill logo are registered trademarks of Tyndale House Publishers, Inc. *Wander* and the Wander logo are trademarks of Tyndale House Publishers, Inc. Wander is an imprint of Tyndale House Publishers, Inc., Carol Stream, Illinois.

The Deception

Designed by Dean H. Renninger

Edited by Sarah Rubio

Published in association with the literary agency of D.C. Jacobson & Associates LLC, an Author Management Company. www.dcjacobson.com

Some Scripture quotations are taken from the *Holy Bible*, New Living Translation, copyright © 1996, 2004, 2015 by Tyndale House Foundation. Used by permission of Tyndale House Publishers, Inc., Carol Stream, Illinois 60188. All rights reserved.

Some Scripture quotations are taken from the Holy Bible, *New International Version,*® NIV.® Copyright © 1973, 1978, 1984, 2011 by Biblica, Inc.® Used by permission. All rights reserved worldwide.

Some Scripture quotations are taken from the *Holy Bible*, King James Version.

The Deception is a work of fiction. Where real people, events, establishments, organizations, or locales appear, they are used fictitiously. All other elements of the novel are drawn from the author's imagination.

For information about special discounts for bulk purchases, please contact Tyndale House Publishers at csresponse@tyndale.com, or call 1-800-323-9400.

Library of Congress Cataloging-in-Publication Data
Names: Gallier, Laura, author.
Title: The deception / Laura Gallier.
Description: Carol Stream, Illinois : Tyndale House Publishers, Inc., [2019] | Series: Delusion series ; [2] | Summary: A year and a half after the horrific Masonville High mass shooting, Owen is determined to uncover why the Creepers have converged on his land and the school—a necessary step toward his ultimate mission to drive evil forces out of Masonville.
Identifiers: LCCN 2019011057| ISBN 9781496433923 (hc) | ISBN 9781496433930 (sc)
Subjects: | CYAC: Good and evil—Fiction. | Demonology—Fiction. | Christian life—Fiction.
Classification: LCC PZ7.1.G34783 De 2019 | DDC [Fic]—dc23 LC record available at https://lccn.loc.gov/2019011057

Printed in the United States of America

25   24   23   22   21   20   19
7   6   5   4   3   2   1

PRAISE FOR *THE DELUSION*

Impressive debut.
   PUBLISHER'S WEEKLY

A complex and gripping tale that carries a powerful punch.
   MIDWEST BOOK REVIEW

I encourage you to read *The Delusion*. It triggers your imagination about the realities of spiritual warfare.
   JACE ROBERTSON, *Duck Dynasty*

Laura Gallier's book *The Delusion* is a very entertaining and thought-provoking read. It's full of relevant content no matter your faith perspective. I am excited to see its impact on bookshelves as well as on the big screen.
   MAURICE EVANS, former NBA player

The Delusion is a great book that allows both teenagers and adults to dive in and get captivated by Owen's life. I couldn't put the book down as I found myself visualizing the details and looking forward to what happened next. The truths behind this fictional book are outstanding.
   RODNEY BLAKE COLEMAN, M. ED., assistant principal,
   Anthony Middle School

The Delusion is a page turner that I couldn't put down, and neither could my husband and teenage son. Laura Gallier has a firm grasp on the challenges that our students face today, and her novel reveals challenging, eye-opening truths.
   KELLY MARTENS, president and founder, Lighthouse for Students

As a film producer, I'm constantly looking for great stories. With *The Delusion*, Laura Gallier has delivered on all levels.
   CHAD GUNDERSON, Out of Order Productions

I appreciate Laura Gallier taking the time to help us remember where the real battle is. *The Delusion* was a priceless reminder that we must be constantly exchanging the lies of the enemy, and our culture, with the truth of God's Word. The book is a fresh perspective on where our true power comes from: PRAYER. That's where the real victory is gained.

WADE HOPKINS, former NFL player and regional vice president, Fellowship of Christian Athletes

Laura effectively depicts the day-to-day battle between good and evil through powerful story and imagery. As a father, it is a wake-up call to the responsibility I have as the spiritual leader in the home, to recognize the battle that is raging and to stand firm for the sake of the next generation. *The Delusion* is a must-read for every father.

RICK WERTZ, founder and president, Faithful Fathering, faithfulfathering.org

---

Other books in the series:
The Delusion

Dedicated to the thirteen fearless women who stand shoulder to shoulder with me, shields up, relentlessly storming no-man's-land:

Anna Adkinson

Kelley Allison

Brandy Brokaw

Suzie Brown

Rachael Donohoe

Dana Grindal

Debra Hicks

Michelle Knapton

Jessica Lantrip

Kelly Martens

Miriam Moore

Taylor Saracho

Stephanie Swann

The biggest challenge with exploring the topic of spiritual warfare is the spiritual warfare we must then endure.

DR. DAVID FLEMING

ONE

THE SPRINGTIME SUN was beginning to melt into the dense shrubbery as I ran through the trees, sneaking quick glances over my shoulder. Eleven months after Dan Bradford hid in these woods, my property behind Masonville High, then stormed the school with two rifles on his back and a demonic army by his side, there was still no fence line to keep people off my land. No barrier to stop trespassers, human or otherwise.

I had to get off the foot-worn trail fast. Find a secluded hiding spot and stay there.

I darted behind a thick oak and pressed my back against the bark. I worried that my heavy breathing would give me away, so I shut my eyes, working to calm my nerves by focusing on a familiar mental image. My all-time favorite . . .

Ray Anne's sweet face, inches from mine, smiling up at me. Her captivating blue eyes, so full of life. A snapshot-style memory that time could never erase.

It had been 321 days since she'd offered up her life to protect another. Two others, actually—Jess and her unborn child.

I heard someone approaching, jogging toward me on what was becoming a popular trail. My eyes flashed open. I couldn't help but hope it was the glowing old man in overalls, coming to find me and teach me something vital and profound. But I knew better. There'd been zero trace of him or his white vintage pickup since my senior year. Besides, I could hear that whoever was headed my way was dragging chains. Even after months of hearing it everywhere, the clanking sound made me cringe.

The jogger passed, unaware I was there. Also unaware that a shackle groped his neck.

A hush settled over the woods again, inviting me to return to my thoughts. Ray Anne's image came right back to me. As much as I admired the courage she'd shown on the day of the shooting, I was just as impressed with her bravery every day since. Multiple surgeries and an exhausting, painful recovery—through it all, she stayed strong. She'd even made up her mind to try to start jogging, even though walking was enough to make her wince at times.

My legs were getting as stiff as the tree trunk behind me, but I didn't budge. If Ray Anne saw me or any trace of the golden glow that surrounded my feet, it would ruin my plan. Any minute, she'd pass down this winding trail just before dusk like she did most days lately, praying and willing herself to keep going. And she'd see my sign—a neon-orange poster board I'd nailed to a moss-covered tree arching over her pathway. Surely she'd stop when she noticed the photo glued on there, a picture we'd taken the night we skipped out on our senior prom.

I'd used a ruler and a fat black marker to draw a left-pointing arrow under the picture, directing Ray Anne to a less-traveled path through the rustling trees, where she'd soon discover another sign, then another— and more pictures of us with mysterious arrows.

Any second now, she'd round the bend, no doubt dressed in one of her crazy-bright exercise tops, with running shoes to match. And I'd hear her labored breaths, the battle cry of a determined young woman.

That's when Custos interrupted.

I wasn't surprised that the familiar armored Watchman showed up— he did that most days. It was his timing that concerned me. If Ray Anne spotted him, he'd completely steal her attention away from my sign, and also, she'd know I was nearby.

This particular Watchman, with blond hair, tan skin, and piercing-light eyes, came around me so often that some months ago, I'd figured he needed a name. When I asked him what it was, his only response was a polite grin. A Watchman had spoken to me the night I shed my shackle, but after that I'd never heard one utter a word, so I had no choice but to name him myself. I decided on Custos—Latin for "keeper."

And right now, that *keeper* was in the way. I knew better than to ask him to move, though. Who was I to boss him around?

I heard the steady sound of shoes pounding the dirt—no metal. As if on cue, Custos disappeared. That was the one and only time I was grateful he left me.

A smile crept across my face as I leaned out and sneaked a glimpse of Ray Anne, out of breath and walking now, bracing her abdomen. The glow emanating from her made a perfect circle of light on the path, highlighting her neon-orange running shoes. She glanced up at the arching tree, did a double take, then stood still, peering up at my handiwork.

Her jaw dropped, then she giggled. I grinned. Sure enough, Ray followed the arrow.

I wove through the bushes, trying not to snap any branches as I headed to the space I'd prepared in the woods. I could hear Ray Anne gasping and sighing as she followed the unfamiliar course I'd set for her.

I arrived at the small clearing—Ray Anne's final destination. It had taken some time to get rid of the lifeless ground cover left over from winter. I was glad to see that all my candles still held flames despite the breeze.

I hid in the trees off to one side, anxious to see Ray Anne's expression when she beheld my romantic gesture. I'd gotten the idea from a picture I'd happened to see on the back of some girls' magazine; only, in that picture, the candles were scattered all around. Mine were arranged in a heart-shaped pattern—100 percent my own inspiration, thank you.

Ray Anne approached with careful steps, crunching leaves. Before I could see her face, I heard her inhale, hold her breath a second, then gush, "Oh my goodness!"

She came to a stop right where I'd hoped she would, in the center of the candle heart.

That's when I stepped up behind her. She spun around and smiled up at me, stealing my breath away, as usual. We'd officially been a couple for three months now, and I'm not ashamed to admit that I still got butterflies around her.

To be honest, I envisioned being with Ray from here on out—like, for the rest of my life. First, though, I had to prove I could be a good boyfriend.

Even though I'd rehearsed my speech over and over, in the moment, it all went out the window. I just spoke as the words came. "Ray Anne, I nearly lost you, and not a day goes by that I don't thank God that you survived—that we have the chance to be together. And today, on your nineteenth birthday, I want you to know how much I care about you. That you're in my heart."

Surprisingly smooth, if I do say so myself. I took her hands and pulled them to my chest. "You mean the world to me, Ray."

Her eyes got glossy, and she gave me the biggest smile I'd ever seen. "I feel the same way about you, Owen."

She hugged me, and the aura on the ground around us was twice as bright now that we stood so close. It was a perfect moment.

But then Ray stepped back, her grin replaced by straight lips. "Owen, there's something I really need from you—for our relationship."

"Okay?" I was prepared to do anything.

She gripped my shoulders and stared me in the face like a coach about to give a key play. "Quit blaming yourself for what happened to me."

I instinctively turned my head, as if she could see shame welling up in my pupils. Of all the things she could have asked of me . . .

"Ray Anne, you got shot because I couldn't take Dan down. Nothing will ever change that."

"I chose to do what I did." She craned her neck, keeping her face in mine so that I had to make eye contact. "It's not your fault, and it breaks my heart to watch you beat yourself up about it. And believe me, I know what guilt does to a relationship." Her voice cracked with emotion.

"You know my mom still blames herself for my brother's suicide, and it's destroying my parents' marriage."

I'd seen the way Mrs. Greiner pulled away when her husband tried to hug her or take her hand, like she didn't deserve the tiniest amount of affection.

I sighed and raked my fingers through my gelled hair. This was far from the first time we'd had a conversation like this. I had no idea why it was so hard to let go of a grudge against myself.

I guess Ray could tell I was struggling. She put her hand on my chest, over my heart. "Owen, I'll say it for the millionth time, even though I never once blamed you to begin with." Her palm on my chest was warm. It felt like kindness was spilling from her soul into mine. "I forgive you. Completely."

I wanted to believe and accept her words this time, but it felt like they slammed into a steel wall that kept anything from getting to the guilt and shame I carried inside me.

Still, I was determined to work this out. "Look, I don't know how to force regret away, but I can make you a promise." I cupped Ray's soft face in my palms. "I will do my very best to quit torturing myself over what happened."

It was all I had to offer. I searched Ray's face for a sign that she was satisfied and believed me, especially given my track record. I'd broken some major promises to her before. But that was the old me.

Finally, she nodded, her grin coming back. "I believe you."

And suddenly I could exhale. I tried to keep my huge smile on the right side of stupid.

A normal couple would have sealed the deal with a long kiss, but Ray Anne was still saving her first kiss for marriage. I'd mostly learned to live with it. I held out hope that someday, I'd be the guy who won the right to give her that first kiss.

I fantasized about that sometimes. Okay, maybe a lot.

I settled for another hug, then changed the subject. "I have something for you." I pulled out a gift bag I'd hidden in the brush. No tissue paper, but at least it was sparkly.

Ray Anne reached inside and gasped when she saw the photo book I'd made especially for her.

"Your mom helped me gather the pictures."

She stared at the cover, her bottom lip quivering, but still smiling. Nearly every photo she'd ever taken with her brother was in there, from Lucas's birth until a month or so before he died.

"I've been wanting to make something like this." She flipped through the first few pages, taking deep breaths. She cleared her throat. "This is incredible."

She brought the book closer to her face and stared at a photo taken when she looked to be about four and Lucas was a toddler. They were looking up at the camera, peeking out from inside a toy box. Ray Anne pressed a balled fist to her lips, and a tear spilled down her fingers.

She closed the album. "I can't wait to look at this from cover to cover later, by myself."

"Sure. I understand."

"How can I ever thank you?" She blinked fast, working to dry her eyes.

"I'm just glad you like it." I reached into my pocket. "I want you to have this, too."

I pulled out a small velvet bag, then opened it and held up the silver chain necklace I'd bought for her, a choker with two cool-looking, interlocked loops. "The circles symbolize eternity," I told her, "and things that last forever." Like my feelings for her, I wanted to say, but I didn't want to come on too strong.

Ray Anne turned around so I could fasten the necklace around her neck, then faced me again, running her fingers back and forth over the chain. "I love it, Owen. Seriously, I'll wear it every day."

It was another kissable moment, but oh well. Instead we stood there hugging, swaying in the mild breeze until we were basically slow dancing. We didn't need music.

The sun had nearly set now, and the trees were shadows against the darkening sky. Still, neither of us was anxious to leave—until a chilled gust ushered a rancid smell our way. We let go of each other and looked toward the last shred of sunlight barely visible through branches. We were downwind from a Creeper.

"We should go." Ray Anne started blowing out candles, and then so did I. It's not that we were scared—we knew our light repelled Creepers. But who wants to hang out in the woods at night with a demon, maybe more than one?

Our own illumination lit our immediate path as we walked hand in hand down the main trail toward our vehicles, keeping a pace that was comfortable for Ray Anne. I shined my cell's flashlight around and above our heads. I admit I tensed up when a pair of glowing eyes shined back at me from a tree, but it was only an animal. A raccoon, I think.

Ray Anne covered her nose. "There's definitely more than one Creeper here." The putrid smell was so strong now, I had to agree. But where were they? They usually stuck close to Masonville High, and we were over a mile from there.

Ray Anne stopped walking. "Listen."

A low, ominous, monotone hum made the hairs on the back of my neck stiffen while rousing my curiosity. Ray Anne grabbed my hand and pulled me off the path. "This way."

I let her lead the way as we followed the creepy chorus, fighting through a dense section of woods where entangled vines made it nearly impossible to walk. The mammoth cobwebs didn't help.

Finally we crouched behind a boulder, spying on a bizarre, disturbing scene in the moonlight.

TWO

Six wide concrete steps led up to a large, flat platform—like a cement stage with no backdrop or curtains. A campfire smoldered in the center of the platform, somehow burning without any brush or logs—just flames. Equally strange, a ring of towering Creepers loomed at the back of the stage, beyond the fire, bellowing out a low-pitched moan without ever pausing for breath.

Creepers don't breathe.

"What are they doing?" Ray Anne whispered.

I had no clue.

The nine Creepers faced inward, toward the center of their circle, each with its grotesque head cloaked in a hood that came to a point like a witch's hat. That was new.

The Creepers swayed in unison, like they were all lost in the same eerie trance. They rocked back and forth in a slow, circular motion, and occasionally they twisted their necks in impossible directions, as if their heads were detached from their torsos.

I should have known better by that point than to become intrigued by evil, to fix unflinching eyes on the kingdom of darkness for so long.

If they were consuming our attention, we could be sure we were drawing theirs. But it took an icy chill creeping up our backs to remind Ray and me of that.

We both turned fast and faced a disorienting wall of darkness. Except for the golden glow encircling our shoes, it was solid black in front of us—not a single moonlit tree limb or leaf was visible. Then from above our heads came a bestial grumble—a deep, threatening growl. A smell like raw sewage filled the air.

A Creeper hovered in the dark, just beyond our aura, its tall, gaunt frame blocking the scenery.

For a split second, I wondered if Molek had returned. I hadn't seen his pale face since the day of the mass shooting, when he'd prowled around me like a lion before I was rescued right from under his nose. But surely if the Lord of the Dead had been standing anywhere near, the Creepers would have fallen facedown at his arrival.

Also, Molek had a stench all his own, like sulfur mixed with burnt flesh and decay.

Most Creepers kept their distance from Lights—shackle-free people like Ray and me—but some weren't as intimidated. This one had dared to walk right up to us. We knew it couldn't harm us, but it was still unnerving to have one an arm's length away, staring us down in the dark.

"Let's go." I didn't whisper. We had a glowing advantage, so why cower?

Ray Anne grabbed my arm, and we turned our backs on the Creeper—and on fear itself. It let us go without a chase, making me thankful all over again to be a Light.

As we made our way back to the jogging trail, Ray Anne tried to make sense of what we'd seen. "It looked like a ritual or something."

"Wouldn't be the first out here." I reminded her of what I'd learned about my mom's parents. This land they'd willed to me had seen its share of dark ceremonies. According to the mysterious old man, who'd never been willing to tell me his name, my grandparents used to participate in secret occult gatherings out here, doing . . . whatever warped, sadistic people do at those.

Why get involved in something like that? I'd have demanded an answer if my grandparents weren't both dead.

With my cell light leading the way, Ray Anne and I were nearing the edge of the woods when something colorful caught our attention. Splashes of bright red peeked through a pile of earth-toned foliage. Ray Anne went for a closer look.

"It's a sweater." It was deeply tangled in the brush. We didn't think much of it—just kept moving until we'd exited the woods and reached the makeshift parking area where Ray Anne had left her silver Hyundai and I'd parked my Ducati behind shrubbery and tall weeds.

I opened Ray's door for her. When she started the car, her headlights shined bright on the wall of hill country trees. A black figure wove through the woods, its head turned toward us. Then came the sewage smell.

Ray leaned against her steering wheel, peering at our stalker. "It followed us."

I stared hard too, trying to see the evil word carved into the Creeper's face—its assignment—but it was moving too fast, like a snake among sticks. "It doesn't matter," I said. "We're leaving."

I didn't want to lose sight of what this evening was supposed to be about. Unbeknownst to Ray Anne, there was more in store for the birthday girl.

We agreed to meet up at her house. I mounted my motorcycle and took a last long gaze into the woods. The Creeper had disappeared, but I knew it was still there somewhere, polluting my land and the town of Masonville with its toxic presence. I refused to rest until I'd found a way to drive the entire demonic infestation away from Masonville High, off my land—and out of the town completely.

Once Molek had disappeared, the suicide rate went into a steady decline—and not one for six months now. It was great news, and believe me, the community was relieved. Even the psychotic sign-holders who had flocked to the campus had disbanded—as if a suicide epidemic was *ever* something to protest. But here's the thing: at least a half dozen Creepers with the suicide assignment were still stalking students. They had just grown lethargic. I'd been inside the school recently and witnessed a suicide Creeper struggle to close in on a girl, lacking the stamina to attach to her cuffs and cords.

Ray said it was because of our prayers, and I agreed, but I also considered it a side effect of Molek's absence. It was like the longer the Lord of the Dead was away, the weaker Suicide and Violence and Murder and all the Creepers with deadly assignments had become. But Molek was bound to return—any day now, for all we knew. I was sure he'd pick up right where he'd left off, reinvigorating his army to fatally wound students again. Knowing him, it might get worse than before, if that was even possible.

Throughout Ray's recovery, she and I had spent countless hours trying to learn spirit world tactics—specifically, a way to block Molek from ever being able to set foot on my land again. We read books and websites, and of course, the Bible, and yeah, we learned some helpful things, but we hadn't come up with a game plan specific to *our* situation and town, right now.

Lots of times, Ray and I had prayed and asked God to show us what to do . . . well, mostly she would pray, and I would nod in agreement. But we had yet to get an answer.

And there were new threats lately. A sophomore girl had disappeared three months before; then a few weeks later, a boy went missing: a kid from the foster system, eleven years old. A druggie homeless guy in his twenties was reportedly missing too, but it was hard to say if something sinister had happened to him or if he'd maybe just wandered off and overdosed or something.

As far as I knew, there'd been no breaks in any of the cases. The rumor around town was that a hard-core gang out of San Antonio was abducting people, and maybe that was true. Either way, it was clear to Ray and me that somehow Creepers were behind the disappearances.

The authorities put more cops on patrol and organized neighborhood watches, but overall, people around here were breathing easier these days, convinced they'd won the war against suicide and that Masonville was becoming a normal place to raise a family. But they couldn't see the fight—the real enemy—like Ray Anne and I could. We both knew the war was far from over, and it was our job to do something about it—a responsibility that felt like carrying a one-ton barbell on our backs 24-7.

I pulled up to Ray Anne's house not long after she did, and her parents were in the driveway, both holding balloons for their daughter. I picked up on that awesome, sweet scent that happens when a family of Lights comes together. Mrs. Greiner had Ray Anne in a hug and wasn't letting go, even though Ray had only been gone a few hours. Then again, this was the lady who'd sobbed the day Ray moved from her bedroom in the house to the garage after Mr. Greiner remodeled it into a living space.

He gave me what could be called a half smile.

"Hello, sir." I got the feeling he was warming up to me a tad, but I still had a long way to go.

Mrs. Greiner escorted us to their small but perfectly manicured backyard, where she had arranged for some of our friends to surprise Ray Anne—Ethan, Anna, Charles and his girlfriend, Joanne, to name a few. Mostly people who attended the thing for people our age I'd been hosting at my apartment on Thursday nights. It was a Bible study, but I was still somewhat turned off by that term, even though I was more open than ever to reading Scripture.

What can I say? Long-held preconceptions don't vanish overnight.

My mother showed up eventually—forty-five minutes late, but the fact that she came at all was surprising. She hardly left the house anymore. We attempted to hug, but she was too weak to squeeze back. Plus, her numerous icy chains got in the way.

"You okay?" I asked. She'd lost even more weight.

"Oh, sure." My mom turned to Ray Anne. "Happy birthday, sweetheart." She strained to hug Ray Anne, too.

Mom barely ate, but the rest of us feasted on finger foods and fluffy cake while surrounded by tiki torches and tropical-looking flowers. Even the pool floats matched the luau theme. As usual, Mrs. Greiner had outdone herself. Whereas my mom had always tried to drown her sorrows in alcohol and useless men, it was obvious to me Ray's mom worked to silence her hurt with never-ending busyness.

I liked seeing Ray Anne show off her new necklace.

I would have chalked it up as a pretty perfect night, but there were two reasons I couldn't. One, it was times like this when I really wished my dad were alive and actually knew I existed and could have been there, experiencing the moment with me. And two, I caught fast glimpses of that sewage-smelling Creeper from the woods watching us throughout the evening, peeking from behind fence posts and dark corners. Finally, around eleven o'clock—after my mom and a few others had left—it ventured out into the open, spying on us from a moonlit corner of the roof.

Ray Anne tugged on my button-up shirt, leading me away from her guests. "It's still stalking us. I don't get it."

"Did you see its name?"

It turned out neither of us had. I volunteered to go read its face but somehow instead got talked into distraction duty: keeping the conversation going with the party people while Ray Anne got a closer look at the Creeper.

I moved to the patio, where everyone was socializing, and chimed in while keeping an eye on Ray Anne. She took bold steps toward the Creeper, and the thing moved toward her, to the very edge of the roof. When she kept coming, it stepped off, hovering in midair above her head, glaring down between its grotesque feet at her.

Ray Anne came to a sudden stop, like she'd been startled or something. "Leave now!" She said it so loud that a few people looked in her direction, including her mom.

The Creeper snarled, baring its jagged teeth like an angry Doberman. Then it floated over the fence into the neighbor's yard, its eyes cloudy and narrowed. Finally, it drifted away, as best as I could tell.

Some Creepers were quick to flee when we told them to, but others remained defiant—an inconsistency that aggravated Ray Anne and me both.

"What are you doing?" Mrs. Greiner called out.

Ray Anne turned and faced us. "Nothing." She raised her eyebrows, flashing me one of those looks that let me know we needed to talk in private.

Mrs. Greiner scanned my face. Unlike my always-oblivious mom, Ray's parents were growing increasingly suspicious of our odd behavior. Ray and I agreed we'd come clean with them someday, just not now. They were Lights, so we figured they'd believe us, but Ray feared the truth would make them resent me for bringing this visionary curse on their daughter. To be clear, we didn't see it entirely as a curse, but her parents probably would. Never mind that I'd begged Ray not to seek out the supernatural well water from my property in the first place.

I followed Ray Anne to the cake table. "So?"

"It's missing a hand."

"Gross."

"And I saw its name, Owen." She looked pale. I waited for an explanation, but she just stood there, fidgeting.

"What is it?"

She leaned close to me and whispered, "Demise."

We'd been eyewitnesses to the powers of darkness long enough to know that being hunted by one of those is serious. Demise Creepers stalked people in preparation for an imminent, all-out assault. We'd put two and two together a while back. Ray's next-door neighbor died of what doctors had diagnosed as a common cold, a teller at my bank broke her back in a motorcycle accident, and a leasing manager at my apartment complex had a nervous breakdown—all oppressed by Demise before tragedy hit them like a tsunami.

Then there was Meagan. My soul still ached every time she came to mind. Demise had stalked her, with Suicide, in the days leading up to . . .

Well, I tried not to think about what happened to her.

But Ray and I weren't shackled like all those people, and Creepers couldn't just attack us at will. I rested my hands on her shoulders. "We have nothing to worry about, babe. Demise can't do anything to—"

A man's voice called to me, prompting me to turn around. But there was no one there.

I faced Ray Anne again. "Who said my name?"

"Huh? I didn't hear anything."

"What do you mean? It was loud."

Ray Anne's mom called to us from the porch. "Ethan's leaving. Wanna come say good-bye?"

"Maybe it was my mother you heard."

By the time we walked Ethan to his car, a spotless white Volvo, I'd dismissed the random voice. I was busy thinking about what total opposites this guy and I were. He was nearly my same height and happened to also be a Red Sox fan, but that was about all we had in common. Yeah, he'd recently graduated from med school, but I'd given up on becoming a doctor a while back, so that didn't count.

Ethan was a preppy pastor's kid who'd grown up singing hymns on stage with the church choir, and me . . . I still felt out of place sitting in a church pew.

As much as I now believed in God and stood by my life-changing, shackle-shedding experience, I couldn't shake my tendency to question institutional religion, along with certain biblical concepts. I was grateful for Gordon, the easygoing pastor who led the Thursday gathering at my place—Ethan's father, by the way. Out of the two of them, I got a much better vibe from Gordon. He always paid attention when I had something to say, but his son hardly bothered looking at me.

Gordon understood that I wasn't trying to be argumentative, that I just needed reliable answers to my avalanche of faith-related questions. There were Scriptures that made a lot of sense to me, and others I struggled to agree with. Had Gordon not been so patient with me, I don't know that I would have stuck with the Bible study this long. Opening up to a group wasn't really my thing.

Ethan waved a halfhearted good-bye in my general direction, then gave Ray Anne a churchy side-hug. I can't say I particularly liked seeing her in his arms (or arm, whatever), but it's not like I was the raging jealous type.

When it was time for me to leave, I hugged her twice as long as he had. Just sayin'.

I came home to my third-story apartment, grateful all over again to have my own place, away from my mom and her baggage. She had given me my inheritance, a hefty six-figure amount, and I'd splurged on this place—twelve-foot ceilings, granite countertops, and some new furniture. It disgusted me knowing the money had been a bribe from my father's parents to make sure he and I never laid eyes on one another, but not enough to stop me from taking the cash so I could move out of my mom's house. Believe me, I needed out.

I powered on the TV. The same news reporter who had annoyed me ever since I'd moved to this town was broadcasting a story. There'd been another disappearance. A freshman at Masonville High, Tasha Watt, was missing. I didn't know her, but it felt like I'd been punched in the gut when the irritating reporter-lady rattled off more details: "Tasha was last seen walking home from a friend's house wearing jeans and a red sweater."

I couldn't dial the police station fast enough. Wouldn't you know it—my call was transferred to my old pal Detective Benny. I told him how Ray Anne and I had seen a red sweater on my property, and I described the location. I hoped he understood I was only trying to help and had nothing to do with her disappearance.

I guess barely escaping manslaughter charges had left me paranoid.

Detective Benny let me know that if the sweater turned out to be Tasha's, the department's canine unit would be combing my property. Fine with me. I really hoped they'd find the girl alive somewhere, but if her decomposing body happened to have been discarded on my land, I wanted it found and taken care of.

I'd just hung up when the power in my apartment flickered off. No big deal, except that then I heard it again—a man's voice calling my name.

THREE

As QUICK AS THE POWER had crashed, it came on again. I jerked my head in every direction.

"Who's there?"

I sprang off the sofa and flipped on all the lights, inspecting my one-bedroom apartment like a wannabe cop, clutching my baseball bat.

God, please don't let anything lurch out at me. Not exactly manly, but I prayed it anyway.

There was a sudden sound of pounding, and I nearly swung my Louisville Slugger into a wall. Then it registered: someone was at my door. But who? It was one o'clock in the morning.

I stared out the peephole, but all I could see was lots of long, sun-streaked blonde hair and a blurry face I didn't recognize.

I guess the woman figured I was peeking at her. "I'm your new neighbor," she called. "Just need to borrow some scissors, if that's okay."

In the middle of the night? Who does that?

I went ahead and opened the door and just barely kept myself from gasping. She was muscular but curvaceous—I'd say midtwenties—with a gorgeous face and a V-neck T-shirt with a plunging neckline. She smiled, revealing adorable dimples on both sides of her rosy lips.

"I'm Veronica." Her voice was kind of low pitched for a woman, but in an attractive way. She had a bit of an accent, but I couldn't place it. Definitely not Texas, though. She leaned forward to shake my hand, and I fought to keep my eyes from dipping below her chin. "I saw your lights are on. I hope you don't mind me bothering you."

"Not at all." I didn't mean to give such a flirtatious grin.

You're in love with Ray Anne, loser. I wanted to sock my own jaw.

Veronica crossed her arms and leaned against the side of my door frame like she was posing for a photo shoot. "I'm trying to unpack, but my scissors are in one of the boxes, and I can't open the boxes without my scissors." She giggled.

"Here, I'll get you a pair." I went to my junk drawer in the kitchen, and she followed me inside, shooting curious glances around my living room. She had like ten chains hanging from the back of her shackle and at least eight cords coming from the back of her head—a seriously messed-up life, for sure. You would think that would have squelched my attraction, but still, I could hardly focus enough to dig through the drawer.

She stared at me from across the room. "I like how you've decorated the place."

"Thanks." It was pretty posh.

Veronica wandered into the kitchen and stood inches from me. "So, do you have a roommate, or . . . ?"

We were alone—no way around it. "It's just me."

She smiled bigger, but I cut my eyes away, determined to snuff out the spark before it had a chance to ignite.

Finally, my scissors. "Here you go."

She didn't take them. Instead she reached over and started flipping through the Bible on my countertop, stopping to read a verse I'd underlined. "'Do not give any of your children to be sacrificed to Molek, for you must not profane the name of your God.'" She crinkled her nose. "Why'd you underline that?"

"I just . . . did a study on false gods." I knew I sounded like a cult leader or something, but what was I supposed to say? That I'd researched

Molek because it was the name used by the wicked overlord that had laid claim to our town?

Veronica closed the book and ran her hand up and down the leather cover. "I have this exact Bible."

"My girlfriend got it for me." It was the perfect way to let her know I was taken.

"Aww . . ." She pouted playfully. "Who's the lucky girl?"

I felt my cheeks heat up. "Her name's Ray Anne."

I was still extending the green-handled scissors to her, but she stood there, nibbling the corner of her bottom lip, eyeing my face like she was impressed with what she saw. "You want to marry this girl, Ray Anne—am I right?"

I wasn't sure what made her think that, but I had no reason to deny it. "Uh, I mean, if that happened someday, it would be awesome."

She leaned so close, I could smell her minty gum. And a seductive lavender perfume. "I bet you can't wait to be a dad someday."

I hadn't thought much about fatherhood. I shrugged.

Veronica looked past the scissors and reached for my other hand, clutching my fingers—not a huge deal, but for some reason it freaked me out, her touching me. I tried not to let it show, though.

"May I?" She turned my hand over and gazed at my palm.

"What are you doing?"

She ran a manicured fingernail over the surface of my skin, giving me goose bumps all over.

"The lines . . . they tell me a story."

Uh, no thanks. I pulled my hand away. "I'm not into that sort of thing." And it was probably best if we kept our hands to ourselves.

"It's nothing bad, I promise. It's a gift, and I use it to help people."

She reached for my hand again, and this time, I let her take it. She studied every detail, sometimes closing her eyes, like feeling my skin was more important than seeing.

"Life hasn't been easy for you."

I shook my head, aware I should have told her to leave already.

"See this spot right here?" She pressed an area near the center of my hand, prompting another adrenaline rush. Or maybe it was all testosterone. "I'm getting something when I touch you there." She closed her eyes again. "You're about to have to make some big decisions that won't be easy. You'll have to choose sides."

I knew I'd better snap out of it and end this. It's not like I believed her.

I twisted my hand away. "Sorry—I need to get some sleep." I put the scissors in her hand, then walked over and opened the door. "Use them as long as you need. You can just put them on my doorstep when you're done."

She thanked me, then walked past me onto the balcony, the cuffs at the ends of her chains clanking over the metal threshold. I was about to shut the door when she turned around. "There's something else you should know—something I sensed."

"Okay?"

"Someone who loves you very much desires to spend time with you."

I instantly thought of my mother. I'd stopped by to see her a few times after I'd first moved out, but hardly at all lately. Mainly because I hated seeing the way she lived, and most of the time, she was sleeping.

Still, I wasn't buying into this woman's supposed psychic powers, and also, I didn't trust myself. For what seemed like an eternity, I'd been resisting the urge to make a move on Ray Anne. I didn't want to ruin everything with some stranger. Even if she did look like Miss Universe.

I told her good night, locked the door, and collapsed onto my sofa.

And that, guys, is how not *to cheat on your girlfriend.*

I flipped the TV channel to a mindless show and mulled over how, twice that night, I'd heard a man say my name.

I finally dozed off and woke Tuesday morning to a blaring TV commercial and a lingering, invigorating scent. Custos had been there.

I grabbed my cell and read a text from Ray Anne: **Did you hear about the missing girl? I think we saw her sweater!!!**

I texted back: **Already told the police. Crazy!**

She replied saying she was joining the volunteer search team in an hour, and I agreed to meet her there. In the meantime, I forced myself to finish an assignment and upload it. I was an online student at a college that's not worth mentioning, earning my basics for a degree I had yet to settle on. None of the majors caught my interest. It's not like the school offered a bachelor of science in Creeper annihilation.

Ray Anne was on track to eventually earn her nursing degree, but we'd both chosen to stay in Masonville. We had a mission to accomplish. And a mystery that had to be solved.

I'd spent a lot of time online and at the library in recent months, asking the skinny librarian lady all kinds of questions while researching Masonville's history, but there wasn't much information out there. Then again, who would want to write volumes about this random little Texas town? Before the suicide outbreak, the world had never heard of Masonville.

I was especially focused on searching for information about the land I'd inherited. I figured if I could possibly piece together when—and better yet, why—Molek and his Creeper army had flocked here to begin with, maybe Ray and I could come up with an idea about how to make them leave.

"The responsibility to drive out wickedness, that belongs to mankind," the old man had told me.

He'd also revealed that, over a century ago, my land had been a plantation, run by a harsh landowner. But I hadn't been able to find any information about it. Then the other day, the librarian had said she'd found something, an old document she believed was related to my property. She'd said she'd e-mail me about it. After I finished my assignment, I checked my e-mail and found her message.

I opened the attachment, a photo of a tattered piece of paper, stained brown by the passing of more than a century. In flawless handwritten cursive, the document was dated August 7, 1886, and titled "T. J. Caldwell Plantation."

Caldwell. Same last name as my grandparents. My mom's, too, until she turned eighteen and changed it to Edmonds—her way of completely disowning her family.

It was a weird feeling, knowing I was bound to be related to T. J. Caldwell, a plantation owner.

I zoomed in on the next line, written top and center on the paper: "Negro Inventory."

Really? I instantly felt sick to my stomach. I took a deep breath.

Down the left side of the paper was a list of names—just first names, like Harriet, Eliza, Arthur, and Polly. Next came ages, ranging from seven to fifty-nine.

Then—dollar amounts under a heading labeled "Value." Apparently five hundred dollars was the going rate for a seventeen-year-old girl. Two hundred for an eight-year-old boy.

Down the right side of the page was a list of remarks, a comment about each man, woman, and child. I covered my mouth with a clenched fist.

"Good hand."

"Sickly."

"Fair hand."

"Excellent cook."

"Always telling lies."

"Very good hand."

I spun my chair away from my screen and stared out my apartment window.

People were bought, sold, and abused on my land. By my ancestors.

Slavery had been abolished some two decades before that list was written, but that hadn't stopped T. J. Caldwell from making slaves out of people—oppressed souls who probably didn't know their rights and couldn't have enforced them if they had.

This felt different from reading about slavery in a textbook.

Maybe the anguished cries of those human beings were all it had taken to summon Molek to Masonville.

I shut my laptop and left to meet Ray Anne.

It was Tuesday, a workday, but it looked like most of Masonville had gathered under the blazing sun on the east side of my property, all waiting for the police to give instructions and commence the search for fourteen-year-old Tasha Watt. As I wove through the somber crowd looking for my girlfriend, I came face-to-face with a bulky guy in a sleeveless shirt—all muscle. It took me a moment to recognize my former best friend, Lance. It was hard to believe he was that huge now.

We both stood there, fidgeting with our phones, unsure how to react. The last time we'd seen each other, Lance had been bleeding out in the school hallway. I'd gone to see him in the hospital a few days later, but he'd been zoned out on pain meds and hadn't known I was there.

"Hey," Lance said, only willing to look me in the face for brief seconds at a time. We'd never cleared the air after he'd tricked me into an ambush where I was nearly beaten to death on my own wooded property. "It's, ah . . . been a while." Two girls walked past, unable to take their eyes off Lance.

"Yeah." I nodded, careful not to gaze at his shackle. Back when we were friends, I'd told him he had one, so staring at his neck would only make things more awkward.

All this time, I'd thought maybe Lance had become a Light. I was there when he'd cried out to God to save him, but in that moment, he was dying. He obviously had never come to understand he needed a different kind of saving.

He asked how I was doing, then brought up Ray Anne. "I heard she's made a full comeback."

"Yeah, she's good. Looks like you have too." His shoulder was scarred pretty bad.

He nodded, eyeing his impressive biceps. "I'm going to the police academy in the fall."

"You want to be a cop?" That surprised me. He'd always been dead set on engineering.

"My plan is to become a criminal investigator."

I swallowed hard, recalling how he'd chosen to enforce justice on me. My rib cage still ached sometimes.

"So you hear from Jess anymore?" Lance ran a hand through his shaggy brownish-blond hair. He definitely looked like a man now compared to the kid I'd known in high school.

I shook my head. "She used to text me now and then, but she hasn't reached out for months."

"I hear she's a mess. Strung out, dragging her kid with her to parties."

I sighed. I would have thought Ray Anne's willingness to risk her life to save Jess and her child the day of the mass shooting would have inspired Jess to more.

Lance looked back, like he wanted to make sure no one else was listening. "Owen, about what happened . . ." He diverted his eyes to the grass, rolling a small rock in circles with the tip of his tennis shoe. "I'm sorry. For what I did. That day in the woods."

Whoa. I never dreamed I'd get an apology from him. Or that forgiveness would roll off my tongue so easily. "It's in the past, Lance. We're good."

For a second there, it felt like my stomach leaped. Perhaps our friendship had a chance. But the excitement was short lived.

He looked me in the face and lowered his voice. "So you're like . . . better now? No more delusions?"

I crossed my arms and pressed my lips together. Even after my warnings about Lance's girlfriend, Meagan, had come to pass, he still refused to give me the slightest benefit of the doubt. I wasn't willing to lie to him now just to save myself some embarrassment. There was no need, and plus, I'd turned over a new leaf, vowing to be totally honest, no matter what.

"I still see things, Lance."

Oops. My eyes dipped to his metal-clad throat, and I don't think he liked it. He glared at me, then shook his head and walked off, mumbling something under his breath.

I think we both knew it: our friendship would never recover. Too many blows to the face and ego. Two conflicting life perspectives that couldn't suck it up and get along.

The obnoxious reporter was there, shoving her microphone in everyone's faces, prodding them to talk about Tasha. Seemed to me if she really cared about the girl, she'd have come dressed to help with the search. Her pantsuit and high heels didn't fit the occasion any better than the glow around her feet matched her grating personality. Yeah, she was a Light, which had shocked me when I first noticed. What kind of person likes badgering stunned, grieving people for interviews seconds after tragedy has ransacked their lives?

I found Ray, and for three sweaty hours, we combed the woods on foot alongside the army of volunteers, looking for any sign of Tasha. Creepers darted through the trees above our heads like giant bats, swooping down at times on vulnerable souls whose chains and cords were there for the taking.

I *hated* them.

When it was time to call it a day, Detective Benny shook Ray Anne's hand and mine and thanked us for helping. He was bound to still think I was strange—maybe completely deranged—but it was a relief to be on his good side now.

As students sped out of the Masonville High parking lot, I pulled up and parked my bike in my usual spot. I'd taken a job as an after-school chemistry tutor, not because I loved the subject, but as an excuse to get on campus and keep an eye on the spirit world.

It wasn't easy going back after Dan's massacre. Nine students and one teacher were killed that day, and many more injured. But I'd sucked it up and made myself go inside for the sake of my mission.

Unsurprisingly, Creepers swarmed the building like flies on roadkill. There was an obvious countermove: if a significant number of students became Lights, the Creepers would be hard pressed to operate in the school. But that was no solution at all, because it wasn't even remotely doable.

Don't get me wrong—I knew what I'd done to become a Light and knew others could have the same freedom. At first, I set out to save every shackled person I came in contact with. People I knew and people I didn't—*everyone*. But I learned real quick that telling people how badly they need God to save them and begging them to surrender doesn't work. I could only get so frustrated with them, though. I used to despise pushy faith people too.

When I arrived at Ms. Barnett's classroom, my two tutorial students were seated at a lab table, both academically anemic, unfortunately. And shackled.

One of them was Riley, the girl I'd approached in the cafeteria the year before when a Creeper, Hopeless, had attached itself to her. She was a sophomore now, with double the number of chains. She was sweet, but the desperate type.

The other student was Riley's latest boyfriend, Hector. He was loaded down with chains and cords, always walking around with his chest puffed up, showing off his high-dollar Nikes. He liked to blare his music so loud I could hear every word through his earbuds—the same music I used to listen to before Ray Anne talked me into giving up explicit songs. From day one, Hector had an attitude toward me.

He sat facing away from me today, his eyes bloodshot like he was high and disinterested—nothing new. But Riley was unusually quiet, and her head hung low.

I lowered into the chair across the table from her. "What's the matter?"

She glared at Hector. I got the idea she would have shot daggers from her eyeballs at him if she could.

Hector gave me a sideways, cocky grin. "She just don't know how to let go and move on." He dug his hands into the deep pockets of his jeans.

Riley turned away from him and angled toward me. "He dumped me for some older girl. As if she'll ever go out with him."

"She just can't handle that I've moved on to a woman who looks better than her."

Riley shot up from her chair and stormed out of the classroom. Ms. Barnett went chasing after her. Then so did a Creeper—Rejection, if I had to guess. They like teenage girls, especially ones like Riley.

Hector sat there with a smirk on his face, about to laugh.

"You think that was funny?"

He crossed his arms and tilted his head back—his way of looking down on me, apparently. "You're what, three years older than me? I don't need advice from you. And I don't owe anyone an apology just 'cause I found a new girl and friends that are . . ." He cut his eyes to the floor.

"That are what?"

He hesitated, then glared at me. "Powerful." He stared me down like a tiger about to pounce. *Give me a break.* He was a twig compared to me.

"What's that supposed to mean?"

He shrugged. "Don't worry about it. Ain't none a' your business."

Ms. Barnett poked her head inside the classroom and instructed us to carry on without Riley. I did my best to review some test questions, but Hector kept giving the wrong answers on purpose.

I passed through the gate into my apartment complex, hoping to take Ray Anne to dinner, then saw that she was already parked outside my place. I slid my helmet off as I strode toward her car, picking up the pace when I saw that she was sitting with her shoulders slumped, her head nearly touching the steering wheel.

I smelled it, then spied it. Demise stared down at us from a nearby stairwell, eyes as gray as its rotting skin. Like Ray had said, it was missing a hand. Ugh. Nothing but a broken bone protruded from its right forearm.

I threw Ray's car door open. "Look, no Creeper is going to touch us. I don't know what that pathetic thing is planning, but you and I . . ."

Ray Anne furrowed her brow, perplexed. I shut up.

"Yeah, I saw it too, but I can't worry about that right now." She wiped her nose with a tissue.

I grabbed her hand and guided her out of the car, staring into her flushed face. "Ray, what's wrong?"

She shook her head. I wrapped my arm around her shoulders and led her up the steps toward my apartment. She had a self-imposed rule about not coming inside—at least not for long. "Being alone makes it easy to compromise," she'd say. But it had been a long time since I'd seen her this upset—I figured she'd make an exception.

She lowered onto my sofa and pulled more tissues from her purse. I glanced out my living room window. Demise hovered in the parking lot below, peering up at my apartment. I closed the blinds, knowing it could still hear us. I had more than enough proof that Creepers could eavesdrop from zip codes away, but what could I do about it?

I faced Ray Anne. "Please tell me what's going on. I'm here for you."

"You might not be after this."

I swallowed hard. "What is it?"

She exhaled, slow and shaky. "I'm afraid to tell you."

I lowered myself beside her on the sofa and gripped her hand, small compared to mine. She pressed her eyes shut, then out came the tears, streaking her cheeks.

My heart sank.

Cancer?

She has feelings for someone else?

All I could do was gnaw on my bottom lip and wait for her to tell me.

FOUR

RAY ANNE TURNED SIDEWAYS on the sofa, facing me. "Owen, I know you care about me . . ." She took another prolonged breath. "But promise me you won't feel like you have to stay with me after this, okay?"

"I don't understand. What happened?"

She stared at a random spot on the wall. "I went to the doctor this afternoon, and he told me . . ." She rolled the necklace I gave her between her fingers, still stalling.

I tensed up, as if I could somehow physically lessen the blow of what she might say. "Ray Anne, whatever it is, you know I'll still—"

"I can't have children, Owen."

Oh.

I wanted to say something, to comfort her, but the words wouldn't come.

She struggled to speak through an outpouring of tears. "There's too much scar tissue, after the shooting."

All I could do was stare at her.

She raised her voice. "Say something!" She seemed to be taking my lack of response as rejection, as if I would actually dump her because she was injured.

I fumbled for something to say. "I—it's okay, Ray Anne. I mean, I know it's not okay for you, but it doesn't change things for me. I mean, maybe it will someday, but not when it comes to us. Okay?"

She wiped her eyes, then finally looked me in the face. "I can never have a baby, Owen. You could never have children if . . ."

It was hard enough to process how the diagnosis impacted her. I couldn't begin to consider how it potentially affected me.

I pulled her toward me, letting her soak my shoulder. All I could think to do was hold her and stroke her hair.

She was still in my arms when the grating of chains scraping cement came from outside, clanking up flights of stairs, followed by a way-too-chipper knock at the door. "It's me. Veronica."

Could she have worse timing?

"Who's Veronica?" Ray Anne wiped smudges of makeup from under her puffy eyes.

"A neighbor. She's bringing back some scissors I let her borrow. I don't need to answer."

Veronica knocked again.

"Go ahead." Ray Anne closed her eyes and sucked in air, working to gain her composure.

I figured I'd get the scissors back and be done with it. I opened the door halfway.

"Hey, handsome." Veronica grinned at me.

Ray Anne bolted off the sofa and leaned in for a look. One peek, and she started rearranging her ponytail, visibly self-conscious about her appearance.

Veronica's striking green eyes lit up as she looked past me and focused on my girlfriend. "You must be Ray Anne." She held out her hand.

Ray Anne approached the door, wiping her red-blotched face with one hand while reaching for a handshake with the other. Veronica clutched Ray's palm, tilting her head to the side as if analyzing her.

How long did Veronica expect Ray Anne to stand there like that? Ray finally grimaced and pulled her hand away. Meanwhile, I tried to figure out where to plant my eyes so that my girlfriend would know I wasn't staring at this woman's miniskirt.

"I'm Veronica. Owen mentioned you last night."

Ray Anne searched my face. I spoke slowly and deliberately. "Like I said. Last night. She borrowed my scissors."

Veronica grinned. "He was telling me how much he's looking forward to getting married someday and becoming a dad."

Ray Anne gasped like the wind had been knocked out of her. I glared at Veronica.

"I said I'm looking forward to getting *married* someday. Marriage. That's a long-term goal of mine, not . . ." There was no good way to finish my statement.

Veronica looked back and forth between Ray and me. "Is everything okay?"

Anyone could see we were in the middle of something. But Veronica didn't seem willing to take a hint and leave us alone.

"We're all right, thanks." Ray Anne could still be kind, despite the knife in her heart.

I was about to close the door when Veronica had the nerve to place her sandaled foot inside my apartment. "Ray Anne, when I shook your hand, I sensed something."

Not this again.

"What do you mean?" Ray Anne asked.

"The word *twins* kept coming to me." Veronica's eyes opened wide, like this was great news. "Ray Anne, you're going to have twins someday."

My girlfriend's mouth dropped open, and I stood there in disbelief, wondering how in the world to make Veronica shut up and go.

Ray Anne crossed her arms and huffed. "I'm not sure what makes you think that." It was more attitude than I'd seen from her in a while. "But believe me, you're completely wrong. I can't even . . ."

I was glad Ray Anne got choked up and couldn't finish her sentence. Her trauma was none of Veronica's business.

Veronica actually took another step forward, stopping just inches from Ray Anne's face. "I'm not wrong about this, Ray."

Ray? Who did this woman think she was?

Veronica placed a gentle hand on Ray Anne's shoulder. "I can tell you more if you like. I have a gift. I can sense things about people . . . about the future."

Ray Anne's eyes narrowed. "Only God knows my future."

"Who do you think gave me this gift?" Veronica's smile wasn't the flirty kind she'd been giving me, but a close-lipped, sweet one. "It's so I can help people. And I'm sensing that you're in need of help right now. I picked up on a deep desperation the moment I touched your hand."

Oh, give me a break. It didn't take psychic powers to see Ray Anne's puffy eyes and guess she'd been bawling.

"God sent me to you," Veronica said.

Time for me to intervene. "Veronica, this isn't a good time, okay? I'm gonna have to ask you to leave now."

She stepped back and cleared her throat, the way people do when they're embarrassed. But then she looked at me and twirled a thick strand of hair around her finger. "That's okay, Owen. I'm sure I'll see you soon." She flashed me a playful wink.

Ray Anne furrowed her brow at Veronica, then stared a hole through me.

My face felt like it was on fire. I basically shut the door in Veronica's face, then turned the dead bolt. "She's an absolute freak." I hadn't done anything wrong, but I still felt guilty, if that makes sense. "Ray, you know there's nothing going on between her and me, right? I've only spoken to her once before now."

My conscience told me to stop there, but I bullied past it. "I'm not attracted to her." There was some truth in that, right? I didn't *want* to be attracted to her. I could feel my pulse pick up. I turned away from Ray Anne and stepped toward my sofa, trying to decide if I'd just blown my vow of honesty.

Ray Anne stayed by the door, staring at me. "I trust you, Owen." Phew. "She didn't return any scissors though."

I took a seat, hoping Ray Anne would too. "Yeah, I guess she's keeping them. I don't know."

"Did you see how many chains and cords she had?" I knew that was Ray Anne's way of warning me to stay away from Veronica, which was fine with me, because I was going to.

"Yes, I did. Tons." I let my head relax back into the couch cushion. "I'm sorry, that whole thing was weird. You want to go to dinner?" Whenever I got uncomfortable, I'd change the subject. I had my mother to thank for that.

Ray Anne picked up her purse. "Look, I'm sorry, but I need some time alone to think, okay?"

I understood. I didn't want her to go, but I walked her to her car and hugged her good-bye. How was I going to help her get through this?

I sprawled out on the overstuffed lounge chair in the corner of my living room and thought about how, if I married Ray Anne, I'd never have children. I hadn't daydreamed much about being a parent—just promised myself years ago that I'd do things way different than my mother. But now, I couldn't stop thinking about what it would be like to never have a child of my own.

I pictured Ray Anne's distraught face when she'd told me. I texted her to make sure she was okay and remind her that my feelings for her hadn't changed.

God, how's this fair? She saves a baby, then her injuries keep her from ever having one?

If only he'd answer.

That night, I made the most of what I could find in my almost-bare refrigerator and finished a biology assignment. Around midnight, I had just turned on the TV when the electricity went out in my apartment again. The light around my feet was helpful but didn't reach far enough to light the room. I accidentally knocked a cup of water off my coffee table while attempting to feel my way toward the kitchen, where I kept a flashlight.

Before my eyes had time to adjust to the blanket of black around me, I heard it again—a man said my name.

It sounded like he was right behind me.

I whirled around, heart hammering. "Who's there?"

I blinked and blinked, straining to see. The strips of moonlight seeping through the living room blinds outlined a shadow, what looked like the dark form of a man.

He uttered my name again.

FIVE

"DON'T BE AFRAID." The mysterious figure spoke to me.

"Who are you?" I patted down the cabinet and finally found my flashlight. But when I shoved the switch on, it didn't work. "What do you want?"

"Only to speak with you." His voice was low and calm. "May I?"

I grabbed a butcher knife from a wooden block by the stove and pointed the blade at him, squeezing the handle with a shaky hand. "Leave me alone!"

And with that, he vanished. The lights flickered on, my flashlight suddenly shined bright, and the TV broadcast returned to the screen—a rerun of a classic Nebraska University football game that struck me as way too cheery right now.

What was that?

I had no paradigm for this.

I rushed to my sofa and grabbed my cell. It was dead and took forever to power back on when I plugged it in. I drummed my fingers on the case, waiting for it to light up so I could call Ray. But when she answered, I could tell she was crying.

"How are you doing?" she asked, obviously trying to stifle sobs.

"I'm . . . I'm good, you okay?" No way I was going to bring up my disturbing experience now. She had more than enough weighing on her.

We talked for a half hour, and by the time we hung up, I'd realized that Ray's diagnosis was not something she was going to get over anytime soon. Maybe ever.

I crawled under my bedsheets even though I wasn't tired. I planned to keep my eyes open all night in case the phantom man came back. But then Custos arrived, poised and on the lookout in my bedroom, so massive his head grazed my twelve-foot ceiling. Relief washed over me, and I became sleepy fast. I still didn't get much rest, though. Custos was too bright and magnificent.

When I woke up at sunrise on Wednesday morning, Custos was gone. But my theory was that he remained aware of where I was and how I was doing at all times, even when he wasn't right next to me.

The whole time I was showering and getting dressed, I kept envisioning the stranger that had trespassed into my living room. I tried to come up with a theory about who he was. What he was.

He didn't look or smell like a Creeper, but he wasn't anything like a Watchman, either. And he was definitely not an ordinary human. He was an apparition looming in the dark, suspending electric currents—and then telling me not to be afraid, for crying out loud.

A pastor might know something about this sort of thing, right? I decided I'd confide in my Bible study leader, Gordon.

Some months ago, Ray and I had started to tell him about our supernatural sight, but right away, Gordon got hung up on asking how we'd gained our vision. The last thing we wanted was to entice someone else to seek out the potentially fatal well water, so we downplayed the whole thing and kept our mouths shut about it from then on. But the supernatural being haunting me now was like nothing I'd ever seen before.

I gave Gordon a call and was grateful when he agreed to meet me for lunch.

I had a nagging sense of obligation to stop by my mom's that morning and check on her. The rank alcohol smell and dark circles under her eyes depressed me every time, but it's not like I could just abandon her completely. And honestly, I was really missing Daisy. I'd wanted to bring my dog with me to my new apartment, but my mom had insisted she needed Daisy around in case someone ever tried to break in. Never mind that her house was ransacked by evil on a daily basis anyway, basically at Mom's invitation. Plus, I needed Daisy way more than she did—to warn me if a Creeper attempted to sneak into my apartment.

I loved driving my Ducati, but Masonville's rural roads had a way of coaxing me into thinking about things—deep things that sometimes made me uneasy. Today I got to mulling over how, just the other day, I'd promised Ray Anne that I'd stop beating myself up about her injuries. But now my guilt was compounded. Her infertility was Dan's fault, for sure, but I never should have allowed him to harm her to begin with. Another irreversible consequence of my failings.

In my experience, carrying guilt around can physically press on your chest, making it difficult to breathe. If only I could go back and do things differently.

There were plenty of things I'd change.

Of course, I'd do absolutely whatever it took to make sure Ray Anne never got shot. I'd gladly take the bullet for her myself.

I'd also try way, way harder to get through to Meagan before it was too late.

And Walt and Marshall . . .

That one was too agonizing to think about.

I forced their faces—and their caskets—out of my mind. Like I always did.

I had to. Otherwise the regret became unbearable, like a wrecking ball bashing my soul.

I parked in the driveway at my old house and zeroed in on the dark Creeper graffiti scribbled above the front door:

infirmity

I had a basic understanding of the word, but an online search on my cell brought up an official definition: "physical or mental weakness." That definitely fit my mom, now more than ever.

I let myself in and navigated through the laundry baskets full of clothes and towels, probably still dirty. Piles of plates and wine-stained glasses, too.

It was 11:00 a.m.—technically morning, so she was probably still in bed. Why hadn't Daisy come barreling to me, jumping up and trying to lick my face?

"Mom?"

I climbed the hardwood staircase, treading over bits of what looked like super-thin shreds of decaying paper, mostly lodged against the banisters—remains of Creeper notes, too tattered to read. I'd seen evil forces use those to communicate about their plans—confirming dates and targets for a strike—so of course I didn't like seeing them at my mom's.

A foul smell hit me as I neared the top of the stairs—like really disgusting body odor, but way worse than any human could ever give off. I covered my nose and kept walking, hoping my mother was all right.

I reached her closed bedroom door and stood outside it for a moment, reluctant to face what I might find on the other side. Finally I clutched the knob and turned it cautiously.

The horrible smell got even stronger. And there was my mother, sleeping, twisted among mismatched sheets like I'd seen her too many times to count, chains and cords flung in every direction. But today, some man I didn't recognize was sleeping with an arm draped over her waist. A large work shirt lay crumpled on the floor a few feet away from me, *Wayne* stitched in red cursive on the name patch.

My jaw clenched. *Will you ever stop letting men use you?*

I'm pretty sure I would have slammed the door had the sound of high-pitched whispers not suddenly echoed through the room. I jumped back when I caught sight of a bony hand poking out from under the sheets at the foot of the bed. A Creeper was intertwined with my mom and the guy. Odor mystery solved. My stomach churned with nausea.

I sighed and walked out of the room, anxious to find Daisy and leave. On my way to the stairs, I happened to glance into my old room, and there she was on the floor, staring at me, panting hard. I could see her ribs.

My fingers clamped into fists. How could my mom neglect my dog like that? Just let her waste away?

I scooped Daisy into my arms, and she yelped like she hurt all over. I stomped down the stairs and out the door, vowing under my breath that it would be a long time before I entered that house again.

At my place, Daisy scarfed down a bowl of dog food, then curled up on the new bed I'd bought her and drifted into a deep sleep. I stroked her ears, feeling guilty for not checking on her sooner.

My mother was so self-absorbed and totally dysfunctional that she'd nearly let my dog starve to death. It was a miracle I'd survived my childhood.

Gordon and I slid into a booth across from one another, both holding plates with cheeseburgers and fries. Gordon rolled up his starched sleeves while making small talk about sports, then set his thick leather Bible on the table and prayed over our meal. Before long, he asked me what was on my mind.

I told him all about the visitation, as I called it, by some sort of paranormal being. Over and over, Gordon nodded and rubbed his chin. Finally, I asked him, "What do you think it could be?"

He sat silent for a moment. "I suppose it could be some kind of demonic—"

"No. I know for a fact it's not that." I may not have earned a doctorate of divinity like him, but I knew very well what a Creeper looked and smelled like, thank you very much. "What else could it be?"

He scanned the room, maybe paranoid that a church member might be overhearing our bizarre conversation.

I leaned in across the table, careful to keep my voice down. "Do you believe in ghosts?"

Gordon looked at me like I might be kidding.

"I'm serious."

He sat up taller, his expression all business now. "Look, Owen, I don't know what you're seeing, but I can tell you that God warns us in the Bible not to consult with the dead."

"You think that could be it? Some dead guy with, like, unfinished business who wants my help?" I'd seen a movie once that had made that plot seem semirealistic.

Gordon looked away and exhaled. I got the impression he was really weighing what to say next. "Owen, I have to ask, are you sure what you're seeing is really there? It's not your imagination?"

I leaned back and crossed my arms. I'd gone out on a limb and trusted this guy, come to him for answers, and now he was questioning my sanity. I didn't think—just popped off. "Do you really believe it's all in my head, or are you just embarrassed because you don't have all the answers?"

I instantly regretted being rude. I lowered my chin. "I'm sorry. I didn't mean to—"

"No, it's fine." I didn't deserve the smile he gave me. "It's a valid question."

I wondered if I'd ever have even a shred of his humility.

I wasn't sure how long Gordon would be willing to continue our discussion, but in between munching on fries, he kept it up. "I can admit that when you've talked to me about this sort of thing in the past, and also now, I do feel somewhat at a loss for answers, and that does frustrate me. But here's what I'm certain of: mediums, psychics, spirits of the dead—all that stuff—it's not from God."

Interesting. I hadn't mentioned Veronica or her psychic predictions. But I never took her seriously to begin with.

Gordon pushed his plate aside and leaned in toward me. "Owen, I see it as my responsibility to do everything I can to protect you and help you mature in your faith. And my best advice is that you commit to living your life according to God's Word." He put his palm flat on his Bible. "You'll never regret following these instructions, no matter the situation."

His advice seemed sincere and all, but trite. Like telling a cancer patient to take some Tylenol and have a great life. I gave up on the subject and asked if I could run something else by him. Of course Gordon didn't mind. He was the second-best listener I knew, after Ray Anne.

"It's about my girlfriend."

Gordon knew Ray Anne. He was a pastor at the church she'd attended all her life, where I went now too. I shared her bad news with him and admitted I didn't know what to say to her, much less how to help. I was also dealing with how the situation could potentially affect me, but I struggled to put that into words. Anyway, I was far more concerned for her than for myself at that point.

Gordon spoke for a few minutes, ultimately suggesting that I trust the Lord and follow his leading. That sounded good and all, but . . . how? I might have asked, but Gordon got a phone call and had to run. "Let's meet again soon," he said. I told him I'd give him a call later in the week.

I stopped by Ray Anne's that afternoon, and she was still weepy. We sat side by side on lounge chairs in her backyard, staring out at the pool. I'd brought my guitar, and I attempted to play her a song. I'd been trying to teach myself how to play, and I seriously stank, but that was fine because it made her laugh a little.

She mentioned that Gordon had left her a voice mail telling her how sorry he was to hear about her situation. "Did you tell him?" she asked.

It hadn't felt like a betrayal to confide in him at the time, but now that Ray Anne was questioning me, I worried she'd be angry at me for blabbing. "No."

Well, that was an outright lie.

"Oh. Well, I guess my mom did." She left it at that.

Hard as I was trying, I was failing miserably at being honest—about as badly as when I'd been shackled. Add that to my guilt pile.

"Owen?"

I could tell Ray Anne was about to say something important. I set my guitar down and looked at her.

"I really, really want to be a mom someday." She stiffened her bottom lip. "But I can't let this consume me. We have a mission to accomplish."

I squeezed her hand. "How about you let me worry about the fate of Masonville for a little while? You deserve some time to deal with this."

She rested her head on my shoulder. "Spiritual forces don't lose focus," she said. "Neither can we."

I caught a glimpse of Demise peering down at us from the neighbor's roof. I popped my knuckles. "Believe me, Ray Anne, I won't."

That evening, I sat on my sofa and used my cell phone to search for *prayers that keep evil away*. Like all the times I'd googled that before, some suggested prayers came up, but they were mostly meant for when a person suspected an evil presence was near—maybe lurking in their house or lingering in a hotel room or something. I needed to know how to prevent a high-ranking principality from ever coming around again. How to enact a spirit-realm force field over Masonville.

That got me thinking about T. J. Caldwell's plantation. I seriously wished I could go back in time and take in the scene with my supernatural vision. Witness for myself when and why Molek set his heart on that land in this town. Not that he has a heart.

At some point, out of curiosity, I typed, *are ghosts real?* When I hit search, my phone lost power, along with my entire apartment.

SIX

I IMAGINED THE SHADOW figure watching me as I rushed to the front door and pressed my back against it, ready to bolt outside if it came to that.

Even with the power out, the setting sun provided enough light for me to see past the aura on the floor around me, across my living room. I kept my eyes fixed on the window, the spot where the ghostly man had last appeared. I struggled to quiet my breathing.

Seconds passed, maybe a couple of minutes, and I saw nothing. More time ticked by—still nothing there. It crossed my mind that maybe the power had simply gone out in my apartment without any supernatural cause. But my phone had died too.

I loosened my grip on the doorknob but didn't let go. My other hand pressed against my heart, as if I could calm it. I kept scanning the living room—until a voice called to me from the dark hallway across from me.

His voice.

I'd had enough. I rushed outside and slammed the door, sucking in the crisp spring air.

"You okay?" A female voice spoke from the bottom of the stairwell. Veronica, of all people.

"I'm fine." I tried to sound convincing.

She began climbing the steps, playfully sliding her open hands along the metal banisters. "You sure?"

"Yeah." I was in no mood for this. "Just getting some fresh air."

She kept climbing until she arrived at the bottom step of the third-story stairwell. From where she stood, grinning up at me, there was an easy vantage point down the front of her blouse, and I think she knew it. I struggled to keep my eyes where they belonged.

"You know I'm here for you, right?"

I gave a halfhearted nod, trying to decide which was worse: dealing with her or the power-sucking prowler in my apartment.

Her brow furrowed. "Something happened in there, didn't it?" Her gaze darted back and forth between my front door and me.

"No." My vow of honesty was officially a thing of the past.

"All right." Her playful tone hinted that she didn't believe me. "Can I give you some advice, Owen?"

I didn't respond, but she did it anyway.

"Don't be afraid of new experiences." She gestured to herself. "Or new people."

I shook my head. "I'm not."

She puckered her lips. "If you say so." Finally, she went clanking back down the stairs. "Nothing's a coincidence," she said over her shoulder.

Whatever.

I stood on my balcony, staring out past the parked cars into the grassy open field behind my apartment complex, assessing my situation. Had I really let this mystery man scare me out of my home?

Veronica made it to the parking lot, then turned and looked up at me. I know this sounds crazy beyond belief, but when she and I made eye contact, I felt like I heard her speak to me, only not with my ears. Inside my head.

Go back inside, Owen.

Did you just . . . talk to me? All I did was think it.

She grinned, then walked away.

I paced my small balcony for a while, until the sun had set, thoroughly confused and weirded out by what had just happened. But I forced myself to let it go for now. I had to deal with the situation inside my apartment. I needed to confront it head-on, like a man.

I stepped inside, willing myself to stare my fears in the face. I even shut the door.

I peered into the hallway, squinting, anxious for my eyes to adjust to the dark. Sure enough, there stood the shadowy figure, his form even darker than the black space around him.

SEVEN

I ATTEMPTED TO STUDY the shadow's frame in the darkness. He seemed built about like me—maybe even slightly taller. "Who are you? What do you want from me?"

"Nothing." His tone was quiet and gentle. "I'm here for you."

"What for?"

"To help you find your way—if you'll let me."

He sounded like an adult, but I had no real sense of his age—if age even applied to a being like him. Exhilaration washed over me, followed by anxiety. "Tell me who you are."

He moved to the edge of the hallway, but I didn't run. "I was once alive," he said. "A human, just like you."

"So you're . . ." I didn't want to say it.

"Dead." His calm admission sent shivers scampering down my spine. "But death is not the end of life, Owen. It's a passageway to another life, an alternate realm."

"I know." I was still tense. Still breathing hard. "How do you know my name?"

"In my realm, all things are known. And you're important to me."

"I don't understand."

He offered no explanation. We lingered in the silence a moment, then he turned his back to me. "I'm going now, but I'll return to you."

"When?"

By the time the word had left my mouth, my lights and electronics were powering back on, and the shadowy man was gone.

I collapsed onto my sofa, wide eyed, startled by the sound of my printer tapping and spooling as it turned on. I dropped my head into my hands, trying to piece together what in the world was going on.

I powered on my phone and noticed my hands were jittery. Fear-derived adrenaline mixed with the rush of surviving danger. I started to call Ray Anne—but no. It still seemed selfish to talk with her about anything except her sorrow.

I called Gordon but hung up when I got his voice mail. Like I was going to leave a message about this. For all I knew, he'd forward it to Ray Anne's parents and warn them to protect their daughter from me.

I was too hyped up to sit around. I went to the grocery store. I needed some fly traps anyway—my apartment had been infested ever since I'd brought Daisy home. Thanks to my mom, there'd probably been some maggots in her skin. But what I wanted most was candles and matches. The next time my power went out, I'd be prepared.

I came home and set candles in every room. It was weird: I was definitely dreading another visitation, but I was a tinge excited, too.

I couldn't let the situation derail my focus, though.

That night, I flipped through my Bible, looking back at portions of text I'd underlined related to Molek. I zeroed in on a passage I'd highlighted in Deuteronomy—one of the driest, most unrelatable books in the Bible, I'd decided.

Let no one be found among you who sacrifices their son or daughter in the fire.

Hard as it was to stomach, I'd learned that, back in the day, the Ammonite people would sacrifice their children to their man-made god Molek on a fiery, blazing altar. I wondered if the Molek I knew—the local Lord of the Dead—had named himself after that idol, inspired by a twisted, unfathomable fascination with the incineration of young lives.

I'd never paid much attention to the rest of that passage and hadn't bothered highlighting it, but tonight, it drew me in.

> *Let no one be found among you who sacrifices their son or*
> *daughter in the fire, who practices divination or sorcery, interprets*
> *omens, engages in witchcraft, or casts spells or who is a medium or*
> *spiritist or who consults the dead. Anyone who does these things is*
> *detestable to the Lord.*

I'd never dabbled in witchcraft or spells or any of that stupid stuff, but the part about consulting the dead . . . Did that apply to *me* now? It's not like I had initiated the encounters with the spirit man. And I'd hardly classify our conversation as me *consulting* him.

Despite the time of night, bright light shined through my living room window. Custos was on the balcony, his back to the door.

Over the next three days, Custos came and went, but the shadow man never showed. I figured maybe Custos was keeping him away, which was fine by me. Well, kind of. My curiosity about the afterlife wanderer was at an all-time high.

Unfortunately, at night, whether Custos was around or not, I heard things in my apartment, like something was brushing against the walls. Daisy would pop up from my mattress and look around awhile before dozing off again. But nothing paranormal could get past my vision, so I knew there had to be a simpler explanation.

By Sunday morning, the restless nights had caught up with me, and I silenced my cell alarm for more sleep. Around noon, I woke to Ray Anne knocking. There was a certain way she knocked—fast but not too hard. I opened the door, and she handed me a white cardboard box. "Chocolate doughnuts left over from church."

My favorite.

I followed her outdoors, onto the balcony off my living room, and we sat beside each other in my wobbly folding chairs, both marveling that the temperature was a comfortable seventy-something degrees. But then she got quiet. As in, completely silent.

"Ray Anne, I wish I knew what to say about the situation you're in. Just know that I'm in it with you, and no matter how long it takes for you to—"

She put her flexed hand in my face. "Please stop. I'm done talking about it."

My mouth stayed gaping open. I didn't have any solutions to offer, but I knew that ignoring the whole thing was no way to cope. "You can't just block it out."

She scooted her chair, angling toward me, her brow raised in determined concentration. "We've got a job to do, Owen. Once we figure out how to drive evil away from our old school—out of this town completely—we can move on and help other towns too." She threw her arms up, exasperated. "I don't have time to sit around wishing I could have children someday."

I wanted to hold her hand, but she was too tense. "Ray, our mission here is super important, for sure. But that's not all there is."

She turned her gaze away from me, past the parking lot and chain-link fence into the grassy, windblown field. "I know." Her dramatic tone was gone. "I still want to get married someday, to a good man." Her eyes pooled. "He may be the only family I'll have."

I felt heavy, like I needed a sturdier chair. I was hoping she'd look at me, a sort of *you're-definitely-in-the-running* kind of affirmation, but instead she cleared her throat and kept her eyes diverted, her voice flat and disappointed. "I missed you at church today." I was sure it didn't help that I'd slept in the previous two Sundays as well. "You still want to get baptized, right?"

"Of course." I tried to sound enthusiastic, especially since baptism was a requirement for becoming an official member of Ray's church. I didn't see any real point in religious ceremonies, but I kept that to myself. Ray Anne wanted to be with a church-loving guy, so that's what I needed to be—traditions and all. I really did want to learn everything I could about spirituality; it was just hard sometimes to relate to the formalities that went with it.

I set the box of doughnuts on the cement floor of the balcony. "I'm sorry I didn't make it this morning, but I have a good reason this time."

She raised a curious eyebrow, fidgeting with the silver necklace I'd given her.

"I haven't gotten much sleep because . . ." How was I supposed to word it? "A man who used to be alive has made contact with me."

That's all I said, but she completely freaked. She jumped to her feet, firing questions at me faster than I could answer. By the time I was done explaining every last detail of my encounters, including a word-for-word recount of every syllable the man had spoken, Ray had her cell out and was typing notes like a court reporter.

"You're telling me it's a dead guy?"

"That's what he said."

She managed to pace back and forth on my narrow balcony. "But he had no light?"

"No. But he didn't stink, either. And Daisy didn't bark one time."

Ray Anne sat, only to pop back out of her chair. "Maybe we should talk to Gordon about this."

"I already did."

She studied my face like she didn't fully believe me. "What'd he say?"

I shrugged. "Not much. You know—do what the Bible says."

Ray Anne sank into her chair and stayed this time, focusing so hard she closed her eyes. "Owen, I gotta say, I think you're in way over your head with this one."

Uh oh. I could feel a lecture coming on, likely coupled with a Scripture verse I couldn't even remotely question without being labeled a full-blown rebel. The undeniable fact was, like the growing fly problem in my apartment, the rules of Christianity were starting to irritate me:

Give money to the church, or you're greedy.

Keep your hands off your girlfriend, or you're a pervert.

Avoid any spiritual experience that happens to be outside the Bible box, or you're evil.

No, Gordon never said it quite like that, but he might as well have—that's what he meant. But like Gordon and his preppy son Ethan, Ray

Anne loved the rules and followed them without question. And since I couldn't imagine my life without her, I had to find a way to follow along too. Or at least pretend.

"Ray Anne, you and I can smell danger coming—literally. We can see evil as clear as day. I admit, this experience has definitely been frightening, and I'm not saying I trust the man. But I don't necessarily think I should run from it just because it's new and different."

Was I really parroting Veronica's advice?

Ray Anne pulled out her little pink leather Bible from her purse and started flipping through it like her life depended on finding a certain page. "I don't know where it's at, but I swear there's a verse about this."

Just like I thought. "I've already looked it up, Ray—you don't have to quote Scriptures at me. It's not like I'm gonna sell my soul or bow down to a ghost." I chuckled, but she kept skim reading pages. "Don't be so paranoid."

I hadn't meant to offend her, but she shut her Bible and glared at me. "You think I'm paranoid? 'Cause I think you're seriously naive."

Anger rose up from my abdomen and clustered in my chest. But I didn't want to argue. Not with her. "Ray Anne, let's not let this come between us, okay?" I reached and wove my fingers through hers, then kissed the back of her hand—the most affection I could get away with.

She stood, then came close. "I told you, we have to stay focused."

I stood too. "I agree."

Right then, a chilling whisper drew our attention in another direction, over Ray Anne's shoulder. Then came the sickening sewage smell.

EIGHT

We already knew Demise was near, watching us against our will, but neither of us expected it would actually come at us.

The thing climbed the brick exterior of my apartment building, passed through the railings lining my balcony, then crouched down in the corner on all fours—or all threes, given its missing hand. Creepers are at least eight feet tall, but this one had crumpled itself into a tight wad within its ragged garments, a confounding cluster beneath its big head. It was like a massive daddy longlegs retracted into a compact ball.

It had been a while since I'd been so close to a Creeper's face, much less in broad daylight, and I'd forgotten how utterly gruesome they were. Disproportionately pronounced cheekbones under an ultrathin layer of rotting skin. Jagged, discolored teeth poking out from a mouthful of brown saliva. This one's black pupils seemed to spill misshapen into a pool of gray, festering with unmistakable hatred like every other Creeper.

Demise growled like a starved grizzly bear, but Ray Anne planted her feet and pointed her finger at it. Then she recited Luke 10:19, a verse that, a few months ago, I'd liked enough to write on a sticky note that was still stuck to my bathroom mirror.

Demise grimaced at us and ground its teeth. Then it shot up and moved above our heads, fully extended now, crawling across the ceiling until it had left my balcony and was clinging to the side of the building.

This next part happened really fast.

There was a blinding light, then a giant hand reached up and plucked Demise from the bricks like a flimsy clump of cotton. Custos had the Creeper by its neck. I got the feeling there was more strength and power in a Watchman's pinkie than in all the world's military forces combined.

Suspended some twenty feet off the ground, my favorite Watchman proceeded to speak to the shuddering Creeper in a language like nothing I'd ever heard. Each syllable flowed eloquently into the next. So he *did* talk. I'd have paid anything for the translation. His commanding voice rattled my eardrums. Ray Anne hit her knees, awestruck.

Demise winced and tried to look away, but Custos gripped its deformed jaw and physically forced it to look at him.

Demise started squealing something over and over and over. Some kind of "Yes sir!" in spirit language, I imagined. Or maybe, "Please don't!"

Creepers began closing in from different directions, a dozen or so, all charging toward Custos with their lips drawn back and fangs exposed. Custos saw them, and without loosening his grip on Demise, faced the field behind my apartment complex. A battalion of armored Watchmen—I counted nine—now stood there.

Glory personified.

It literally took my breath away. The gang of Creepers tucked tail and ran.

Eyes bright with fury, Custos uttered a few more intense words at Demise before dropping down and plunging the flailing Creeper into the ground, pounding him into the earth, away from us. At least for now. Then Custos rose and stomped down hard on the crater, sending a tremor through my apartment building that I assumed only Ray and I felt.

In a matter of seconds, we witnessed the hole in the ground return to an undisturbed patch of grass, like pixels swarming a screen, then settling into a crisp image.

Demise was gone, literally buried in defeat.

Custos looked up at me, and all I knew to do was wave. Tears running down her cheeks, Ray Anne whispered, "Thank you."

I expected Custos to smile, but his face was somber, his eyes narrow with concern. He turned and charged across the parking lot, passing through the fence into the field. Once he joined them, the team of Watchmen left.

I lowered to the cement beside Ray Anne and brushed wisps of hair away from her clammy face, perspiring from the intensity of the moment. "It's okay now."

She caught my hand midstroke and held on tight. "No. Don't you see, Owen? The war is closing in on us and escalating. Something's happening."

Of course I could see that. How long would I continue to try and shelter Ray Anne from harsh realities? She always figured things out anyway, and she'd proven she could handle it. I didn't have to baby her like I'd done my whole life with my mother.

"You're right. We have to step things up." I didn't think it was possible to become more determined than I already was, but I insisted to Ray that we had to dig deeper and look harder for answers and solutions.

Ray Anne nodded, then threw her arms around my neck. I resisted the urge to rely on her to talk to God for the both of us, like I usually did, and asked him myself to please guide us and show us what to do—to help us understand how to drive evil forces out of Masonville for good. "And bring Tasha Watt and the other missing people home," I prayed, "if it's not too late already."

I held out hope we'd get some answers soon.

Tuesday afternoon, it was time for tutoring again at Masonville High. Even before I turned into the parking lot, I knew something wasn't right. I looked beyond the students piling into vehicles and peeling out onto the street, to the school building, where a dark blob was covering most of the roof, shifting like a tattered tarp in the wind. I finally made sense of it. Creepers were piled two and three deep on top of the building, facedown, shoving one another.

By the time I careened into a parking spot and slid my helmet off, the Creepers had spread their arms and legs out, and while lying prostrate, started chanting in one human language after another. I'd seen this kind of thing before, my senior year—the day they'd called to Molek and he appeared, stoking their thirst for destruction. And now they were chanting for their king again.

I looked into the sky and then all around, convinced that this was it—the Lord of the Dead was coming home. On and on the chanting went, until, one by one, the Creepers lifted their huge heads and started scrambling to their feet, gathering into a tight, upright cluster.

They peered into the sky behind me, still pushing and jabbing. I turned, and high in the air, off in the distance, a huge object loomed— something dark and big and bulky with . . . what was that stuff hanging off it?

I stood there staring, expecting Molek to rise out of the mysterious object or lurch out from behind it. But instead the thing hung there, unmoving, untouched, and unoccupied. I looked toward the school again, and the Creepers were reaching toward the contraption, staring at it as if enthralled. Obsessed.

Finally, the Creepers dispersed, seemingly content to carry on as usual while the airborne oddity remained.

I had to carry on too. It's not like I wanted to walk inside that building, but it was time. Past time by now.

I made my way toward the main entrance of Masonville High, contemplating.

It seemed like the harder I tried to make sense of spiritual realities, the more questions I had—an aggravating cycle. I mean, what was that hovering object? I grumbled under my breath on my way to Ms. Barnett's classroom. *I pray for answers but get none. Why do I even bother?* My nagging sense of irritation escalated to all-out anger.

I passed a row of lockers and wondered if I could pound my knuckles into one without getting caught on camera. But then I felt a wave of freezing air against my back. I turned to see Doubt trailing close behind me. It had a double set of fangs and reeked like curdled milk.

Oh. I understood now . . .

That last cynical thought of mine hadn't come from me.

To be clear, Creepers don't have to be attached to a human's chains and cords to target a person's mind—I didn't even have entrapments anymore. All they need is a whiff of human vulnerability, and they'll rush in to test a person's resolve, launching thoughts into the air like spiritual sonar, aiming at shackled people and Lights alike.

To agree with Doubt would provoke it to keep up its pursuit of me, but to disagree required confidence in God—something that, I had to admit, fluctuated in me from one day to the next. Sometimes from one hour to the next. But I'd side with God over a devil any day, so . . .

I didn't say it loud, just loud enough: "I trust God to give me answers. At some point."

Doubt hissed like a territorial cat, then sank into a wall, out of sight.

It wasn't a world-changing victory, but it meant something to me.

I wasn't in the mood to discuss chemistry, but that was the lame part of my job—the downside of being a spy at Masonville High. By this point Hector and Riley could hardly stand to be in the same room together, but I managed to get them to interact enough to redo a lab they'd both failed.

At one point, Riley leaned against my shoulder, trying to make Hector jealous, I think. "Are you going to Spring Scream?" she asked me.

"What's that?"

"Biggest costume party ever—like Halloween six months early, behind the school."

A narrow field of grass was sandwiched between my wooded property and the back side of campus. I wasn't sure if the land belonged to me or the school district, but either way, it was a terrible place to have a party—overrun with Creepers.

Not that I'd ever convince Riley of that.

Apparently determined to talk me into going, she stood and began describing her cat costume, motioning while explaining how strips of black fabric would stretch across her stomach and match a mask she was making herself. She was smiling bigger than I'd seen in a while but stopped when she caught my sudden wide-eyed grimace.

"What are you staring at?" She fiddled with the waist of her low-cut yoga pants, confirming that I'd truly seen what I thought I had—a tiny megawatt glow in her abdomen. A baby on the way.

"Riley . . ." I started to say something, but Hector was right there. Plus, it was none of my business.

Surely she knew by now. Although still minuscule, the radiant shine was twice the size as the one I'd first spotted in Jess our senior year.

No telling who the father was, but my guess was Hector. Poor baby.

I wrapped up our session early. While I made my way down the Creeper-graffiti-stained hallway, I thought about Ray Anne—how she'd never carry a little light.

Suddenly I caught sight of something glistening in my peripheral vision, distracting my attention from my depressing thoughts. There was a trail of gleaming spots on the floor, bright patches of white, shimmering light that marked the tile hallway like dazzling footprints. They faded in and out, but if I squinted and concentrated on seeing them, I could spy them more clearly. That was a first.

I followed the path of illumination, and it took me around a corner, then down another hallway. The alluring spots led straight to a heavyset woman, a Light who was speaking under her breath while unloading a locker full of books and binders into a bag. She was dressed like a professional, in a silky blouse and tailored slacks.

"Excuse me?" I approached her with no clue what I was going to say. "Do you mind me asking what you're doing?"

She looked up at me. Outside her glossy brown irises, her eyes were a tearstained shade of pink. "I'm emptying my niece's locker. Tasha."

"Oh . . . I'm sorry."

She managed a slight smile. "I have faith we'll find her." After a final, lingering glance into the empty locker, she pushed the door shut.

"Me too." I introduced myself, and she told me her name was Betty.

I reached out to shake her hand—the same medium-brown shade as Walt's had been, I noticed with a twisting in my gut—but she wrapped me in a bear hug instead. Her embrace felt more motherly than my mom's ever had. She gave me some heavy, affectionate pats on the back too.

"You're so tall, you must be a senior."

"Actually, I graduated last year."

She looked to the end of the hallway, somber, then back at me. "That was some school year, huh?"

I nodded, the unwelcome image of Dan's face surfacing in my mind. The memory of blood gushing from Ray Anne's abdomen.

Thankfully, Betty changed the subject. She told me she was born in Masonville but left as a child, and she'd recently moved back from Baton Rouge. She seemed proud to tell me that her family had lived in Masonville for three generations before her.

While walking alongside Betty toward the main entrance doors, I offered to carry the bag of Tasha's belongings, but she didn't want to let go of them.

I sneaked a few glances behind us—the floor was blank. Why wasn't Betty leaving any glistening prints now?

She asked if I'd known Tasha, then explained that her niece had recently moved in with her because Betty's sister—Tasha's mom—had become too unstable to function as a parent. I could relate—to the messed-up mom part, not to the part about having a loving aunt.

"So, you moved to Masonville to take care of Tasha?" I asked.

"That's one reason." She waited for some students to pass us before carrying on. "I also knew I had to get back here when I saw the news broadcast of that young man opening fire in these halls." Her pace slowed until she came to a stop in the middle of the science wing. "There's work to be done in this town." She gazed above our heads, then shuddered. "Somethin' strange is going on here—evil on the loose that needs to be put in its place."

I caught glimpses of Creepers scampering overhead and within the walls, but they kept their distance from us, a pair of Lights. "Let me get this straight," I said. Betty eased the bag in her hands to the floor, and I searched her freckled face. "Are you saying you believe there are evil beings here? 'Cause . . . I believe that too."

"Yes, I am, son." She stared long and hard at me, then reached out and grasped my shoulder, speaking in my ear. "My great-great-granddaddy saw things on the land around here with his own eyes. Evil beings. He told my grandmother they were tall and hideous—looked like they hadn't eaten in some thousand years and smelled as nasty as rotten corpses. And they would sneak up on people and bind them with chains around their necks."

Betty let go of me, and I stumbled backward, my mind on over-load. In my peripheral, paranormal vision, Creepers shifted and rushed around us, stirred by our conversation.

Betty sighed and shook her head. "I'm sorry. I know I sound ridiculous—I don't expect you to understand."

I took her hand and squeezed it. "Betty, I don't just know what you're saying." I swallowed hard. "I see it."

She pierced my eyes with a stare that made me never want to lie again. "You better not be feeding me a line, you hear me, son?"

"I'm not lying, I swear. Everything you just described—the chains, the stink, their skin-and-bones appearance—all of it, it's as real to me as you standing here now." I couldn't believe that I had just happened to run into someone who might be able to give me the insights I was look-ing for. My pulse pounded. "Betty, did your great-great-grandfather pass down any more information?" I wanted to know *everything*. *Immediately*.

"Oh, honey . . ." Betty was as wide eyed as a deer facing oncoming traffic. "There's more. A whole lot more."

NINE

ONE DAY IN HIGH SCHOOL, when Lance had talked me into ditching classes for the day, we hid in the oversize cleaning closet on the science wing and waited for the halls to clear so we could escape. I never thought I'd hide in that closet again, much less with a woman in her fifties, but Betty flipped on the light and pulled me inside so we could carry on our conversation in private.

Standing among heaps of mops and industrial-sized boxes of paper towels, she crossed her arms. "I'm concerned that you're telling me fabrications, young man. Seriously exaggerating, perhaps. I'm warning you, this is no trivial matter."

"No, I get that. I'm telling you the honest truth."

She looked me up and down, tapping her index finger against her maroon-glossed lips, then quickly dug through her purse until she found a notepad and pen. "When do you claim to have gained your supernatural sight?"

"A little over a year ago—last March. But my girlfriend and I have promised each other not to tell anyone how we got it, so please don't ask me."

She tilted her head. "You're saying she sees too?"

I nodded, eager for it to be my turn to ask questions. Betty wrote notes in nice cursive. "Describe what you see on people." She touched her neck.

"Thick metal shackles with chains attached—and big cuffs at the end of those. Also cords, in the back of people's heads."

"Well, I'll be." She wrote faster now. "You call them cords. My great-great-grandfather—Granddaddy Arthur—called them tails."

"They do kind of look like rat tails." I spoke up before she could ask something else. "What were you saying when I found you in the hall? I saw you talking."

She pursed her lips. "I was praying—for Tasha and the rest of the students."

Interesting. "Betty, you left a long, like, trail of light down the hall."

She lowered her pen and smiled, her eyes going glossy. "I . . . I did?"

"Yeah. But the thing is, I've prayed and been there when others have too, and I've never once seen anything like that."

She nodded. "Granddaddy Arthur used to say that the more he sought answers—really tried to empathize and understand—the more he began to see. Sometimes just flickers of things at first."

Wow. After all I'd witnessed, could there be more that I was still blind to? "Whatever else there is, I want to see it. Every single bit of it."

She held out an open palm, inviting me to put my hand in hers. "I don't fault you for that, young man, but you need to be aware . . ." She squeezed my hand like she really cared about our conversation—and about me. "The more you witness, the harder things tend to get."

"Harder how?"

Betty's cell phone rang, startling us both. She glanced at it. "It's Principal Harding. I've got to go." We exited the closet—thankfully, no one saw us. I don't know what excuse we would have given for what we'd been doing in there.

After Betty's brief conversation with Harding—something about the record of Tasha's visits to the school nurse—Betty and I resumed our walk toward the main exit. She invited me over to her house on Friday for dinner. "There's someone you need to meet." She encouraged me to bring Ray Anne, too.

I couldn't say yes fast enough.

Finally, it seemed like some major answers were on the way. And to think I'd almost given in to Doubt.

On my way to the parking lot, I called Ray and told her every incredible thing that had just gone down, and she squealed into the phone. She said we should make a list of our most important questions to bring with us on Friday. That sounded good to me. We talked a little longer, and the subject of the dead guy never came up, but she did ask me about Veronica. "Has she come by your apartment again?"

"She said hi from downstairs two days ago, but that's all." For the life of me, I didn't know how to explain having heard Veronica's voice in my head. So I didn't try.

Later that afternoon, my heart skipped a beat when I flipped on my bedside lamp and it didn't light up. But it turned out the lightbulb just needed replacing.

Maybe the man was truly never coming back. I was sure Ray Anne was praying he wouldn't. I was content to let it go—I had enough freaky mysteries to unravel. On top of everything, no matter how I tried to distract myself with to-dos and music and TV shows, I couldn't shake the eerie sense that I wasn't alone, that I was being watched. I'd battled this ever since I'd first drunk from the well, and I'd mostly learned to ignore it. But today, it was noticeably worse. I couldn't go very long without looking over my shoulder.

I'd just finished changing out fly traps around my buzzing apartment when my mom called. I'd been wondering how long it would take her to realize she hadn't seen or heard from me. Or my dog.

After basically no small talk, she asked if she could treat me to dinner tonight. She paused, uttering a soft groan like she was in pain, then added, "Someone will be with me. We want to talk to you."

Ugh. I had a hunch where this was going. "If your new boyfriend—Wayne, is it?—is moving in, you don't have to run it by me."

She stayed quiet, leaving my remark to linger like nasty cigar smoke.

I tried to backpedal toward niceness. "I worry about you, Mom." It was the truth.

"I understand." That's all she said.

"All right, I'll be there, but I'm bringing Ray Anne."

She paused so long I thought she might say no. "Um . . . okay. I suppose you can bring her."

Since when did she care if my girlfriend was with me?

The phone call came and went without her ever mentioning Daisy. For all I knew, she hadn't noticed she was gone.

I parked my bike at Ray Anne's, and we got in her car. It's not like she could straddle my motorcycle in a dress—a stylish black dress that looked amazing on her, by the way. She was backing out of her driveway when we spotted Demise hovering across the street, staring at Ray's house, grinding its razor-like teeth.

"I don't know why it's camping out here," she said, "but I don't like it. I don't think Ramus likes it either. He's been coming around even more."

Ramus—a Latin word, of course—was the name we'd given the armored Watchman who often guarded Ray Anne's house. That was actually a big improvement over what Ray Anne wanted to call him: Bloom. "Because he smells like flowers," she'd said, "and he looks a little like Orlando Bloom, don't you think?"

She might as well have named him Cupcake or Fairy Dust. It was unfitting. Insulting, really. "Let's name him after something strong and sturdy," I'd pleaded. We settled on Ramus, meaning "branch."

"Can we stop by and see Ashlyn?" Ray Anne asked as we pulled onto the freeway. "We have some time to spare, and Central Hospital is on our way."

Ashlyn was yet another one of Dan's victims. The poor girl had slipped into a coma after being struck the day of the shooting—a bullet to the base of her neck. Clinging to her injured body that day, Ray Anne had promised Ashlyn that she'd never leave her, and true to her word, she went to see her a lot. Sometimes several days a week.

I still didn't like hospitals—the dingy air and coats of death dust blanketing just about everything and everyone were beyond depressing—but I agreed to go along. We sat at Ashlyn's bedside, where she'd been lying like a prisoner to her mattress for months now, hooked up to all kinds of machines, including one that breathed for her.

I couldn't imagine having had my nineteenth birthday come and go without being aware of it, lying comatose while every muscle in my body wasted away. On top of that torture, Ashlyn was entangled in a mass of those sickening webs Creepers spawned onto the walls and over the critically ill and dying—another burden of a shackled existence.

Ashlyn's eyes were open today, but open or shut, she was always unresponsive. Still, Ray Anne talked to her as if she were wide awake, and prayed for her too—pretty much the same thing every time, asking God to show Ashlyn mercy and wake her.

How many times did a person have to ask God to intervene before he'd do it? If he did it at all? Seeing Ashlyn had a way of stirring skepticism in me, evoking old resentments toward God that ate away at my faith. I knew better than to gripe about it, but on the inside, I wrestled.

Ray Anne took some pink carnations from a vase and tucked them into Ashlyn's hair, braiding a strand in the process. I whispered to Ray, "You're going to be an incredible nurse someday, you know that?"

She grinned at me, then turned her attention right back to Ashlyn. "I wonder how much longer her mother will hang on." From one week to the next, Ray feared she'd arrive at Ashlyn's room only to discover that she'd been removed from life support. "I'm still holding out for a miracle."

I admired Ray Anne's unshakable faith. Mine was racked by constant tremors.

In Ashlyn's shackled state, the risk of her dying was catastrophic. Ray Anne lost a lot of sleep over it, and it haunted me, too. I didn't know if Molek would be the one to confiscate her soul or some other

Lord of the Dead would show up in his place, but either way, Ashlyn
was in the worst possible danger. Like a sleeping duck drifting toward
a crocodile's den.

Surely God wanted her to wake up, to have a second chance at finding light and freedom. Why wouldn't he?

Ashlyn's mother was a Light—did she assume her daughter was too?
Ashlyn's father had died a few years before; there was no way for us to
know the state of his soul or where he was spending eternity.

Ray Anne moved a framed childhood picture of Ashlyn, taken with
both of her parents, to a tray table within Ashlyn's line of sight, even
though she couldn't really see anything at all. And then we left her there.
Too quiet and still, encased in Creeper webs.

As Ray and I entered the dimly lit steak house where we'd agreed to
meet my mom, I tried to make sense of the nervous pit in my stomach.
I wasn't looking forward to meeting my mom's date, but why was I
dreading it *this* much? It reminded me of when I had to force myself to
leave the house after first witnessing people's shackles. Okay, not that
bad, but still miserable.

The hostess led us to our table, dragging her chains along, but I froze
before reaching my chair. What was *he* doing there, beside my mother?

TEN

"PLEASE, HAVE A SEAT." Dr. Bradford stood, sporting a designer suit with his tarnished shackle. He pulled a chair out for Ray Anne, and she stared at me like she'd seen a ghost. I didn't blame her. This man's son had shot and nearly killed her. Sentenced her to infertility.

No wonder my mom had hoped I'd leave Ray at home. I wished she'd said something, but shocker, she chose to be inconsiderate.

Ray Anne sat, but I still stood there, trying to come to grips with how my mother was in the same room with this man—an evil fake with a major affinity for the satanic world.

"What are you doing here?" I sounded disgusted because I was.

Dr. Bradford gave my mother an affectionate look that made my skin crawl.

"I asked him to be here," she said.

I looked between Mom and him and scowled. "Aren't you a married man?"

My mother waved her hands, nearly knocking over her glass of water. "He's my doctor, Owen—nothing more."

Dr. Bradford nodded in agreement, but the way he looked at her seemed to contradict that. It was a glance that I would have called charming and tender if it had come from anyone else. "I'm here professionally, Owen, to help facilitate a sensitive conversation. But if you must know . . ." He cleared his throat, gazing down from behind his chair into the empty seat. "My wife has left me. Dan's actions have put an immense strain on our marriage." He turned to my girlfriend. "Ray Anne, I'm so very sorry for what Dan has put you through."

"Don't talk to her." I wasn't a kid anymore and felt no obligation to show respect to undeserving adults.

"Son . . ." My mom pleaded with her eyes for me to go along with this. How naive could she be?

"Your parents were his beloved mentors, Mom. You know—the ones who abused you?" I still hadn't told her I knew she'd been raised in the occult, but Bradford's close relationship with my grandparents should have clued her in that she needed to keep her distance from this man.

Dr. Bradford had the nerve to walk over and grip my shoulder. "Owen, your mother and I knew you'd have reservations. It's okay—have a seat and let's talk."

I knocked his hand off. He'd manhandled his son, but I wasn't going to let him touch me.

"Owen!" My mother was barely strong enough to put her fists on the table.

"It's okay, Susan." Calm and confident, Dr. Bradford strode back to his chair beside her. "Don't allow him to upset you."

Me?

He smiled serenely at me. "Owen, you should know, I'm not the man I used to be."

I huffed. "That's the exact line Dan used to feed Jess."

Bradford sighed and lowered his chin like an innocent, misunderstood child. My mom placed her frail hand on the sleeve of his suit jacket. "I doubt I'd be alive right now if it weren't for Brody."

I didn't want to know Dr. Bradford on a first-name basis.

"Your mother is extremely ill," he said. I'd already figured that out, but it was still hard to hear him officially say it. "Sit down, and we'll explain."

THE DECEPTION || 71

I didn't want to be anywhere near him, much less seated at his table, but I needed to hear this. I sat, but my legs stayed tense.

"I'll get straight to the point," Dr. Bradford said. "I'm sorry to tell you, your mother has cirrhosis of the liver, a chronic condition where the tissue—"

"I know what it is." I also knew it was deadly. All my life, I'd feared Mom might suffer something like this.

I wasn't willing to ignore the obvious. "So, I guess being an alcoholic has taken its toll, Mom."

Ray Anne kicked me in the shin under the table.

Dr. Bradford placed his hand on my mother's back, between her bony shoulders.

Is that how doctors touch their patients? I wondered.

"Everyone makes mistakes," Dr. Bradford said, "and sometimes we pay dearly." He focused on Ray Anne again. "My son is in prison, where he belongs, but he was my only child, my one hope of ever having grandchildren."

Ray flashed me a look. Did he not know about Jess's pregnancy? That he was already a grandfather? And was he really making himself out to be a victim?

"Owen." He leaned in toward me, like he really cared. "Are there any questions I can answer for you about your mom's diagnosis or treatment?"

It was too dim in the restaurant for me to study his eyes, to search for the dark stirring of evil I'd seen inside them before, but I still knew not to trust him. "No. She and I will discuss it."

He had the nerve to start rubbing circles on my mom's back. "I'm ensuring Susan gets the best treatment possible. Access to specialists she'd never have otherwise."

Yeah, right. I couldn't pinpoint his motive for being this attentive and thoughtful toward my mother, but I was sure it was selfish. Had to be. This same man had tried to lure me into a mentoring relationship as a guise for instructing me in satanic practices—my grandparents' twisted legacy.

Ray Anne dug her nails into my arm, prompting me to look up. A Creeper came charging toward our table and stopped behind Dr. Bradford. I couldn't read the gashes on its face in the candlelight, but it was easy to see it strumming through the cords hanging from the back of Dr. Bradford's scalp, now roused to life and contorting in its hand. It examined my mother's cords too.

Ray Anne stood, no doubt about to attempt to drive the monster away with her light. But I gripped her arm, determined to have the situation play out another way. She sat as I came out of my chair.

"Mom, I want you to leave with Ray and me, right now. I understand you're in serious need of medical care, but you can't trust this man."

"Owen . . ." Her eyes pooled. "I need Dr. Bradford—can't you understand?" She cupped her mouth and sucked in air.

"For once, Mom, trust me over what some man is telling you."

She shook her head.

I took some slow breaths to ease my rising temper. I'd never told her everything I knew about this man, and clearly, it was time. "Leave with me now, and I'll explain everything to you."

That must have made Dr. Bradford nervous. He stood and glared at me. "Your mother is very ill—she doesn't need this kind of stress, Owen."

I narrowed my gaze. "Then maybe she doesn't need me in her life to begin with."

Ray Anne gasped and clutched my fingers. "Don't do this," she whispered.

The frustration of years of enduring my mother's willingness to trust everyone *except me* was reaching a breaking point. I spoke loudly. "We'll find other ways to get you the treatment you need," I assured my mother. "Don't let him manipulate you with that." I reached my hand out. "Please, Mom, come with me."

She winced, then turned her face away from me and clung to Dr. Bradford's arm.

I shook my head. "Fine."

I grabbed Ray Anne's hand and pulled her up. We left my mother sitting there, being accosted by evil alongside Dr. Bradford.

Ray Anne scolded me the whole way home. "Did you hear what your mother said as we walked away? Dr. Bradford pulled strings to get her onto the transplant list. I'm not saying he's a good man—I'm saying your mom is really, really sick, Owen."

I couldn't care anymore. She'd been ill my whole life, in lots of ways. I was tired of it. Weary of watching men take advantage of her—because she allowed it.

Ray's lecturing didn't stop when she pulled into her driveway. "Do you know the last thing I said to my brother before he died? I told him to shut up and get out of my room. Trust me—you don't want to say things you'll regret. Tell your mom you're sorry and—"

"When are you going to stop telling me what to do?" I'd never copped an attitude like that with her. Or exited the car and slammed the door that hard. But I didn't appreciate being bossed around like an incapable child. Like my opinions were dumb and irrelevant.

She slammed her door too. "I'm trying to help you, Owen. Don't you see? You're making a mistake."

My frustration grabbed the reigns of my tongue. "Stop. I already have one mother too many."

Ray Anne gaped at me for a second, then spun away from me. She rushed up her driveway and locked herself inside her garage apartment, even with me on her heels apologizing, begging her not to go.

I dragged my feet to my motorcycle. Ray Anne wasn't mad at me very often, but when she was, my whole world felt off.

It was two o'clock in the morning, and I had yet to fall asleep. I was desperate for the sun to hurry up and rise so I could go beg Ray Anne again to forgive me. She wasn't returning my texts.

I guess Daisy got sick of me tossing around on my mattress; she'd hopped down and settled for the floor. Lying on my back, I pressed my eyelids shut, willing myself to get some rest.

Even with my eyes closed, I could tell my night-light had flickered off. I popped up onto my elbows. Another burned-out bulb or . . . ?

I couldn't see a thing. I was reaching toward my cell on my night-stand when I felt the lower corner of my mattress dip, weighted down by something I couldn't see.

I sat straight up and pulled my knees into my chest, my heart thumping so hard beneath my sternum, I could feel it against my legs.

"Come."

The sound of the dead man's voice made me feel like my stomach was full of ice, like old times. My mattress sprang back up, then came the soft, swishing sound of the man striding out of my room. I fumbled to grab a candle and get it lit, then held it by my chin. I took one small, reluctant step at a time into the hallway, tormented by the thought that I might bump into him.

What would he do if I didn't follow? I was as scared to defy him as I was to obey.

I made it to the living room, trying to mentally piece together that verse out of Luke, wondering if it would work on a ghost and make him leave. But when my candle's flame extinguished without a gust, my concentration derailed.

"Give your eyes time to adjust, and you'll see me."

It took half a minute and a lot of blinking, but his form came into focus in the pale blue moonlight pouring in around the blinds in my window. He was seated on my sofa, on the corner farthest from me, a breathing shadow.

"Your heart is heavy tonight."

"Yes," I admitted. It was like I was living a nightmare. Or had been sucked into a scary movie where there was no way to distinguish special effects from reality.

"It's your mother. And Ray Anne as well. You've hurt and angered them both."

I swallowed hard even though my mouth was dry as chalk. "How do you know?"

"I know you well." He stayed completely still. "I'm often with you, even when you're unaware."

That's when I started trembling. There was no way a spiritual being could get near me without being seen. But I also couldn't deny the plaguing sense I often had that I wasn't alone.

"Come, sit with me."

I didn't want to, and he knew it.

"You've been warned to stay away from me. Those people have good intentions, but they've been taught to fear what they do not understand. Don't be like them."

That didn't sit well with me, the idea that I shouldn't aim to be like Gordon or Ray Anne. "Out of everyone I know, I admire them the most," I admitted.

"So much that you would surrender your destiny to their mere opinions?"

I would have needed time to come up with a rebuttal for that.

"I mean you no harm," the man said, beckoning me again to sit near him on the sofa. "I'm one of several messengers the Source has sent to you."

"The Source?"

"God, as you call him. Have a seat, Owen. Relax."

I wasn't about to sit next to a dead guy, but I did muster the courage to lower myself onto the edge of the lounge chair across from him. His silhouette was visible in the dark, but hard as I tried, I couldn't make out any defining features.

"Ask me anything," he said. "I'll withhold nothing from you."

Frightening as the experience was, I liked the sound of that. "What's your name?"

"As it is written in Isaiah 62, when we die and stand before the Source, he gives us a new name that far exceeds that bestowed by our parents. The Source calls me Faithful."

I felt like I was hallucinating, like I was strung out on mind-altering drugs even though I'd never taken any. "When did you become a ghost?"

"No, Owen. I'm not what you think of as a ghost. I'm spirit, made in the image of the Source, as are you and all of humanity."

I was still nervous but no longer shaking so noticeably. "How did you escape hell?" I was testing him. There was only one right answer.

"I surrendered to the Source—to the Cross—just as you have."

Correct. Slowly, I eased back into my chair, relaxing just enough to rest my fingertips on the armrests. "Why don't you have light?"

"Oh, but I do." Beneath his feet, a golden aura grew bright as fire.

I shielded my eyes. Then all went dark again.

"I have no need to bear light continuously like you do. I'm one with the Source now, untouchable by forces of darkness."

My heart was racing again, but mostly with invigoration. I'd prayed for answers, and I was getting them in heavy doses now, however unexpectedly. "What's the Source like?"

"Ahh . . ." He seemed to savor my question. "Powerful beyond description. And more forgiving than you can possibly comprehend. And the Source is self-contained, Owen, and has no need nor desire for love the way people do. Humanity craves love. Focus on extending compassion to mankind, and all you give and sacrifice will be reciprocated back to you."

There was no uncertainty in him, no vagueness or dodging my questions. So I asked more—many more. He was a patient listener, empathetic yet quick to correct my misconceptions. "Don't believe the lie that your mother is no longer worthy of your love," he instructed at one point. "Stop judging her, and you'll discover that the Source has placed an endless reservoir of mercy inside of you."

Over time, I'd developed a bond with Gordon, but this . . . this was a connection all its own. A whole other level. At no point was there any hint in this man of selfishness, impatience, boasting, arrogance—none of the negative qualities that sabotage relationships and appear on peoples' cords. I didn't claim to fully understand his existence, but as sunrise neared, I'd settled at least one thing: his motive toward me was good.

I could hardly believe it when the morning's first golden-orange hues pierced the windows. How had time passed so quickly? The man and I sat still, content to be quiet for a while. I wanted so badly to see his face, and finally, as black shadows lifted to gray, he began to come into focus. Dark hair. A defined jawline. Strong, young-looking hands.

The more the darkness surrendered to the light, the more intently he stared back at me. I got the feeling he was trying to tell me something, only not with words. As I beheld his face, becoming increasingly visible every minute, it was like an out-of-body experience. Like his heavenly realm had completely engulfed mine.

I became lost in the moment, suspended between the duality of the living and the departed. I was no longer aware of what day or time it was. I couldn't have told you much about anything in that moment, I'm sure, except one thing. The only thing that mattered.

I recognized the man sitting across from me.

ELEVEN

I WAS SO STUNNED I could hardly form the words. "I've seen you, in pictures."

"Yes. It's me, Owen."

My father.

He stood. "You have no idea how grateful I am to be given this time with you." Then he walked toward my front door, his image blurring and fading like night steadily giving way to dawn. I sat staring after him in awe.

Then I closed my eyes. "Thank you, God."

I said it over and over.

I woke that afternoon, a Wednesday, to Daisy's whines and her wet nose nudging my arm. Her bladder was probably about to explode. I'd been so in shock over the identity of my mysterious visitor that I'd forgotten to take her out before I fell asleep.

As I stood in the grass, getting soaked by a springtime shower while I waited on my dog to do her business, I texted Ray Anne: **Please accept my apology and I have something INCREDIBLE to tell you!!!**

I was so elated about last night's encounter, I feared it was too good to be true. Just a dream, maybe. But when my wet dog and I returned to my apartment, my candle was right where I'd set it when the wick went out. That was enough tangible proof for me.

I had to wait another hour before Ray Anne got out of class and I could tell her the awesome news. I knew she'd have a new attitude about the spirit man when she found out who he was. And hopefully she wouldn't hold yesterday's harsh words against me much longer. She'd always been fast to forgive.

I was too amped up to do anything productive. I kept replaying pieces of last night's conversation, rehearsing my father's wise words and sympathetic advice. He hadn't said he'd be coming back, but surely he would. Maybe he was somehow looking down on me right at that moment. The thought no longer scared me.

I was standing at my living room window, watching the downpour, when I had a radical idea. Was there a way to call my dad?

I knew that passage in Deuteronomy warned against consulting the dead, but that clearly didn't apply in this situation. My father had come to me, on assignment from God. I thanked the Lord again for sending him.

I knew if I called on my father and he showed up, he'd knock out the power, so I turned off all the lights and the TV to begin with. The soothing sound of rain made me sleepy all over again, but the chance of seeing my dad was all I needed to fight off exhaustion.

I sat in the same lounge chair as the night before. "Father . . . are you here?"

I waited.

"Please, come back."

He didn't leave me waiting long. He entered through the front door, passing through it like spiritual bodies do, and returned to his spot on the sofa. "The next time you seek me, light a candle. You've seen my face—I won't extinguish the flame ever again."

"Okay. Thank you for coming."

"Thank you for inviting me."

I lit my big three-wick candle and set it on the coffee table between us. I was still uneasy—this was all still so new—and I hated that he was bound to pick up on that. It felt rude.

Trying to cover my awkwardness, I asked about my mother, and he shared all kinds of things—how they'd met, what he'd liked about her, how he could barely eat or function after she'd walked out on him. For the life of me, I couldn't picture her with him—I guess because I'd never seen her with a good man.

"I didn't know I had a son until I crossed over," he said. "Nor that, to this day, your mother still loves me."

"How can you tell?"

"I feel what's in her heart." His smile looked like mine. "She still has the wedding ring I gave her. It's in a green box on the top shelf of her closet."

I wasn't surprised my mother had never told me about the ring. She was a vault of secrets.

Our conversation flowed effortlessly into the night. At one point, my dad congratulated me for having been such a strong athlete in high school, something I'd longed to hear from my father my entire life. But as much as I just wanted to sit and talk to him like a normal father and son, I had to make the most of having him here, with his wealth of supernatural information.

"Have you heard of Molek, the Lord of the Dead who claims this town as his territory?"

"Of course. He's known throughout the universe and by all in the vast expanses of the spirit realm."

"Did he name himself after that man-made idol in the Bible? The one people sacrificed children to?"

"No, Son. That detestable idol was named after him. He was there, receiving those sacrifices as offerings to himself."

The realization twisted my stomach into knots. "Do you know where he is right now?"

My father tilted his head back, as if he were pulling information from a database in the air. "He's patrolling another region for now, a mountainous area." He kept concentrating. "You know it as Colorado."

"What can Ray Anne and I do to stop him from coming back—to rid this town of him and his army for good?"

My dad sighed and shook his head. "How can you and Ray Anne conquer any foe—much less a force like Molek and his legion—if the two of you are divided?"

I felt heat creep up my neck as I remembered the way I'd spoken to Ray the night before. "I know I was harsh, but believe me, I'm going to keep apologizing to her, and I know we'll get back on track soon."

"I'm concerned that she's going to hurt you."

I shifted in my chair. "What do you mean?"

"You've made such sacrifices for her, suppressing your desires and conforming to her restrictive way of life. And yet, Owen, there's someone else she fantasizes about, envisions herself marrying."

It was like he'd buried an ax in my heart. "I don't understand. Who?"

"I'm sure it will be obvious to you very soon. Just be careful."

I stood. "You said you'd withhold nothing. What's his name?"

He formed that gentle, calming smile that was becoming familiar. "I'm not here to disrupt the natural course of your life, Son. Only to guide you as it unfolds, as long as you desire."

I lowered myself back into my chair, stunned, Ray Anne's betrayal throbbing like an open wound in my chest.

I wasn't afraid of my father—not really—but when he rose and walked toward me, I couldn't keep myself from tensing up. He stopped an arm's length away. "May I come closer?"

I liked that he respected me enough to ask for my consent. I said yes, of course. He approached my chair and leaned over me.

"It's okay," he whispered. "Rest." He held his palm above my forehead, and a menthol-like chill washed over my face, like I'd smeared VapoRub on my skin. I became tingly all over and wonderfully sleepy. "Remember what the wise proverb says, Owen. 'If you faint in the day of adversity, your faith is small.'"

I tried to nod, but my head felt too heavy. My eyelids collapsed.

I was completely disoriented when I woke. I didn't even know what day it was. My cell wouldn't power on. The power losses had somehow fried the battery.

It seemed like it should have still been dark outside, maybe early morning. But when I powered up my laptop, I saw that it was Thursday afternoon, and I was already late for my tutorial session. I hurried to get showered.

I was rushing down the stairwell outside my apartment when Ray Anne pulled up and exited her car without turning off the engine or closing the door. "Where have you been?" She hugged me tight. "My calls have gone straight to voice mail since yesterday—I've been so worried about you."

I put my arms around her, but it felt kind of weird, after what my father had shared. Still, I explained that I needed a new cell battery, then apologized again for the way I'd treated her the other night.

She squeezed my hands and stared up at me. "I can't stand it when we're mad at each other."

I hugged her again, but it only made my heart ache. "Ray Anne . . ." I started to ask her about the guy but decided to hold off on confronting her until I figured out who it was. I'd never seen her flirt with anyone but me.

"So what's the incredible thing you texted me about?" She was all smiles, our falling-out a thing of the past.

I was in danger of completely missing my tutorial by this point but too excited to put off telling her. "Ray Anne, you're never gonna guess who the man is—the one who appeared to me."

She crossed her arms and frowned. "He came back?"

"Yes, but it's not what you think. It's way cooler than you could imagine!" I couldn't have forced the grin off my face if I'd tried. "It's my father, Ray!"

At first she just stared at me silently, but that didn't last long. She started lecturing me again like she had the other night, this time using words like *danger*, *forbidden*, and—the real biggie—*abomination*. I couldn't believe what I was hearing. The more I tried to reason with her, the more spastic she got.

"But he can help us, Ray. He knows so much."

I tried to talk some sense into her, but all she did was insist I find a way to stop the visitations immediately and promise her I'd never interact with my father again.

Why couldn't she just be happy for me? Trust me to navigate the situation and determine what was right and wrong for myself?

After a few minutes of going back and forth but getting nowhere, I finally caved and promised to cut things off with my dad—as if I had a clue how to stop him from appearing whenever he wanted. That was enough for her to calm down and hug me again. I sighed with relief.

But I could hardly wait to call on my father again.

Ray and I weren't hitting on all cylinders, and for the first time, it felt like we were starting to drift apart. Like each of us had secret interests that excluded the other.

I hated it—but I had no idea how to fix it.

I rushed into Ms. Barnett's classroom twenty minutes late, figuring Hector and Riley would be long gone. Shockingly, they'd stayed. Riley sat at a lab table smacking her gum with her back to Hector. I asked them to fill me in on what they'd done in class, but no surprise, neither had paid attention.

Riley had no color in her cheeks and kept putting her hand over her mouth. Sick from her pregnancy, if I had to guess.

As I was reviewing how the periodic table works for the millionth time, I noticed Hector pulling something partway out of his pocket, rubbing his thumb over it, then concealing it again. A minute later, when he reached for his cell, an object fell out and hit the floor—some kind of light-purple crystal trinket thing. Hector picked it up fast and shoved it back in his jeans.

"Careful! You don't want to lose your precious *vocatus*," Riley taunted him.

He shoved his face in hers. "Shut up."

I held my hand between them. "Hey, chill out, guys."

Hector glared at me but finally sat back, away from Riley.

"What's a vocatus?" I recognized it as Latin, but I couldn't recall the meaning.

He crossed his arms and smirked, looking me up and down. "Ain't none of your business." That's the PG version.

"Oh, come on, Hector. Tell him where you got it." Riley leaned toward me, then spoke in a loud, dramatic whisper. "That older girl he likes gave it to him, so it's super special." Hector stared her down, jaw clenched, popping one knuckle at a time.

She huffed. "What? You think I'm scared of you?"

"You oughta be." Hector was a skinny guy, not exactly threatening. But there was something in his eyes . . .

I knew evil when I saw it.

"Riley—"

I wanted to tell her to chill, but she got up in his face. "You can't do anything to me."

I stood, expecting to have to keep Hector from shoving her. But this time he stayed planted in his chair, his expression more matter-of-fact than irate. "Girl, you're gonna regret every word you just said."

"Is that a threat?" she asked.

"More like a curse."

And that's when I learned that a curse is a real thing. As in, *alive*.

TWELVE

Something crept out of the corner of Hector's mouth. A black, tube-like creature about as thick as a garden hose, squirming against his cheek. And it kept coming—a foot long, then two—emerging from between his teeth, then slithering down his shackled neck, beneath his shirt collar. It was all I could do to keep from puking.

Finally, the thing cleared Hector's mouth. I swear, it was four feet long.

Riley huffed and plopped back down in her chair, and Hector started typing on his cell like nothing had happened—as if he hadn't just spit out a monster.

I watched with my jaw gaping as the thing kept snaking down under Hector's clothes.

Riley must have seen the look on my face. "Hey, are you okay?"

Then Hector. "What's your problem?"

"Um . . ." How many times did I have to endure this? Trying to explain the unexplainable?

Ms. Barnett stopped by her classroom. "Hector, Ms. Keith wants to see you about your research paper. Go ahead and go."

With a final scathing look at me, then Riley, he stood and walked to the door. As if I wasn't already worked up enough, I endured another jolt of adrenaline when the giant black parasite crept out from Hector's pant leg, slithering onto the floor. It had no eyes or scales, but it did have a serpent's mouth—forked tongue flickering in and out. It was coming straight toward us.

No . . . toward Riley.

"Move!" I tried to pull her away, but she stood and jerked her arm out of my grasp.

"What are you doing?"

I stepped toward the serpent thing, but it dove down through the floor, slithering beneath the tiles. It was like watching a fat water moccasin swim just below the tide. It resurfaced beyond my aura, within striking distance of Riley, and squirmed forward, brushing over her shoe and climbing up her leg.

How was this possible? Hector's flippant curse had come to life.

"Are you going to Spring Scream next Friday?" Riley was talking about the costume party again, as if we weren't smack in the middle of something really worth screaming over.

"Riley!" I couldn't help it—I pointed at it. Then I dared to grab it off her, but my fingers passed through it like it was only a shadow. The same way Meagan's trembling hand had gone through mine.

Riley gave me a playful, flirtatious push. "What's your deal?"

The thing slithered up her thigh, over her high-waisted jeans, then began climbing her fitted shirt.

I cupped my hands over my mouth, holding my breath.

What was that passage? Luke nineteen. No, chapter ten, verse nineteen. Something like that . . .

Think, Owen!

The serpent thing caressed Riley's shackle, working toward her chin.

"The enemy . . . I mean, all power over the enemy has been given to me, and . . . you can't . . ."

Riley plopped down on the lab table and held her cell in front of my face. "Congrats. You're on my story, weirdo."

Her lips were barely parted, but I watched in revulsion as the slimy intruder pried its way through them, burrowing inside her mouth twice as fast as it had left Hector's.

Is it sliding down her throat?

"Riley . . ." What would that thing do to her now—to the infant soul she carried? "I'm sorry." It was my job to stop evil, and I'd failed.

She was engrossed in her cell. "Don't worry about me. Hector's all talk."

I came close, eyeing her mouth. "You should stay away from him." It was like I was back in high school, begging Jess to beware of Dan. "Hector's dangerous."

She scoffed. "Give me a break. That stuff's stupid."

"What stuff?"

She paused to send a text, then told me about a new meditation and relaxation class that Principal Harding hoped would teach kids to cope better, aka, not kill themselves. "We do breathing patterns, mental focus exercises—just different stuff," Riley said. "The instructor has us get completely still and silent and listen for our inner voice."

"Okay?"

"We can go to that class instead of PE, so duh? Lots of us go. And I mean, it's kind of cool. When we all close our eyes and focus on the energy in the air, it feels like the temperature in the room drops." Riley had no clue that a sudden paranormal dip in temperature was a bad sign. "A few weeks ago, the instructor started handpicking some of her favorites and inviting them to do stuff after school. Guys, mostly."

"Including Hector?"

"Yeah."

I waited while she returned another text.

"Anyway, he was so proud he'd earned that vocatus from the instructor, but it's some big secret how he got it—he won't tell. All I know is, he's different now. He's on some power trip 'cause Miss Snow pays attention to him. He's a 'chosen one.'" She made air quotes with her fingers and rolled her eyes. "So moronic."

Riley exhaled and slumped her shoulders, frowning now. "Hector thinks she's beautiful. All the guys do." She scrolled through her camera roll, then held her phone in my face. "Miss Snow."

The instructor was beautiful, all right—especially in an image, where shackles and chains and cords didn't show. But then again, I already knew she was gorgeous.

Because I knew Veronica.

What were the odds?

I climbed onto my motorcycle in the school parking lot and searched the word *vocatus* on my phone. I was right—Latin: *an urgent call; to summon or invite.*

Hector wasn't willing to talk about it, but maybe Veronica would. I figured she'd come around soon enough. What was she pushing on these students?

By the time I'd gotten my cell battery replaced, grabbed some food, and taken an online quiz I hadn't studied for, it was almost seven o'clock, and people were about to fill my living room, Bibles in hand, like they did every Thursday evening. I had twenty minutes to spare and wondered if that was enough time to call on my father and get his advice on some things. I saw it for what it was—a growing dependence—but guys rely on their fathers, right? I mean, guys who have one.

Granted, mine was speaking from beyond the grave.

I glanced at the clock again and decided to wait until the meeting was over.

I waited in the parking lot for Ray Anne, hoping she'd come a few minutes early like she usually did. Hoping she still wanted to be with me. I still had that troubling, uneasy feeling, like something wasn't right, but I wasn't any closer to knowing what to do about it. Finally, Ray Anne parked and approached me, and I squeezed her in my arms, silently begging God to keep us together.

Mr. Church Boy, Ethan, headed our way, aura glistening around his preppy loafers. "Hey, Ray Anne." His smile reminded me of a Ken doll—annoyingly perfect and chipper. I searched Ray's face. Could *he* be the one?

Ethan handed me a bag of Chex Mix, then struck up a conversation with Ray, leaving me to walk behind them. It's not like I blamed him for being attracted to her—I'd clued in to that a while back—but being so obvious about it right in front of my face was kind of low. I just held out hope that she didn't feel that way about him.

We went inside, and Ethan made a joke about the flies in my apartment. I blew it off and set the bag of Chex Mix on the kitchen bar as he continued chitchatting with my girlfriend. It felt like I'd swallowed something rotten when I saw her chuckling, playing with a strand of her curled hair, overly amused by Ethan's lame story.

How had I missed it? Completely overlooked the chemistry between them?

I wanted to push Ethan out the door, then hurl him off my third-story balcony, but I was sure even *that* wouldn't have wrinkled his perfectly starched polo shirt and khakis. Besides, all he had to do was land on his mammoth-sized Bible and he'd be fine. Not a broken bone or scratch on his pretty-boy face.

More people arrived, and at one point, I realized I was squeezing a can of ginger ale so hard it was deforming. I'd never felt jealousy like this. It was painful, like a malignant tumor filling my chest cavity.

Gordon arrived and asked me how I was doing. I said I was fine, even though I was in agony as his son and Ray Anne stayed so engrossed with each other they didn't even acknowledge the other people arriving. Sixteen total—a mix of shackles and Lights.

When it was time for the meeting to start, I sat next to Ray on the sofa. Gordon asked who would like to open in prayer but didn't glance my way. You'll never guess who volunteered.

As Ethan launched into an eloquent display of spirituality—eyes closed and head bowed—I spied on Ray Anne. Her head was bowed too, but then she looked up. At him.

I bit down on my bottom lip.

The group had just said amen when there was a knock at my door. I got up and answered—it was Veronica, dressed in a pale-pink sweater that struck me as way too soft and modest for her taste.

"Hey. Just returning these." She handed me the green-handled scissors, then looked past me at my guests. "Oh, I'm sorry—am I interrupting?" She stood there all wide eyed, like a puppy on adoption day.

Gordon stood. "Owen, would you like to introduce your friend?"

No, but . . . I opened the door wider. "Guys, this is Veronica Snow."

She didn't seem to notice that I just *happened* to know her last name. Everyone voiced a hello except Ray Anne. Was it wrong that I liked that she might feel some jealousy over me?

Gordon was his usual overly welcoming self. "Owen, should we invite Veronica to join us?" He was big on teaching us to include people.

Before I even agreed, Veronica walked over to the empty spot on the sofa next to Ray Anne. I had to settle for a chair in the back of the room, at my breakfast table.

Ray Anne shared her Bible with Veronica as Gordon taught on the parable of the Prodigal Son and then posed questions to the group. I found it interesting that tonight's topic was about a son reuniting with his father. A sign from God to me, maybe?

As usual, Ethan captivated the room with his profound knowledge of all things Bible, making a stunning comparison between physical and spiritual blindness. Ray Anne hung on his every word like a padawan at the feet of Obi-Wan Kenobi.

My father had been right—and Ethan was the one, the contender ripping her heart away from me.

By the time the discussion was winding down, my face was hot, and my shirt collar felt tight.

What's the matter, Owen? You seem agitated.

There it was again—Veronica's voice trespassing in my head. She was looking at me, but her mouth wasn't moving.

Stop it.

She looked away, and all was quiet in my head.

But I couldn't leave it alone. *How are you doing that?* I directed my thoughts toward her, as messed up as that sounds.

I have a gift, remember?

I saw something now, a blurry streak that reminded me of how gas fumes can make the air look like it's boiling. It shot from her to me as quickly as her remark hit my brain.

I knew it was probably a bad idea, but we kept talking—communicating as if we were conversing out loud, the freaky force field traveling back and forth between us. Ray Anne might have seen it if she'd looked at me at all.

And how totally crazy is this? All I had to do was envision that crystal Hector had, and Veronica "said," *Ah. A vocatus.*

What's it for?

Wouldn't you like to know. She winked at me. *You want one?*

I want you to tell me about it.

Just tell you? It doesn't work like that. You should come to my class sometime.

So she somehow knew I'd already been made aware of her class.

How cool is this, Owen? You and me, connecting on a higher, intimate, spiritual level?

That made me think of my father. I tried not to envision him and worked to hide the image of his face from her, but I was helpless to suppress it.

She looked at me, eyebrows raised in excitement. *He was here, visiting with you, wasn't he?*

Yes, I reluctantly responded, resenting that my soul felt naked and on display before her. *You know him?*

Didn't I tell you? She spoke loud and clear inside my head. *Someone who missed you was hoping to see you.*

"What do you think, Owen?" Gordon's question prompted the whole group to look at me.

"Um . . ." I had no idea what they were talking about. I floundered, trying to come up with something halfway intelligent to say, but how could I? Ray Anne stared at the pen in her hands, rolling it back and forth, humiliated, I'm sure, to have such a moron for a boyfriend. I needed to make my best impression on her right now, not be an epic disappointment.

I glared at Veronica as she scanned Ray Anne's open Bible. If she hadn't intruded on my mind, I wouldn't have been in that situation to begin with. Gordon must have sensed my uneasiness. He called on someone else. I kept watching Veronica, wondering what she was whispering to Ray Anne. I tried to tap into her thoughts, but it wasn't working now.

I bolted into the bathroom and locked the door.

Are you okay? She was in my head again.

Quit it! Leave me alone.

I splashed cold water on my face until I sensed she was truly gone from my psyche. I couldn't wait to get her out of my apartment, too. By the time I left the bathroom, the meeting was over, and people were socializing and starting to leave. Veronica was talking to one of the guys, a Light who'd recently graduated from Texas Tech, and eventually, she followed him and the flow of people out the door.

Finally, it was just Ray and me. She was putting her belongings in her Vera Bradley bag, getting ready to go. I only knew the name brand of her bag, by the way, because I'd bought it for her.

"What was Veronica saying to you?" I asked.

"She said she was sorry for upsetting me the other day." Ray Anne pulled a silver necklace from her purse. "Then she gave me this—like, as a token of her apology." Ray held up the long chain, and an ornate, antique-looking locket swung back and forth. "Kind of weird, huh?"

Veronica was so weird, I didn't even know where to begin—especially with Ray. She was already unhappy about the father visitation stuff; what would she have done if I'd have told her about my telepathic conversations with Veronica?

Ray Anne studied the locket, running her fingers over the swirly pattern. "It's really old fashioned." Hard as she tried, she couldn't get the locket open. I felt like a loser when I couldn't either.

"Oh well." She dropped it in her purse. "Maybe my mom will want it."

It was nice to see that she still wore my necklace. Surely that meant Ethan hadn't stolen her heart completely.

I blurted it out: "Ray, there's no one else you'd rather be with besides me, right?"

She smiled and huffed like I was being ridiculous. "Of course not."

I liked the sound of that but struggled to believe it. "It's just that you and Ethan seem really . . . drawn to each other."

She grabbed my shirt sleeve. "He's a friend, Owen. That's all." But then she got her serious, crinkled-brow expression. "It's you I'm worried about."

"Why?"

She let go of me and crossed her arms. "You weren't being up front with me earlier, were you? When you promised to stop communicating with that spirit?"

I frowned. First of all, he was my father, not some spirit, and second, that look of disappointment on her face wasn't fair. I hadn't done anything wrong. But I always said and did what it took to make Ray Anne happy. I couldn't be honest, not if I wanted to stand a chance at keeping her as my girlfriend.

I was about to reaffirm my less-than-sincere promise when she prodded, "Please, Owen, don't lie to me about this."

I sighed, contemplating how to find some middle ground. "Well . . . what if I'm not quite ready to completely cut him out of my life just yet?"

Not middle ground enough. She scowled and started rummaging through her purse, hunting for her keys like she couldn't wait to leave. It wasn't like her to let things go unresolved.

"Don't you want to talk about this?" I asked.

"Yeah, but I have to go. My study group is meeting at Starbucks." She turned and opened my front door. "Besides, you've made up your mind. I don't think you really want to listen to why it bothers me anyway."

I followed her out my front door, onto the balcony. "I do, I just . . . this experience is one of the most significant things that's ever happened to me, Ray."

She faced me. "That makes it worth lying to me about it?"

"I'm sorry." What else was I supposed to say?

She attempted to smile but couldn't fake it. "That's just it, Owen. I don't think you are." She fiddled with her keys a moment. "It wouldn't bother me if I didn't care about you so much."

She turned to go, and for once, I didn't chase after her—just stood on the balcony and watched her drive away. I caught a whiff, then a glimpse, of Demise spying up at me from the bottom stairwell. I slammed my door and locked the dead bolt, refusing to give evil the attention it wanted.

I sat in my quiet apartment, thinking. Praying . . .

"God, show me what to do."

I could call on my father, and I was sure he'd be there for me.

Or I could go to Starbucks, pull Ray Anne away from her study group, and listen to her with a really open mind this time. Even if she failed to convince me, I owed her that much.

It didn't take long to decide. I sped to Starbucks, parked next to Ray Anne's Toyota, then hurried toward the door.

And there she was, at a table with Ethan. Just the two of them.

THIRTEEN

I DIDN'T BOTHER GOING inside or letting Ray Anne and Ethan see me. I gave them the space they clearly wanted and drove home fast, running red lights.

I barged inside my apartment and gathered all my candles, way too on edge to sit still or pray or—God forbid—cry. I lit the wicks, then paced my dark living room. "Father, please come."

That was all it took.

"Oh, how I wish I could have spared you this pain, Son."

This time he emerged from my kitchen. We stood face to face. Man to man.

"Does she love him?"

He gave a single, confident nod, crushing the last shred of hope I had. "Her heart has turned away from you completely tonight. And she desires to turn you away from me."

"I won't let that happen."

He grinned. "Of course not. Loyalty runs in your veins. And Owen, there's a way you can recapture her heart. Win her back and even change her feelings toward me."

"How?"

He pointed to the desk across my living room without turning his head. "Open the drawer and remove the blue pen and a sheet of paper."

I thought he'd give an explanation, but he just waited in silence, so I did as he said.

"136 Sycamore Lane."

I wrote it down.

"Go there tomorrow, at midnight. When you arrive, turn right and park at the end of the road. Then wait under the oak tree."

He turned and strode toward my living room window. "Don't be late." He passed through the window. I peered through the blinds, but there was no sign of him—just a random Creeper stalking a guy in the parking lot.

"Father, come back. I have more questions." I asked a couple of times, but he didn't return. I told myself not to take it personally. I was sure he had his reasons.

I powered up my cell phone and sent Ray Anne an impulsive text: **My father was right about you.** Then I silenced it and slammed it facedown on the coffee table, almost hoping it would break.

I lay on my sofa, lonely, tempted to despair. My living room was a soothing yet unsettling mix of candlelight and shadows. All was quiet, except for that unnerving sound of rustling inside the walls.

I could have used the comfort of Custos's presence. Why hadn't he come around the last couple of days?

At least I had Daisy. I called for my dog, but she didn't come to me. That was a first.

I sat up and flipped on a lamp, then called to her again. Still no sign of her.

I looked around—behind the sofa, under my bed—but she wasn't there. I turned on my kitchen light and finally spotted her hunkered in the corner by the pantry, trembling all over.

"Daisy . . ." I tried petting her, but she still shook inconsolably.

My father came from the kitchen tonight.

I'd been taking comfort in the fact that my dog had never growled or barked at him, but it had never occurred to me that maybe it was only because she was paralyzed with fear.

I sank to the floor and tapped the back of my head against a kitchen cabinet over and over, as confused as I'd ever been.

Friday was a beautiful, sunny day, but it didn't cure the loneliness bearing down on me. It seemed like it had been forever since I'd had a close guy friend to hang with, but it was my discovery that Ray Anne was falling for someone else that was causing the most agony.

She called multiple times that morning, but I ignored it. Then she showed up at my door.

"What's going on?" She walked past me and stood in the center of my living room with her hands on her hips. She stared at last night's burnt candles scattered on the floor. "So . . . you're into séances now?"

"So you're into cheating now?" I yelled.

"What are you talking about?" She put on a shocked, innocent face.

"I saw you with Ethan last night. Nice study group."

She reached toward me. "No, you've got it all wrong." Her tone was soft and persuasive. "You know Ethan's doing his residency at Central Hospital. He was there last night to help our group with some calculations in our pharmaceutical class. But no one showed up but me." She forced her fingers between my folded arms. "We talked for a while—mainly about my classes and his hospital rotations—then we left. It was nothing."

I wanted to believe her, but I could hardly look her in the face.

"Why'd your text say your father was right about me?"

I was getting tired of constantly downplaying truth to keep her happy. So for once, I didn't. "He says you have a divided heart. That you fantasize about marrying someone else."

She let go of me and stepped away, averting her eyes. "No . . . I . . . that's not fair."

"It's true, isn't it?"

She meandered to my sofa and sat, staring into the distance. "Okay, it's true that I have *thought* about it, but—"

"About Ethan?"

She lowered her head and sighed. "Yes. I've allowed my mind to wander and think about what it would be like to be with him—I admit that. But I always end up coming to the same conclusion." She stood and came close again. "He'll probably make someone very happy someday, but he's not the one for me. I was convinced that you were." Sadness poured over her face. "But I feel like I don't know you lately, Owen. Like you're into things that are scary and dark and losing interest in the right things."

I hesitated, but then gave myself permission to be completely transparent. "Ray, what if I'm not cut out for church? What if I want to relate to God in my own way—a way that happens to be a little different than you and Gordon and . . ." I didn't want to say Ethan's name. "And what if I *do* think it's a waste of time to get baptized and sing hymns and take Communion? I mean, it's wafers and grape juice, for crying out loud." I clutched her shoulders. "I don't have all the answers, but I'm sincerely looking, Ray Anne. I'm exploring what comes my way—can't you accept that?" I pulled her toward me. "Can't you still care about me?"

"Of course." She didn't hesitate. "But as for our future . . ." She shook her head.

"Why?" I threw my hands up. "You see that I'm a Light, that I have God in my life—why do I have to jump through hoops to earn your approval?"

"They're not hoops, Owen." She raised her voice too now. "They're important aspects of a life of faith."

"I don't see it that way." Finally, I'd come clean.

Her eyes pooled. "I know."

We stared at one another with longing, both wanting what the other wouldn't give.

"I can't keep pretending to be someone I'm not just to make you happy, Ray Anne."

"No." She wiped her eye before a tear could escape. "You can't."

We both knew what this was—that we now stood on opposite sides of a mile-wide chasm that demanded a breakup. But I wasn't willing to say it. Neither was she.

"I'll see you at Betty's tonight." She made her way out the door.

"Want to ride together?" I was already battling regret.

"I think we should probably just meet there."

"Fine."

She left, and I collapsed into my lounge chair, wishing I could rewind the last ten minutes and do things differently, but the longer I moped, the more I realized I was acting just like my mother.

How many times had I seen her alter her personality in a pathetic attempt to keep some guy from leaving? It never worked. And yet I'd been living like my world would implode if Ray Anne didn't stand by me.

I still didn't want to lose her, but I made up my mind. I was no longer willing to lose myself to keep her.

It was freeing.

And excruciating.

Betty's house was small but nicely decorated with bright colors and so spotlessly cleaned, even I noticed.

Ray Anne was already seated at the dinner table when I arrived. I sat next to her, enduring the awkward silence that now hovered like a fog between us. Betty's grandmother sat across from me—she said Ray Anne and I could call her Dorothy. Betty called her Dot. She was a tiny, wrinkly old woman who looked a century old. Maybe more. Her brown eyes were cloudy, and she felt all over the table for her silverware, then her cup, straining not to spill.

Betty had prepared a delicious meal that we all enjoyed between periods of talking too much to take bites. Ray and I learned that Betty had never been married and had no children of her own, but she'd grown close to many of her students during the nineteen years she'd worked as a professor at Louisiana State University. As for Dorothy, she didn't say much—just tapped her plate with her fork, searching for more chicken and potatoes.

After Ray Anne complimented Betty on her homemade peach pie, Betty pushed away from the table and stood. "Now, did you two come over to chitchat or to hear my great-great-granddaddy Arthur's astounding life account?"

Ray Anne shot out of her chair. "We want to hear it!"

Betty looked at Dorothy, who grinned at all of us. "Dot tells the story best," Betty said. "She heard it directly from her grandfather—from Arthur."

Betty and Ray Anne helped Dorothy scoot her walker about an inch at a time to a wingback chair in the living room, then braced her as she eased onto the seat cushion, adjusting her granny gown to cover her legs. Ray and I sat on the floor by Dorothy's pink house shoes and surrounding glow like preschoolers at show-and-tell.

Dorothy stared into the distance and spoke slowly, as if each word was of great importance—which it was to Ray and me. Her voice was so soft and wavering that we had to hold our breath and lean forward to catch her words, but the story . . .

I was completely fascinated. And horrified.

FOURTEEN

"My granddaddy told me this story lots of times and made me promise never to forget it." Dorothy lifted a shaky finger. "Not to forget a single part—and never tell it to the wrong people."

Betty smiled at Ray and me from the sofa. "Like I told you, Dot, I believe these two are the right people."

I was definitely grateful that we were about to hear this, but Ray Anne looked so over-the-top happy, I thought she might start clapping. We hung on Dorothy's every word.

She told us that Arthur was born in 1879 in a one-room shanty—kind of like a run-down shack—on Caldwell's plantation in Masonville. My property, but I had yet to tell Betty that. "Master Caldwell bought and traded people like folks do nowadays with baseball cards."

Had Dorothy's statement not been so troubling, I might have smiled at her outdated analogy.

She described T. J. Caldwell as a bloodthirsty man with eight children—three ruthless daughters and five violent sons who treated black people like animals, barely providing for their most basic needs. "If the slaves got sick or hurt, it was a death sentence. Same if they tried to run."

Dorothy's shoulders hunched as she explained how Caldwell would make examples out of runaways, executing them and any family they'd left behind just for daring to try to live free.

Ray and I learned that, as a small boy, Arthur was put to work with his parents and siblings, doing hard physical labor from sunup to sundown, polishing shoes and saddles and whatever else needed to be shined—also cutting down trees and piling logs and doing every kind of chore related to Caldwell's household and livestock. He wasn't paid at all, obviously, and was just fed measly table scraps more suitable for hogs than humans. But like the others suffering under Caldwell's tyranny, Arthur's family saw no way out.

"Some of them got so beat down, they took their own lives," Dorothy said.

Ray cut her eyes at me.

"But Arthur's mama and daddy, they made up their minds to be strong for their children."

Young Arthur couldn't read or write and didn't own a single book, but his mother knew some psalms by heart. Her words would soothe Arthur to sleep, even though he didn't have a mattress or pillow or blanket.

The only break Arthur ever got from his hellish life was when he'd dare to sneak across Caldwell's property on Saturday nights and meet up with a group of kids—maybe twenty of them—who gathered deep in the woods, "around a dry well," Dorothy said.

Ray and I looked at each other, wide eyed.

"White kids came from neighboring farms, and black kids came from Caldwell's place. They were good friends, those children—had none of that hate grown-ups had in their hearts."

Eight-year-old Arthur and his little sister Pearl were among the youngest in the group, Dorothy explained. The black kids taught the white kids gospel songs while the white kids passed along leftovers from dinner and things like socks and medicated ointment when they could. Sometimes the kids would say prayers, but mainly they swapped stories and played around as friends, often dreaming up ways, however unrealistic, to stop Caldwell and his abuse.

Dorothy closed her eyes a moment and took a deep breath.

Then she explained how, one scorching day in July, Caldwell brought home several black children, all bound by chains to his horse-drawn wagon. They'd been forced to run for miles; to slip or faint meant getting dragged over unpaved roads. "Nothin' new, except these little ones were all sick and starving—come straight from the African slave trade." Ray Anne had to ask for a tissue when Dorothy told us the kids were too dehydrated even to cry.

Caldwell put ropes around the new arrivals' necks and pulled them along like dogs, shoving them into a vile cage he kept on a concrete auction block not far from the Caldwell family cemetery. I shuddered at the thought that the graveyard might still be somewhere on my property. The cage was an iron-barred death trap designed to imprison human beings until they were sold to the highest bidder. The ones who survived, anyway. I'd known my ancestor Caldwell had been a monster, but this . . . I was speechless.

Caldwell gave the caged children nothing—no food or water—and no one dared risk trying to help them.

The next night, when the group of kids met up at the well in the woods, the plantation kids told their friends about the caged children and asked for help. The white kids handed over some morsels of food they'd brought, and Pearl hid them in her tattered apron. But the kids hadn't brought anything to drink. "Those kids gathered round that bone-dry well and prayed for a miracle." Dorothy sniffled, and her blind eyes swelled with moisture. "But nothing happened."

She explained how some redheaded boy suggested they take Communion; the enslaved children had never done such a thing. The boy led them through the steps as well as a little kid could. They all pretended to eat bread and drink wine, saving the food they had while swallowing the only thing in their hands—air. "Then the kids prayed one more thing." Dorothy looked down toward us even though she couldn't see. "They said, 'Lord, let Caldwell's eyes be opened so he'll finally see and regret the evil he's doing to people.'"

Ray Anne grabbed my hand, and we both squeezed.

According to Arthur's account, right then, a sloshing sound began stirring under their feet. Shocked but excited, Arthur hopped up and turned the crank on the dry well—and up came a bucket full of water.

Arthur filled some glass bottles the kids had found discarded in the brush and vowed to come back soon with clay jugs to get more. He and Pearl ran as fast as they could go, ahead of the others, arriving at the plantation at sunrise and rushing to the cage. The children inside could barely lift their heads.

Little Pearl began handing out bits of food, but as Arthur extended a glass bottle of water, Caldwell's oldest son—a strong and ruthless young man—rushed over and kicked Arthur in the side of the head. Arthur yelled for Pearl to run, but she refused to leave his side.

"So brave," Ray Anne almost gasped.

Dorothy described how T. J. Caldwell came charging over on his horse, joined by three more of his sons. Together they snatched the food away from Pearl and devoured it themselves, laughing about how those who don't work shouldn't eat. Then Caldwell demanded that Arthur hand over the bottles of water, but the boy defied him, flat out refusing. That's when Caldwell seized Pearl and Arthur, ready to punish them by the harshest of means.

Arthur and Pearl's father came running, their mother too, and soon a crowd gathered—the slaves shouting and begging for Caldwell to relent, while Caldwell's sons insisted he show no mercy.

Ray and I sat still as statues as Dorothy sighed, then folded her delicate arms into her chest. Betty stood and wrapped a throw blanket around her grandmother's shoulders. "Arthur wouldn't say exactly what happened next," Betty explained. "Only that Caldwell doubled over in agony and collapsed to the ground."

Both Ray and I knew *exactly* what had happened. T. J. Caldwell had to have drunk some of the well water. He'd probably ripped a bottle from Arthur and guzzled it down as a demented form of torture against the painfully thirsty caged children.

"Soon Caldwell started raging," Dorothy said, "talking about beasts all round him. He begged for mercy and told his sons to let the slaves go free. But those boys wouldn't do it."

Betty took over for Dorothy, explaining how, during Caldwell's rant, as the angry mob swelled, Arthur's father managed to grab Arthur and tell him to run, to hide in the woods until it was safe to come back—if it ever was.

So that's what Arthur did, even though it meant leaving his injured little sister behind.

Dorothy cleared her throat and attempted to sit up taller, but she kept her eyes closed. "When Arthur came back some few days after, most of the blacks were gone—others were dead, their battered bodies scattered round the property. Caldwell was lying dead in the dirt too. Folks said he fell dead the day Arthur left." The water had killed him, no doubt. "And Arthur saw the monsters too. Roaming all round Caldwell's land. Climbing up 'n' down trees and in and out of the main house. Moving above his head in the air too."

Arthur had obviously swallowed the water—either from one of the bottles or the well itself.

Dorothy pointed toward her house shoes. "He saw light shining round his feet, and those creatures didn't come near him, but he saw Caldwell's sons and daughters with chains and tails in their heads and shackles round their necks, gettin' tortured by evil without them realizing."

I'd already learned a lot, but this next part was key. Dorothy trembled as she told us that as Arthur spied on the scene, he saw Caldwell's daughters do some kind of strange ritual around a bonfire, trampling chicken bones and splattering goats' blood on the grass. He refused to ever speak of what he saw the young ladies do next.

"But Arthur said what he saw after that was almost as bad." Dorothy clung to the quilted blanket draped around her. "A giant devil came down from the air and stood in the fire. Skin pale as death. Long, milk-white hair. Eyes filled with enough terror to make a grown man holler. And he brought lots more of those monsters with him."

"His name's Molek," I said with certainty.

Dorothy glanced my way but kept going. "That wicked thing roared like a beast, and the rest of the evil spirits fell facedown around him and those women—those witches."

"So . . ." I needed to process things out loud. "Creepers were drawn to the land because of all the hatred and violence and death. But Molek showed up and brought even more when Caldwell's daughters did that weird bones-and-blood stuff."

Betty nodded.

I didn't know if Ray Anne had come to the same conclusion as me, but I felt sure I knew the unspeakable thing Arthur had witnessed—the act that had drawn Molek to Masonville and incited his preoccupation with Caldwell's property. It was the same unthinkable act that had drawn him to the land of Canaan thousands of years ago, like I'd read about in the Bible. But like Arthur, I didn't want to bring it up.

We all stood, except Dorothy, and Ray Anne leaned in to Betty's embrace. I felt like I might dry heave as I admitted, "The Caldwells were my ancestors. I own all that land now."

Dorothy reached toward me, and I lowered to one knee in front of her, letting her take my hand and pat it. "You've got the chance to do right with that land now, young man."

"She's right," Betty said. Then she added, "The Caldwells' plantation home was eventually leveled. Now the high school sits in its place."

Whoa. There really were no coincidences.

Ray Anne swayed back and forth, too keyed up to stand still. She pulled out the list of questions she'd brought. "Where do you think Molek has gone? We haven't seen him since our senior year, but we don't know where he went or when he'll return."

"I knew it." Betty angled her face toward the heavens and smiled. "Think about it. The day that boy shot up the school, it was on every news channel across the nation. People of faith from coast to coast hit their knees, lifting up Masonville High, and some of us have never stopped. If Molek's gone from Caldwell's old land, it's prayer that kicked him out."

I had a ton of respect for Betty, and it couldn't be denied that she had a lot of wisdom about spiritual things, but I wasn't convinced she was right this time. Based on my father's firsthand knowledge, Molek had left Masonville of his own volition to go hunt souls in Colorado.

Now wasn't the time to explain where I'd gotten my intel, so all I said was, "Maybe Molek left on his own—you know, to tend to another one of his territories."

"No, young man." Betty furrowed her brow at me. "If you haven't seen the reigning spirit of death at that school, you can be sure he's trying *everything* to get back on that property—stalking and searching for any possible entrance point."

"What do you mean?" Ray asked.

"A vulnerable soul or two with hearts consumed by darkness, who'll call him back to the land."

I actually took comfort in that. "We're the only ones who even know his name, so that won't be an issue."

Betty patted my shoulder. "Things aren't always so simple, young man."

Exactly. She had no way of knowing I was getting inside information from a contact immersed in the supernatural realm.

That's when Betty, Ray, and I noticed that Dorothy was holding her wobbly hand in the air, trying to get our attention. Her mouth was hanging open, like she'd gotten some shocking news.

"What is it, Dot?" Betty asked her.

"Did you just say that the spirit of death left this place?"

"Yes," Ray Anne said.

Dorothy shrank even lower in her chair. "Betty? I need to talk to you. Alone."

Ray Anne and I looked at each other. I could tell she wanted to hear what else Dorothy might have to say as much as I did, but we clearly weren't invited.

Betty apologized for the abrupt good-bye and said she'd be in touch very soon. "And by the way—" She stopped Ray and me as we were headed out the door. "Arthur always warned that no one should seek out that well. I'll never ask you where it is."

We thanked her, and she hugged us both.

I walked Ray Anne to her car and opened the door for her as she fiddled with her keys, stalling. "That was a lot to take in, huh?" she said.

"Yeah. We should talk things through. Sometime soon, I mean." Even though we were standing only a few feet from each other, it felt like there were miles between us. It wasn't right. "You and me—we need each other, Ray Anne."

She smiled—the sad kind of smile where a person wants to look happy but can't. "I was about to say the same thing."

I hugged her, wishing I could hang on forever. "I'm still committed to our mission," I told her. "And to you."

She nodded. "I needed to hear that."

As she drove away, a tiny spark of hope flared in my heart—maybe our relationship could still get back to normal.

I got onto my bike, grateful that the answers Ray Anne and I had prayed for were finally coming to us. Arthur's story was depressing and tragic, but also invigorating. It was like we were part of a legacy, not just lone rangers in our bizarre, extrasensory world.

I was back at my apartment, typing newly discovered facts into a notes app on my cell when I happened to pay attention to the time—nine minutes until midnight. And that's when I remembered, 136 Sycamore Lane. Could I even get there in time?

I had no idea why my father had given me that address or what going there had to do with helping me win Ray back, but I typed it into my GPS, willing to check it out.

I pulled up at 12:03 a.m., killed my engine, and slid my helmet off. *No. Way.*

FIFTEEN

Masonville Memorial Funeral Home and Cemetery. Of all the places.

All was still and quiet, except for the occasional scurry of leaves. I took in the moonlit scene. Ornate tombs. Endless rows of headstones. A fleet of older-model white hearses parked side by side like piano keys on an eerie, antique piano.

Just as my father had described, there was a long road that stretched to the right, extending to a grassy cul-de-sac where a sprawling oak tree stood, swaying in the breeze like it was grieving the dead. But I only knew that because I walked my motorcycle through the cemetery entrance and pointed my headlight that way. I didn't drive down there.

No way.

Graves had always creeped me out. I wasn't looking forward to explaining to my father why I'd bailed on his instructions, but surely he'd cut me some slack. I mean, the realm of the dead was his turf, not mine.

When I pulled up to my apartment, Veronica was a few parking spots down, standing beneath a streetlamp next to the open driver's-side door of a red BMW 4-Series. A pricey car for a breathing class instructor, but whatever. She was carrying on a conversation with Detective Benny, of all people. And it was 12:30 a.m.—I couldn't decide if that was weird or not.

When they saw me, Veronica smiled and waved, then got in her car and drove off—no telepathic comments aimed at my brain this time, thankfully. While I secured my helmet to my bike, Detective Benny made a beeline from his squad car to me, his open metal cuffs scraping the cement. As usual, he practically broke my fingers while shaking my hand.

"So, you know Veronica?" I asked him.

"Tasha Watt was in her program at school. Miss Snow has been very helpful in the investigation."

I nodded. "If there's anything I can do to help—"

"There is." He silenced an incoming message on the radio strapped to his belt. "We need to do some excavating on your property—along the side opposite Masonville High. We'll have to bring in a bulldozer and other equipment."

A rush of light-headedness came over me. "Did you . . . locate a body?"

"I'm not at liberty to discuss the situation." To me, that sounded more like a yes than a no. "Do I have your permission?"

"Of course. Do I need to sign something?"

Wouldn't you know it—another crushing handshake. "That won't be necessary. Your word is enough." He turned to go, then stopped. "I'll need you and everyone else to stay off that end of the property for the time being. We'll section off the perimeter."

"No problem."

As I trudged up the stairs to my apartment, I held out hope that the cops would exhume centuries-old bones, left over on my land from Caldwell's brutality—not someone killed recently. Against all odds, Betty was counting on Tasha being found alive.

I took Daisy out to do her business, then tried to relax in my bed, but my arms and legs were throbbing and restless. That annoying rustling sound was stirring in the walls—including the one behind my head—and also in the ceiling, but I'd pretty much learned to tune it out. Something else was bothering me tonight. Since his first appearance, my father had been nothing but kind and patient with me, yet I worried: What if he didn't sympathize with my decision to ditch the cemetery and ignore his instructions?

I'd lost the confidence to call out to him and dreaded that he might close in on me any second, unannounced and angry.

Lord, help me.

Lying on my back, I was massaging my forehead and cheeks, working to calm the stress, when a seemingly random childhood memory played like a movie reel in my mind. I had to have been about four years old when I'd accidentally pedaled my tricycle into the bumper of a car that belonged to one of my mom's exes. I think his name was Todd. I'd watched his drunken grin snap into a rage-filled scowl as he ripped me by my arm off my trike, shook me, then dropped me facedown on the pavement. My mom charged at him, but he knocked her to the ground too.

How could the mere memory make me tremble? Why was I even thinking about this?

I NEVER TREAT MY CHILDREN THAT WAY.

Whoa. An indescribable voice spoke—not through my ears but, like, in my heart. The words seemed to have bubbled up from deep within, infusing such peace that the bothersome restlessness was instantly gone.

"God . . . ?" I whispered, staring at the ceiling, motionless and mesmerized. "Did you just . . . *speak* to me?"

At first, I thought I was imagining that my bedroom was getting brighter, but then I looked toward the foot of my bed—the light around my feet was becoming blinding.

There was no analyzing my situation or planning how to react. Out of pure instinct, I released my head onto my pillow and raised my hands into the luminescent air, thanking God out loud for being so powerful and wonderful and real. This feeling, this absolute *knowing* that the God of the whole universe was present with me . . .

There's no adjective good or grand enough to describe it. No description for the all-over sense of safety and satisfaction. I knew right then that if heaven feels anything like that—even a little bit—it's an utter waste of energy to dread your eventual death.

If you've shed your shackle, that is.

Like a soothing heater steadily yielding to a frigid AC unit, my illumination faded back to its normal golden ring, and the comforting serenity all but evaporated. I knew better than to think that God—the Source—had left me entirely, and yet my bedroom felt abandoned now.

I wrapped my arms around a pillow and turned onto my side, still marveling that I'd heard the Lord speak. That he'd addressed *me.* It wasn't that long ago that I'd have branded a person insane for claiming to have heard the voice of God, and yet tonight, I was sure it was him—that he'd made a point to tell me he was nothing like Todd or Charlie or any of my mom's ex-boyfriends. Had I assumed he was?

Come to think of it, it was the exact mistake I was making with my earthly father—well, my *un*earthly father.

I lit a candle, ready to call out to him now, but the moment was ruined when Veronica showed up at my door. I didn't know who else it could be, pounding like it was broad daylight instead of two o'clock in the morning. I hurried into my living room and spied through the peephole.

Oh . . .

I swallowed hard, then opened the door.

"Jess . . . what are you doing here?"

SIXTEEN

"Hey, Owen." She was even thinner than in high school, and her smeared makeup and sloppy hair didn't fit the Jess I knew. But she was still beautiful. "I stopped by your mom's the other day. She told me where you live."

Her baby boy was sleeping in a neon-orange stroller with his head slumped to one side, a dazzling tiny light emanating from his heart. He had to be around three or four months old by now. Despite his tiny facial features, there was no doubt he was Dan's son.

"Can we come in?"

I swung the door open, and she sighed in relief, then parked the stroller by my sofa and let her purse slide off her shoulder and hit the floor. She walked straight to the kitchen and flung the refrigerator door open, swatting away flies. She stuck her head in and surveyed the empty shelves. "Seriously?"

"I eat out a lot."

She slammed the fridge door, then walked past me and dropped onto my sofa. She'd had four shackle-tethered chains in high school. She had six now.

I stood looking down at her. "What's going on with you?"

"I'm super tired." She rolled over and, with her back to me, tucked a throw pillow under her head.

"Um, I'm good. In case you're wondering." I hadn't spoken to her in months—hadn't laid eyes on her in nearly a year. "What are you doing here, Jess?"

"I just need to crash here for the night. I'll be gone in the morning. Promise."

"Where do you live now?"

She grabbed another pillow and covered her head with it, then waved her hand in the air, dismissing me.

"So that's it?"

"I'll talk tomorrow." Her words were muffled against the couch cushions.

I was less than thrilled with Jess crashing on my couch, and I knew Ray Anne would like it even less than I did, but what could I do? I couldn't turn an infant out onto the street at two in the morning, even if he was Dan's kid.

I tried to lie down in my bed but couldn't relax.

"Jess, why don't you and the baby sleep in my room, and I'll take the sofa?"

She didn't move at first, but then sat up fast and pushed the stroller into my room, next to my bed. She got under the covers but left the baby snoozing in his chair. I closed the door, and Daisy and I tried to get comfortable on the sofa—until my dog suddenly bolted up. Her shaggy ears raised like antennae as she froze, listening as intently as she could. I sat up to pet her and calm her, but she leaped off the couch and hunkered down behind the lounge chair across the room.

"What's the matter?" I whispered, bracing myself. Something was about to go down.

Sure enough, a Creeper passed through my closed front door like smog billowing through a screen, so tall I had to tip my head back to take in its full frame. Its arms were folded tight against its chest, its hands squeezed into malicious fists. The rank smell of burning flesh reminded me of when I'd singed my finger on a soldering iron, yet my apartment was subzero now. Like the mysterious Creepers Ray and I had spied in the woods the evening of her birthday, this one wore a pointed hood that draped over half its face.

As quickly as I jumped up from the sofa, a single-file procession of them advanced past me like a train of terror, moving so quickly I lost count of how many there were. Within seconds, they'd passed through the wall into my bedroom.

I ran into the hallway and flung my bedroom door open. My heart leaped with elation. Heaven's army was on the scene. Three armored Watchmen seized the seething Creepers by their throats and limbs, pinning some to the ground and suspending others in midair. But these hooded Creepers didn't shriek and run. They growled and roared and howled so loud, I covered my ears in a useless attempt to muffle the noise. And they fought back, working to claw at the Watchmen's flawless faces while attempting to sink their fangs into any piece of illuminated skin they could find.

It was like watching skyscrapers go to battle, slamming one another with colossal blows. And yet Jess slept, undisturbed. The baby did too. A robed Watchman with a shield fastened to his back draped himself over the child, his arms long enough to embrace the entire stroller.

I'd slipped into useless spectator mode, in awe of the combat. I wondered if Custos would eventually join the fight. My jaw hung wide open as a Watchman whose skin looked deeply tanned managed to plunge a Creeper through the outside wall, banishing him outdoors. Hands free now, the warrior reached back between his shoulder blades and unsheathed a sword I hadn't noticed he'd been carrying. But instead of wielding the massive blade against forces of darkness, he looked right at me, then slid the sword my way. The ornate, jewel-laden handle landed at my feet.

There was no way I could pick it up—the blade had to have been five feet long, and the handle was nearly as thick as a gallon jug. But I knelt down, compelled to try.

It might as well have been cemented into the ground. I couldn't lift it at all, yet that same Watchman kept glancing at me while he continued battling, like he expected me to use it.

I tried again, harder this time, marveling that my hands could even grasp a spirit-realm object to begin with. But I didn't have the strength.

Not even close.

I stood as the last remaining Creepers were overpowered and expelled from my bedroom. The Watchman swiftly retrieved the sword and, with the armored battalion, charged out of my apartment, as if duty had called them elsewhere.

The sudden stillness and silence was deafening, power-packed action replaced by the delicate rhythm of Jess inhaling and exhaling. And yet the baby's protector remained, seemingly content to kneel next to the stroller and watch the infant sleep. His fragrant aroma filled my entire apartment.

I stood there awhile, taking in the sight of the fierce yet gentle Watchman. Seeing them never got old.

At some point, I wandered over and sank onto the sofa, finally falling asleep, only to wake a short while later to the stressful sound of Jess's baby crying. The midmorning sun glared in my face. I opened my eyes and realized there was more than sunlight enveloping me. That radiant robed Watchman was standing in my living room, looking back and forth between my bedroom and me. I got the feeling he didn't like the baby squalling and wanted me to do something about it.

I poked my head into the room. Jess had piled every one of my pillows over her head. The little guy caught sight of me and arched his back, flailing his miniature arms and legs. His thin brown curls were pasted to his clammy head.

I couldn't help but wonder if Dan had ever laid eyes on him. I couldn't imagine Jess having ever gone to see him in prison.

"Hey, your baby's upset." I peeled the fluffy sound barriers away from her. "Jess."

She was in a deep sleep—not the kind caused by an intense dream or exhaustion from a hard day's work but the type where a person's body is on overload after being strung out and abused. The way my mom so often slept.

After several failed attempts to get her up, I turned to the flushed-faced baby and managed to hoist his fragile, squirming body into my arms. I'd never held an infant and was sure I was doing it wrong, but considering how closely that Watchman was eyeing us, I think he would have swooped in and caught the kid if I'd started to drop him. The little guy's cotton-soft hair smelled like cigarettes, and his clothes like mildewed laundry when it's left in the washer too long. He labored to catch his breath, his bottom lip quivering.

All I knew to do was call Ray Anne and beg her to come help me. Obviously, she was surprised to hear Jess and her kid had stayed at my place, but she agreed to come over right away. Before we hung up, she asked me to do the unthinkable. "I'm sure he needs his diaper changed." I didn't see any diapers in Jess's purse, so I was off the hook. But I did find bottles of OxyContin. I shook my head.

Ray showed up a short while later with grocery sacks full of baby stuff, including formula, nail clippers, a thermometer, and a stuffed koala bear. The robed Watchman remained in my living room until Ray walked in—then he smiled and vanished, looking as relieved as I was to have her take over for me. She took the baby from my arms and went into mother hen mode, feeding him a bottle, then bathing him in my kitchen sink and dressing him in a new jumpsuit thing she'd bought.

I told her about everything that had gone down the night before, and she half listened while playfully counting each one of the baby's minuscule toes. I'd assumed she'd know how to make the baby stop crying—and she did—but I'd seriously underestimated how natural she'd be at caring for an infant. The irony stung: Ray Anne would never have her own baby because of this child's father. But Ray didn't seem concerned with that right now.

It was after noon when Jess finally woke and wobbled into my living room, still clumsy from her comatose sleep. She spotted her son sleeping peacefully on Ray Anne's shoulder and got defensive. "You don't have to do that." She reached for him. "Here, give him to me."

Ray Anne assured her it was okay, but Jess snatched him up anyway, waking him and sending him into a crying spell. Jess attempted to shush him with stiff, impatient pats on his back.

"What's his name?" Ray Anne asked.

"Jackson."

"He's adorable."

Jess nodded, not making eye contact.

Ray Anne cleared her throat—and the air. "Just so you know, Jess, I don't blame you for what happened to me. I'm glad you and Jackson are okay."

Jess thanked her but still didn't look her in the face.

Eventually Jess explained that her parents had kicked her out and cut her off financially when they'd found out she was pregnant, and she was having a hard time finding a job. "My goal is to save up and go live with my cousin in New York," she said. "I've been accepted to a fashion design school there."

It sounded like one of those pie-in-the-sky careers, but then again, Jess could be a really determined person when she wanted to be. Maybe she could actually make it work. If she quit popping pills. Hadn't she worried about Ashlyn when she was into that in high school?

Jackson was only getting fussier, but Jess raised her voice above his whimpers, telling us how she'd finally found an evening job waiting tables but couldn't afford child care. Without pausing to think, Ray Anne offered to babysit Jackson for free. "He's an extra-special little boy," Ray said. "You can't have just anyone watch him."

There's no way Jess understood that, but I did. Jackson was an infant, and already, kingdom powers were warring around him. Last night's battle had been intense.

It took some prodding, but Jess eventually agreed to Ray's offer. I marveled at the scenario—my girlfriend babysitting my ex-girlfriend's baby. I never saw that coming, but then again, it had been a really long time since anything in my life had gone as planned.

Soon Ray Anne had to go, and even though Jess said she was leaving too, she kept stalling. Daylight came and went, and she was still there. It was getting more awkward by the minute.

I tried to keep the conversation light, but Jess kept baring her soul. She shared intimate details of her life—how she'd been with this guy, then that guy, which I already knew based on the number of chains she had now.

Eventually, she turned up the heat. "Do you ever miss me, Owen?"

I refused to go there. "I wonder how you're doing sometimes and hope you're okay."

She twisted her long hair into a loose knot. "I'm trying to get my life together."

I nodded halfheartedly. I wasn't convinced.

"I have to say, I'm surprised you're still with Ray Anne." Jess shook her head. "You two are nothing alike. She has a big heart and all, but she's a little *too* nice, don't you think? I'm surprised she doesn't want to be a nun."

There was no point in getting defensive. Ray Anne had agreed to watch Jess's son for free, not to mention taking a bullet for her—if Jess didn't already have a good opinion of her, nothing I said would change that.

Around ten o'clock, Jess asked if she and the baby could sleep in my bed one more night. I reluctantly agreed but made it clear that this had to be the last time.

I was back on the sofa. The walls rustled out here as much as they did in my bedroom.

This time, the robed Watchman traipsed through my living room into my bedroom and assumed his post before evil even had a chance to descend. I waited, wondering if another battle would break out—wanting to see one, to be honest—but everything stayed so quiet, I fell asleep.

Nightmares were nothing new to me, but this one was off-the-charts petrifying.

I dreamed I was lying on my back, asleep in my living room—like I actually was—and I fell from my sofa onto my hands and knees. I landed in a swamp of tar-like sludge. I tried to stand and walk, but the tar was too sticky and thick to lift my legs. The harder I tried to move, the angrier I got, until I was seething with a ferocious sense of bitterness and vengeance—like the swamp was my enemy and I hated it with all my being.

But then a real enemy invaded my dream. Molek closed in, encircling me, staring me down with those hollow white pupils suspended in darkness. His long, wispy white hair was adorned in that black crown of thorns. He roared in my face, then suddenly I was on my back on the sofa again.

That's when Murder, the Creeper that first stalked me after Walt and Marshall died, came charging through the wall in my dream and crouched over me, hissing. Then came Regret, a ghastly Creeper with a huge mouth and extra-long fangs. It hovered over my face, dribbling saliva on my cheeks and bare chest that stung like corrosive acid. Then a third Creeper arrived—Demise. The same one that had been hunting Ray and me in real life.

Despite the barrier of light encircling my feet, the three assailants pressed in tight around my body as I lay there so that I could barely move. I wanted to cry out, but Demise slapped its grimy hand over my mouth. Then Regret dangled a tattered black sack a few inches above my face. My initials were slapped on it like a blind seamstress had sewn them. There was nothing inherently scary about the bag, but the sight of it still struck terror in my soul.

Digging inside, Murder pulled out long chains and wrapped the freezing links around my throat so fast and tight I could barely breathe. I saw Regret reach into the neck of its own garment and pull more chains out, binding them around my throat too, but it also wrapped them around my arms and legs until I was completely bound. Having fully restrained me, Murder used its jagged fingernail to etch words on the cuffs secured to the ends of the chains. I couldn't tell how many there were.

Regret reached deep into the bag—deeper than seemed possible—and pulled out two cords, both much longer than the typical ones that droop from people's heads. One end of the cords burrowed into Regret's grossly large palm while the other ends squirmed until they found the back of my scalp, then started digging into my skin like leeches. It hurt so bad I tried biting Demise's corroded fingers, but my teeth chomped down on air. And my aggression only seemed to excite Regret.

While I thrashed in a useless effort to break free, Demise let go of my face and shoved its only hand into the black bag, pulling out a fistful of ashen grossness I'd come to know as death dust. It spit into the nastiness and massaged it into a muddy concoction until it looked like the gooey tar from the swamp. I was stiff with dread, convinced Demise was going to refit me with a shackle, but instead, it rubbed the rotten-smelling gunk all over my face, covering my lips and nostrils so that it became impossible to inhale.

I lay there suffocating, enduring trauma no one should ever face, much less a Light, while the horrible threesome grinned and cackled, reveling in assaulting me. I knew my situation was dire—that I stood no chance of survival—but just in time, my father appeared in the dream, beaming all over, from head to toe.

"Release him." Even though he didn't even raise his voice, the Creepers backed away. I choked and gasped as all three of my attackers ran away from my father, fleeing my apartment. My dad pulled the chains and cords off me like they were measly cobwebs, then grabbed chunks of the black mud from my forehead, nose, and mouth and flung them away.

While struggling to catch my breath, I thanked him over and over. He sat next to me on the sofa.

"What just happened?" Even in my nightmares, I wanted to understand.

"That bag holds your bondage from the past."

I knew that. I'd seen Creepers bring out Ray Anne's and try to hurt her with it back in high school.

"Because you are weak, they're using it against you."

I didn't like being called a weakling. "Is there a way to destroy it?"

"No." He was always calm and confident. "It's indestructible." He was still glowing. It reminded me of the Watchmen's illumination, only not so blinding.

"Do you trust me yet, Son?"

I was sitting upright now in the dream. "I'm learning to."

"Then go to the address I gave you. Be there tomorrow at midnight."

He leaned forward and set an object on my coffee table. It was too dark to make out what it was.

"How'd you get those Creepers to obey you like that?"

"Don't worry about them. They're harmless in my presence. When you're with me, you're safe."

"But I want to have that power too—to free others during attacks, like you just did for me."

"Owen." He smiled peacefully. "You can't free yourself, much less others. You don't have the authority."

"Well, how can I get it?"

Sitting next to my father, I felt waves of reassurance flowing from him, alleviating my anxiety. "Abide with me," he said, "and in time, I'll empower you. I'll show you how to do the works that I have done, and even greater."

I had more questions, but my attention shifted over my shoulder. Jess was standing across the room from me, holding a lit candle. "I need to use the restroom, but the power's out." She squinted at me. "Who are you talking to?"

I glanced toward my father, but he was gone. "Um . . . it's just me."

I didn't know how or when I'd woken from the nightmare, but I seemed to no longer be sleeping.

"The power should be back on now," I told Jess. She stepped into the bathroom, then flipped the light on and closed the door. I was disoriented and confused but took comfort in knowing that in real life, Creepers could never attack me like that.

I turned on a lamp and saw that my father had placed a small square mirror on my coffee table. I recognized it as Ray Anne's. She'd left it here a while back, and I'd tossed it into my bathroom drawer. I didn't understand how or why my father had it, but when I caught a glimpse of my reflection in it, I shuddered.

There were black, tar-like streaks all over my face.

SEVENTEEN

THE NEXT MORNING, I was still on edge. Hard as I'd scrubbed, my face was still smudged, but when Jess didn't say anything about it, I knew it was only visible through a spiritual lens. She stood by the door, loaded down with all the new baby stuff, Jackson strapped into his stroller. But she kept hesitating to grab the doorknob and leave.

"Thanks for letting us crash with you like this."

I handed her a baby sock that had fallen behind a chair. "Sure."

"You've always been there for me when I need you."

I gave her a polite smile—the we're-just-friends kind.

"By the way, why won't you tell me who came over last night? I heard you and a man talking."

"You did?" That threw me.

"Yeah. I wasn't, like, eavesdropping. I just happened to hear. Something about an address, I think?"

"Oh . . ." I nearly dropped my phone.

"What's the big deal?"

I paced my living room. "You have a history of not believing me, Jess, remember?"

Jackson started fussing, but she ignored him. "How about you give me another chance?"

I got the feeling that's what she'd been wanting to say this whole time—about us.

Jackson arched his little back and protested until she finally scooped him up and held him. "Okay, tell me." Jess was never one to let me off the hook.

I sighed then lowered myself to the floor, sitting on the carpet across the room from her. "Did I ever tell you that I figured out who my father was and that he was presumed dead?"

"Yeah?"

"Well, he's definitely dead."

"Okay?" She came and sat across from me with the baby in her arms.

"He's been . . . visiting me." I braced myself for a sarcastic remark, but she didn't say anything. "He's who I was talking with last night. I'm surprised you heard him."

More silence, then— "How cool! Owen, that's incredible! I mean, I've seen this stuff on TV, but wait—can you hear him *and* see him, or just hear him?"

"Both."

"Crazy! Do you think I could see him too sometime?"

My sacred experience was starting to feel like a circus sideshow. "I don't know about that."

"'Cause I would love to meet him. I would try not to freak out." She put Jackson on his back on the carpet, then stood and practically galloped around my living room, dragging her cuffs along. "So you're saying that voice I heard last night, that was a *dead* guy?"

Her question rubbed me the wrong way, but what she said next was about the most uplifting thing I'd heard in a while.

"Owen!" She sprawled out in front of me. "I'm so happy for you. That's so great that you get to connect with your father, after all this time. I bet you're super excited."

Finally, someone was celebrating the miracle of my reunion.

"I am," I said.

"Then why do you look so bummed?"

It surprised me that Jess could still read me so well. "Not everyone is thrilled about it."

"Let me guess—Ray Anne?"

My lack of an answer was answer enough.

"Oh, please." Jess turned on her side and propped her head up with her elbow. "What, like, ghosts are against her religion?"

"He's *spirit*—not a ghost. And she's asked me to stay away from him."

"Do you do everything she says?"

I glared at Jess. "I was talking with him last night, wasn't I?"

She smiled, visibly pleased with my defiance of my girlfriend's wishes. At least I hoped Ray Anne still considered herself my girlfriend.

Jackson clawed at his tired eyes and started fussing all over again.

"You want to hold him?" she asked me.

There was no point in playing house and toying with her emotions. "That's okay." I stood and gathered her sacks of stuff. I was tired of company and wanted her to leave—for real this time.

Finally, she and her metal appendages were headed out the door.

"You never told me where you live."

She shrugged, trying to look carefree, I think, but she didn't pull it off. "I have a friend who says I can move in with her for now—you know, until I get my own place."

It was an odd turn of events. Jess had lived her whole life in extravagance, and now she was basically homeless. With a baby on her hip.

I had the money to help her get on her feet, but I knew better than to swoop in and try to rescue someone in her situation. She needed to grow up on her own, and I needed to keep my distance. Our season together was over, and I had no desire to rekindle things. I still found her attractive, but her life was a hurricane of bad choices and noisy chains. I wanted nothing to do with her.

In spite of everything, my heart remained with Ray Anne.

I gave Jess the thirty dollars cash that was in my pocket, and she took it without hesitation. I could only hope she'd spend it on her son.

That afternoon, I hammered out a portion of a research paper, but it was torture because, as usual, my mind was consumed with other things—mainly last night's assault against me. *Thank you, Lord, for sending my father.*

I hadn't heard from Ray Anne since she'd left my apartment yesterday, and I didn't know if it was because she wanted time and space away from me or because I'd missed church again this morning. Either way, it irked me. But I didn't text or call her. I had to prove I wasn't desperate. Mainly to myself.

That night, I made up my mind to go to 136 Sycamore Lane and follow through this time. As if the graveyard scene wasn't eerie enough, a thunderstorm had rolled in. I'd get soaked on my motorcycle, but I wasn't going to let that stop me. I stuffed a flashlight inside my jacket pocket and left.

I was on my balcony when an oppressive thought came: *Demise is out to get me, and there's nothing I can do about it.*

I approached the stairwell, and there was the one-handed Creeper, moving toward me in the driving rain, walking in midair above the parking lot as if on the same third story as me.

I'm too weak to endure this.

I knew the thoughts were being launched at me like darts at a bull's-eye, but they felt true. Like I was thinking them up myself.

I'm outmatched. Every thought stirred crippling emotions. *Defenseless.*

Demise kept tracking, moving toward me faster than its steps alone were taking it. It stopped abruptly just beyond my balcony, then extended its index finger, curling it back and forth, coaxing me over the railing. Then came a vivid mental picture of me climbing up and over, breaking my neck on the wet cement below.

Is this what Demise had done to Meagan? Plowed the soil of her soul so Suicide could rush in and finish the job?

A forceful thought pierced my mind: *True freedom and power are found only in the afterlife.*

Suddenly the idea of suicide was not about escaping this life but deliberately upgrading to another, shedding my flesh to advance to a superior realm. I knew the notion was evil, and yet I couldn't deny the appeal—the longing for a passageway to an existence where weakness would be eradicated forever. But it had to be a lie. All Creepers do is lie.

"Get away from me."

Demise thrust itself forward, through the banisters, and its companions from my dream, Murder and Regret, came rushing to its side. All three surrounded me, their disfigured feet just outside my aura. The rest of their towering bodies pressed in so close I shivered, hardly able to stomach the stench. I was living my nightmare all over again, only completely awake.

Why were they able to torment me like this? To physically badger a shackle-free person?

I'm serving the wrong side, the losing kingdom. It was such a strong thought, it was practically audible.

I intended to call out to my father, but another word echoed in my mind and sprang from my mouth—two syllables I'd thrown around all my life, mostly sarcastically or as part of a string of curse words. I figured God must have put the word on my tongue, because the instant I said it, all three of my attackers shrieked and jumped back. Demise contorted its neck disgustingly low and hissed at me with a wide-open mouth, then gave an order to the other two in their hellish language. They raced away, disappearing in the pouring rain.

The warmth of victory rushed through my veins. If my father was aware, he had to be proud of me right now—and God, too. There was nothing weak about what I'd just accomplished.

Who would have thought the name of Jesus could be so potent? So threatening to evil forces intent on threatening me? As cliché as it felt to admit, evidently there really was power in his name.

Even in the rain, I could see in my rearview mirror that the black smudges were fading from my face—another relief. I turned into the cemetery on Sycamore Lane one minute before midnight and drove right, then parked against the curb at the big cul-de-sac with the mourning oak tree.

I'd been told to stand under that tree, so using my flashlight and the aura around my feet, I trod through the wet grass toward it, passing rows of headstones—and corpses—but I suppressed that thought. I faced the street and waited beneath the massive branches, putting up with big droplets tapping my soaked head.

Nothing happened.

In my nervous boredom, I shined my flashlight on the headstone nearest me, heart-shaped granite. A woman's name was engraved with dates: 1952–2009.

Fifty-seven years old. Cancer, maybe? A car accident? Sick as it may sound, I wished the cause of death had been listed. It bugged me not knowing.

I found myself thinking about my mother and the possibility that she might be buried in this place someday—probably sooner rather than later. Could I live with myself if we never spoke again?

I pushed the morbid thought aside.

Ten minutes passed, and I wondered if I'd missed the point of all this somehow. But then an echoing sound caused me to jerk the flashlight in every direction while the hairs on the back of my neck became stiff. It was a boy's laughter, like a young guy was running in circles around the tree, cracking up in the night rain.

I was done.

I'm aware that what happened next sounds like a scene from a low-budget horror movie, but that's how it went down. As I started back toward my motorcycle, I fumbled my flashlight when I needed it most. I bent down to grab it, and it was illuminating the headstone a foot in front of me.

Lucas Benjamin Greiner.

I was kneeling at the grave of Ray Anne's younger brother.

EIGHTEEN

"OWEN!" It was my father. I stood up, leaving my flashlight on the ground. It flickered and went out. Two figures approached in the rain. Neither appeared damp.

Next to my father stood a thin young man, barefoot, wearing what looked like a white T-shirt and jeans. It was too dark to make out his facial features, but I'd seen enough pictures of him to fill in the blanks.

"You know who this is, Son."

"Yes."

Lucas stepped forward. "I want to talk to my sister. Tonight."

"I . . . I don't know. She's leery of all this."

"We understand," my father said. "But you must plead with her. Tell her that her brother is calling—longing to commune with her. And we mean her no harm. We care for her."

"You're asking me to bring her to you?"

"Please," Lucas said. "To the woods behind the high school."

My stomach dropped. "Why there?"

My father wrapped an arm around Lucas's shoulders. "That's where Lucas ended his life. It will give Ray Anne solace to see her brother out there, so full of eternal life now."

I'd never asked Ray Anne where or even how her brother had committed suicide because I knew it would hurt her to talk about it, and I'd never wanted to think about it long enough to research it. But I never would have imagined it had happened on my land.

Surely Ray Anne would be relieved to know her brother wasn't trapped in eternal suffering. She hadn't had spiritual sight before he'd died and couldn't be sure whether he'd been a Light—a redeemed soul who, in a moment of weakness, had fallen prey to Suicide's lies.

"It's good to finally meet you, Owen." Lucas's tone was casual, like we were both alive and our paths just happened to cross.

Maybe it was just the situation—me standing in a cemetery, talking to two deceased people—but I felt uneasy. "I should go."

My father nodded, giving me his blessing, and I dodged headstones on the fast walk back to my bike. I felt like they were both watching me as I drove away.

Thankfully, Ray was awake—not a drop of makeup on, but she still looked amazing. She handed me a towel and spread several on the floor of her garage apartment for me to sit on. Slowly, she lowered into a beanbag chair across from me, clutching her abdomen like her scars were throbbing.

"Are you okay?" I asked.

She nodded. "I'll be fine. What are those dark smudges on your face?"

Oh yeah. She could see what remained of the tar streaks. "I'll explain that later. There's something more important I need to tell you."

How was I supposed to word this? I wrapped my soaked jacket in a towel, then took my shirt off. She stared for a moment, then cut her eyes away. I'm not bragging—just stating a fact: I looked good. But the chemistry between us wasn't important compared to what I'd come to say to her.

"Something happened tonight, Ray Anne, and I admit it was a little scary, but it was mostly incredible. A miracle, really."

"Okay?"

I stared at her adorable face, knowing that what I was about to say would either bring us closer or deepen the valley between us. "I met someone tonight. Someone who means a lot to you."

She leaned away, suspicious already. "Who?"

There was nothing I could do to prepare her. So I just said it. "Your brother." I bent forward and clutched her fingers, speaking softly. "Lucas appeared to me."

She jerked her hand away, jumped to her feet, and—I'm not kidding—threw her beanbag chair at my head. "Why would you say something like that?"

I freed myself from the blob and stood up. "I know it's unusual, Ray Anne. Freaky, even. But it's real, and he's asking for you. He wants to see you."

She dug her fingers into her scalp and started crying.

"He's not shackled, Ray. You can finally rest in knowing he's not suffering." She sobbed harder. "And he wants me to bring you to him . . . tonight."

I stepped toward her, my hands out. She reared back and pushed me as hard as she could. "Owen, you're sick! You're being deceived . . . falling for evil!"

Between quick, frustrated breaths, I told her, "They're not evil, Ray Anne. My father and your brother—they're coming to us as family."

"How do you know?" She stomped her foot, sniffling. "Demise has been tracking us—what if it's him, huh? Posing as your dad, and he's got some other Creeper playing the part of Lucas?"

"What!" I was really trying not to get annoyed, but this? I huffed in her face. "Creepers don't shape-shift, Ray Anne. My God, this isn't Transformers."

"Don't take the Lord's name in vain."

I crossed my arms, resisting the urge to pop my knuckles. "Are you kidding me? I tell you that I've just seen your brother and he's asking for you, and all you can do is call me out for breaking a rule?"

She started crying harder, then started coughing and couldn't stop. I took a much-needed deep breath, then grabbed a bottled water for her out of her minifridge, hoping it would help her chill out. But after multiple sips and me rubbing circles on her back, she was still coughing. I hated seeing her gasp.

"I'm sorry," I told her. "I didn't mean to upset you. Take your time—we don't have to go right this second."

She cleared her throat the best she could. "Owen, I'm not going *anywhere* tonight. I want nothing to do with this. Ever."

Here we were again, at the same crossroads. I knew I'd get nowhere by pressuring her, so I gave up, my hands raised in surrender. "Okay, Ray Anne. If that's what you want."

Her eyes dropped from my face to my bare chest and she flinched, then squinted.

"What are you staring at?"

She blinked fast, then shook her head. "Nothing, I guess."

It was weird, but I let it go.

She handed me my wet clothes, still teary and coughing. I took the hint. I was out the door when she called to me. "I think you should know, when I left your apartment Saturday, I saw Custos."

"Where?"

"In the field behind your apartment building. He was looking at your place, but standing back, behind the fence."

"Huh. I wonder why."

"Your choices are pushing him away."

I shook my head. "You're the one pushing people away, Ray Anne."

I thought for sure that would make her pause and at least think a minute, like any reasonable person would. Instead she dropped her chin and closed the door in my face.

And she accused *me* of being deceived?

NINETEEN

By TUESDAY MORNING, Ray Anne and I still weren't talking. We hadn't officially broken up, but we might as well have. I missed her, of course, but I tried playing it cool, hoping she'd reach out to me in a moment of weakness and apologize and want to mend things. But I was still out to prove I could live without her if I had to. Instead I got a call from Pastor Gordon.

"Ray Anne told me what's going on," he said. "How you've been interacting with spirits. Is that true?"

I didn't deny it.

"You and I already talked about this, Owen. It's a very bad idea, and God specifically prohibits it in the Bible. I'm extremely concerned about you."

I knew Gordon was probably sincere, but I felt like Ray Anne had tattled on me to the church principal and I was being forced to sit in the bad saint's chair. "Gordon, I get that you probably won't believe this, but I have very strong instincts about what's good and evil, and I'm telling you, I'm not doing anything sinful." I had more than mere instincts, but I couldn't elaborate on that.

"This is not a gray area, Owen. God has made himself very clear, and you're going against him. I get the idea you think you're in control of the situation, but sooner or later, you'll realize you're not. I wish you would trust me on this. I wish you would trust God."

Excuse me? My relationship with God was fine—better than ever—and I didn't need Gordon criticizing it. And I hadn't given up any kind of control. He'd overstepped his role as a pastor. I knew right then I probably wouldn't keep hosting or attending the Bible study.

Gordon sighed. "You know where to find me if you change your mind. Now, you're more than welcome to continue coming to our Thursday gatherings, and I hope you do. But if you continue with this defiance, I can't have you hosting us at your apartment."

Well, there was that problem solved, anyway.

"Ethan has offered to host. We'll be at his place this Thursday night."

Yeah, *definitely* not going.

I'd just pulled into the Masonville High parking lot when Betty called to tell me she was at a relative's house in Louisiana, searching for something very important that Dorothy had remembered while Ray and I were over the other night—something Arthur had instructed her to write down that Dorothy thought could shed some light on what was going on with my land and how to deal with it.

Man, I really hoped she found it. That supernatural floating object—big and boxy with dark, seaweed-looking stuff trailing off it—had moved closer in the sky toward Masonville High. I had no clue what it was, only that it had something to do with Molek. If it was closing in, I feared he soon would be too.

The clock was ticking.

Hector skipped tutorials that day, and Riley was completely checked out—sitting next to me, toying with the ends of her light-brown hair, but mentally not there. She admitted she was having a hard time concentrating and blamed it on a headache. My guess: that serpent was slithering through her brain. Not to mention the stress of her pregnancy. She sat so close to me today, I kept having to inch my chair away.

"What's wrong, Riley?" I finally asked.

She kept her head down. "It's a girl thing. You wouldn't understand." She stayed slumped over, eyes pooling, then yawned, stretching her arms up and out so that her shirt came up. Her jeans sat low on her hips, and I got a decent look at her abdomen—enough to be sure.

The teeny light was gone.

Intentionally, or had it happened naturally? It's not like I could ask.

"Owen?" She doodled random lines on her worksheet. "Have you ever hated yourself for something you did?"

Intentionally, then.

"Yes." I answered honestly, trying to somehow use the situation for good. "I know exactly how that feels."

She still couldn't look me in the face. "What'd you do about it?"

Thanks to my supernatural senses, I had a lot of answers most people didn't. But she'd posed a really tough question—one of the biggest I was struggling to resolve myself. I gave her the best, unfiltered advice I had. "Talk to God about whatever you did, and don't let demons torture you about it."

She looked at me then, one eyebrow raised. But I stood by the validity of my statement, even if I was struggling to walk it out in my own life.

Ms. Barnett approached and handed Riley what looked like a print-out of her grades and instructed her, "Be sure to have your grandmother sign this."

So apparently Riley's parents weren't around.

A text swooshed on her cell, and as she read it, she grinned and gasped. "I got invited!"

"To what?"

"The after-school thing with Miss Snow." It was like she'd won the lottery. And forgotten all about her turmoil.

"I thought you said it was stupid."

"Well . . . that was before, when I wasn't included." She rushed to stuff her binder inside her backpack, then hurried into the hallway.

I followed her. "I'm coming too." I wanted to see Veronica in action, observe how she interacted with the students. Tasha Watt had been in her program, and while that didn't necessarily mean anything sinister, it was enough to pique my interest. Also Hector—the only person I'd ever seen spew a slithering curse from his mouth.

Riley paused and glared at me like I was an idiot. "You can't just show up to this. She has to invite you."

"She already did." Through mind-to-mind communication, but, I mean, it still counted.

About a dozen students, mostly guys, huddled in the main foyer, all surrounding Veronica like she was some kind of Pied Piper. Hector stuck especially close to her.

Veronica's face lit up when she saw me, and she hugged me so tight, my heart rate felt like it doubled. "You're joining us?" she asked me. I caught some envious glares from the guys.

"Yeah."

She grinned.

Veronica addressed the group. "Okay, I'm taking you somewhere awesome today, but it's a long walk." Even the girls were trying to press past one another to stand as close to her as they could.

I hung back, perplexed. The foyer was freezing and saturated with the intolerable smell of Creeper bodies, but as I scanned every direction, I didn't spot a single one. Finally, I saw a few darting across the ceiling overhead, but their appearance was faint, like my sight was glitching.

It had never occurred to me that my spiritual eyes might weaken at some point. What would I do if I lost the ability to see into the spirit realm entirely? The same senses that had wrecked my world when I'd first woken to them had become my most vital tool in life. I think I'd have rather parted with my arms than lose it.

Veronica led us out the front doors of the school, around the back of the campus, then through the knee-high grass into the woods behind Masonville High. *My* woods.

Surrounded by picture-perfect cedars and oaks, I picked up on some occasional sinister whispers coupled with blasts of chilled, rancid air. Forces of darkness were near, looming behind the trees. Or were they standing in plain supernatural sight, just no longer seen by me? I hoped that wasn't it.

Riley waited for me to catch up to her. "You know a guy killed himself out here, right?" She tried to look serious, but she couldn't quite hide a crooked smile.

Disgust gnawed at my emotions like a rat chewing through a rope.

"Riley." I latched onto her arm and turned her to face me. "You may not believe this, but I care about you—not in *that* way, but as a person." I wanted to explain everything to her, the spiritual threats and the pitfalls she'd already fallen into. But she wouldn't understand. "Be careful." I took a panoramic glance around the woods—Caldwell's old land. "Bad things can happen." It wasn't nearly the warning she needed, but she nodded like she actually kind of took me seriously.

At first, I didn't think much about the trek we were taking. I owned over a thousand acres and was always up for exploring sections I'd never seen before. But soon we were headed down a path as familiar to me as the layout of my apartment. I hoped we'd change course, but Veronica led the way to a thick wall of brush, instructing us to tear at the vines and branches so that we could all pass through.

To the wooded clearing.

Where the historic, miraculous, murderous well was—the sound of underground sloshing as strong as ever.

"Everything all right, Owen?" Veronica asked.

I couldn't hide the shock on my face. "How do you know about this place?"

She ducked through a narrow hole in the greenery wall, then held out her hand, offering to escort me through. "I felt drawn here recently," she said. "Like energy was pulling me into these woods, to this spot."

Energy?

I barely touched her hand as I stepped inside. "Isn't it incredible?" She glanced up and around with an awestruck smile, like a child at a carnival.

The students—all shackled, by the way—were marveling at the canopy of interwoven branches high above our heads. No one seemed to notice the old water well. Thankfully, it was covered almost entirely in vines and shrubbery. I tried not to look at it, like it wasn't even there.

I wandered with everyone else to the center of the clearing. It was super weird being out here again, in the exact place where Arthur and his childhood friends had gathered and prayed for the dry well to give water. The same spot where the old man in overalls had handed me a cup that forever altered my world. The scene of the crime where I'd served Walt and Marshall drinks that forever sealed their fates too.

I'd also shed my shackle beneath these century-old trees—a soul-warming memory mixed with the bad ones.

Veronica motioned for us to form a tighter circle as she stood in the center, making a slow turn over her shoulder, careful to give each person a welcoming, confident nod. I put my back to the well, secretly guarding it.

Veronica instructed us to release our heads back, let our eyes relax shut, and take deep breaths in unison. I felt like a moron. When the awkward exercise ended, Veronica passed out incense sticks that looked like foot-long matches. After igniting hers with a lighter, she used it to light Hector's, then he lit the girl's next to him, and that continued around the circle. Each time a new flame kindled, the person who lit it would say, "*Ego in pace. Ego aqua, igni, et aer.*"

It was Latin—"I am at peace," then something about being one with the water, fire, and air. Again, my mother's weird insistence on teaching me Latin was paying off.

It was my turn to light the incense stick of the guy next to me. I didn't bother with the phrase, determined to be more of a spectator. After I lit the stick, I noticed something squirming next to the guy's shoe. It was the fattest worm I'd ever seen in my life—as thick as a hot dog.

I wondered if it was paranormal—something like the curse-snake Hector had expelled—but when Veronica saw it and grimaced, I wrote it off as just a gigantic worm. Veronica kicked dirt over it as it burrowed back into the ground.

After that grossness, when the circle of flames was complete, I spotted a hooded Creeper spying down on us, hovering on its stomach some ten feet above our heads. It was posed like a giant skydiver, only not falling.

Seconds later, it faded. I'm not saying it disappeared; I'm saying I couldn't see it anymore. My heartbeat became a hammering thud I felt at the base of my neck.

What's happening to my senses?

Veronica had us lower into deep lunges, still holding our smoldering incense sticks, then reach down, then out, then straight up, over and over until my legs actually started burning. I felt geeky and girly.

Each time we looked up, I squinted, hoping my power to see Creepers overhead would kick in again, but then movement among the trees a short distance in front of me demanded my attention, and I gasped at what I saw.

Who I saw.

TWENTY

THROUGH A NARROW GAP in the greenery wall, between two tree trunks, Lucas motioned with his hand for me to come near. He whispered my name, and it echoed through the clearing. I scanned the group, unsure if they'd heard it. They all lowered themselves to the forest floor and extended their legs out in front of them—business as usual, apparently.

I dropped down, attempting to strike the same pose while contemplating how to dismiss myself in the middle of the yoga session, or whatever we were doing.

Lucas called to me a second time.

Across from me, Veronica cut her eyes over her shoulder, as if she somehow sensed that a supernatural life-form stood a short distance behind her. But then all she did was rest her hands in her lap and lower her chin to begin another breathing exercise.

"Owen. Where is Ray Anne?" The corners of Lucas's mouth drooped. It was obvious to me that he missed his sister deeply.

I was ready to break away from the group and go to him, when a faint melody of whistling reached me. I froze and listened as hard as I could. Even if I hadn't recognized the tune, I knew this was not some songbird.

Could it be?

I sprang to my feet. "I'm sorry, I've got to go!" I turned my back on the group—and on Lucas—and charged through the woods, running toward the musical sound.

Where are you going?

Veronica. In my head again.

Stop it. I'm not doing this with you. My brain got quiet.

The whistling was getting louder. Sure enough, through scattered trees and shrubs, I spotted my old friend, the man in overalls, his signature straw cowboy hat resting low on his forehead. A glow spread around his brown boots.

"Hey!" I waved my hands above my head and grinned wider than I had in a while. "It's me—Owen!" It surprised me how over-the-top excited I was to see him. Yes, he'd proven to have answers to many of the mysteries that had plagued my paranormal life, but now more than ever, I realized I really liked this guy.

Truth was, I'd missed him.

He saw me and smiled, clutching the handle of a large shovel. "It's good to see you again, young man." He wrapped an arm around my shoulders and embraced me. I was dripping with sweat, but his back felt dry as the breeze.

"Where have you been?" I asked him. I'd somehow forgotten how unusual his eye color was—a mix of gold and brown.

"I've been from town to town, working." He motioned with his shovel.

"I've needed your help around here," I admitted.

"People need help everywhere."

Okay, so maybe I'd been a little self-absorbed lately.

I hadn't noticed until then that he was standing next to the skeletal remains of an animal. It had majorly decomposed, but it looked like a dog.

"I figured I'd give this creature a proper burial," he said. "Sound good to you?"

I shrugged. I wasn't really concerned with what he was doing out here

THE DECEPTION || 145

as long as I could get answers to my most vital questions. "Do you know where Molek's gone and when he's coming back? Is he in Colorado? I'm afraid he'll return any minute now, and—"

"Afraid?" He looked me in the face and held my gaze. "Fear is never necessary."

I nodded. "I just don't want to see the suicides and all the terror get worse again."

He plunged his shovel deep into the ground, pulling up a heap of dirt. "Molek can't strike again without mankind's help."

"What do you mean?"

He took his time uprooting another pile of soil. "Molek partners with deceived, darkened people to accomplish his plans. Same way God works through Lights to accomplish his."

"Ray and I call them Lights too."

He nodded, apparently unsurprised. "It's wise to pay attention to what the people in this town are up to. Especially what goes on in secret."

I let out an impatient sigh, wishing he'd shoot straight with me like my father always did. "What kind of secrets are you talking about? And who do you mean?"

He paused digging and looked toward the clearing.

"Veronica?" I'd had my suspicions about her and her unusual, sometimes invasive paranormal communication, but from what I'd just seen, she was teaching the students to stretch and breathe. Not exactly devilish behavior.

The old man said nothing—just used his shovel to tip the insect-infested carcass into the fresh grave.

"Are you saying Molek is no longer a threat?" I asked. "Certain people are now?" Naturally, I thought of the abductions. Maybe uncovering the kidnappers needed to be my top priority.

The man gripped the worn shovel with both hands and searched my face. "Let me be clear: if Molek *ever* mounts his throne again over this town, he will bring terrible, unthinkable turmoil, the effects of which will be felt far and wide for generations. But it'll be people who allow that to happen. Unless you intervene and stop it."

He handed the shovel to me and pointed to the mound of unearthed dirt, motioning for me to cover the critter's corpse, but I let the tool crash to the ground. "Tell me, then!" My jaw clenched tight, my teeth grinding. "Tell me how to stop Molek."

He stepped toward me, allowing me to breathe hard in his face. "You'll know soon enough. In the meantime, be cautious about who you choose to trust."

"Please." I gripped his arm, and it somehow felt as tight and muscular as mine. "Tell me who I should and shouldn't . . ."

And just like that, he vanished—literally faded in an astounding swirl of golden light. It reminded me of the way my father would sometimes dissolve when he was ready to end our visits.

A chill swam down my spine. I suddenly knew why I'd almost never seen the old man anywhere but in these woods, on what used to be Caldwell's land. And how he understood so much about the spirit world and Molek. And why he was able to vanish into thin air. It all made perfect, logical sense . . .

The old man was Betty's great-great-grandfather Arthur, sent by God to help me.

Wow. Like, *seriously* wow.

I marveled my entire walk back to Masonville High, wishing he'd given me time to ask more questions, but also trusting that, like he'd said, those answers were coming soon. Surely Betty would find that old message from Arthur she'd set out to locate, and it would tell me exactly how to stop Molek.

Traipsing through the forest, I looked around for Lucas, lamenting that Ray Anne was so stuck in dogma-driven fear, she was missing out on all this. Yes, the Bible warned not to consult the dead, but there was obviously more to it. It was an Old Testament thing that probably no longer applied anyway, but also, I was convinced it was a question of who initiates. I hadn't sought out any of these spirit people—at least not first. All of them had come to *me*. Because God had sent them.

How could I help Ray Anne understand that? I hated that she was so deceived.

When I reached the parking lot, I called Betty. Her voice mail picked up. "You won't *believe* what I have to tell you!" I imagined the joy she'd feel when I finally got to tell her I had a friendship with her great-great-grandfather. I hoped she wouldn't react in fear like others had.

I stopped by her house, but there was no answer. Not back yet from Louisiana, I concluded.

A couple nights later, I started missing Ray Anne so much, it was like my heart was throbbing. I was tired of this standoff, both of us waiting to see which of us would cave first. At the same time, I was proud of myself for not giving in to pathetic codependence.

I was in my living room getting ready to call out to my father, hoping to run my latest realizations by him, but wouldn't you know it, Jess showed up. I was afraid she'd want to camp out again, so I stood in the doorway and kept her on the balcony. "Where's Jackson?"

"With Ray Anne." She sighed like she was relieved.

Just hearing someone say Ray's name made me miss her all the more.

"Aren't you supposed to be at work?" I asked.

"They let me go early." She held up a white paper sack. "I brought Chinese."

She was clearly hoping that would be her ticket in, and it worked. We sat at my breakfast table.

"Seen your dad lately?" She spoke so casually about it, it reminded me of how Ray and I used to always talk about paranormal stuff. Before things got messed up and complicated.

Without going into tons of detail, I told Jess about seeing my father and also Lucas at the cemetery and how Ray Anne got hysterical about it. I knew Jess wasn't the best person to confide in, but she'd caught me at a time when I was actually in the mood to talk.

"Can I go with you? I want to meet your father."

"We don't have to go anywhere." I drowned my rice in soy sauce. "We can ask him to come here."

She squealed like a rich girl at a shoe sale, but I warned her, "I've only called him by myself. I don't know if he'll show up with the two of us here."

She dropped her plastic fork and crumpled her napkin. "So, what do we do?"

I pushed aside what was left of my meal and grabbed my candles, then handed her the box of matches. We lit the wicks and sat on the floor facing my sofa.

"So do we chant or something?"

I rolled my eyes. "It's not like that." I cleared my throat. "Father, are you here?"

I called to him a few times, and then the power went out. I'd forgotten to warn Jess about that, and she panicked, clinging to me for dear life. "Is he gonna grab me?"

I assured her she was safe and told her to chill out. I thought her drama might drive him away, but he entered from the hallway and took what was becoming *his* seat on the sofa. Jess slapped a hand over her mouth and pointed at him, speechless.

"Don't be afraid, Jessica."

She fanned her face with a hand. "You know my name?" She elbowed me hard. "He knows my name!"

"You go by Jess," he said, "but the Source calls you Jessica—for now."

"The Source means God," I told her.

"God . . . knows my name?"

He smiled, staring affectionately at her in the candlelight. "Of course. All of heaven does."

"Oh." She marveled for a moment—then jumped right in. "So what's it like on the other side?"

"Magnificent. Far more peaceful than physical life."

For shackle-free people, I wanted to add, but I didn't interrupt.

"Do you experience pain?" Jess wanted to know.

"No. Not ever."

The two of them went back and forth like old friends, and Jess finally let go of my arm. "Where's Lucas?" she asked.

I didn't appreciate her bringing him up. That was my business, not hers.

"Lucas is waiting for his sister." My father's polite smile faded as his gaze turned to me, disappointed, it seemed. "He waits in the woods, watching for her, night and day."

"So creepy," Jess said.

I rolled my eyes at her tactlessness.

"Do you know my future?" She wasn't letting me get a word in.

"I know countless things, including how you feel about my son."

Jess looked at me, but I kept my eyes forward, unwilling to go there. Plus, something way more important had just occurred to me—something I wanted Jess to hear from my father, not just me.

I asked him, "Can you please explain to Jess why she needs the Source and what happens when we die if we haven't—?"

He gently extended a flexed hand, silencing me with a compassionate smile. "Of course I will. But now is not the time. She's not ready yet, Son."

"Not ready for what?" Jess asked.

"Until we meet again," my father said to her, "know that the Source approves of you, and you never have to fear him." Then he stood and strode toward the hallway, disappearing into the dark. The power came back on.

Jess turned to me, breathless and wide eyed. "What just happened?"

I raked my fingers through my hair, irritated that I hadn't gotten to ask him much of anything. "Sometimes he leaves like that. All of a sudden."

"I'm freaking out!" She powered her phone on, then apparently felt the need to recap the entire experience to me from start to finish, like I hadn't been sitting right there. "How does he know so much?"

"In his realm, information is out in the open. He can access basically anything about anyone." It felt weird hearing myself say that, like I'd become some sort of afterlife guru.

"Owen . . ." She left her spot next to me on the floor and climbed into my lap, wrapping her arms and long legs around me. Her chains coiled in the carpet around us. I couldn't remember the last time I'd been this physically close to a female, and I felt my body ramping up.

Ray Anne was always so guarded. So prudish, if I'm being honest.

"Thank you for sharing that experience with me." She cupped my face. "I'll never forget it."

I gave a slight nod, then stared down at my cell, avoiding her longing eyes while working to get ahold of myself and muster enough willpower to get her off me.

I saw that it was eleven o'clock. "Shouldn't you go get Jackson?" I asked.

She huffed. "He'll be fine." She leaned her face toward mine, like old times.

"Jess . . ." I turned away. There was only one girl's kiss I wanted, and this wasn't her.

Jess huffed again, then pouted. She slowly unwrapped herself from me and backed away. I didn't give in to any of her delay tactics and had her out the door in under five minutes. I stood lingering on my front balcony, taking in the cool night air, when a brilliant brightness shined from the moonlit field beyond the parking lot. I looked over to see Custos, standing in the same place where Ray Anne had said she'd seen him.

I darted down the stairs and ran toward him. He moved toward the chain-link fence but stopped short of passing through. I stood on the opposite side, inches from him. His radiance rivaled the stars. "Custos, it's so good to see you!"

He lowered to one knee, but I still had to tilt my head back to look into his shining face. Quick glimpses were all I could manage. He'd never made eye contact with me like this.

He wasn't smiling.

"What's wrong?" I asked.

He pressed his massive palm to the fence, and I put both of mine up to his. My two hands looked like a child's compared to his one. Soul-soothing warmth and an indescribable sense of acceptance seemed to flood from his hand into my being, and yet his brows were pressed tightly together with concern.

"Why have you been staying away?"

I knew he wasn't likely to answer, but I kept standing there, wishing he would. His gaze shifted from my face to over my shoulder, to my apartment, prompting me to look back. Several slats of my bedroom blinds lifted, and the bottom dropped out of my stomach. Someone—or something—was looking down at us from my bedroom window. Demise? My father? I had no idea.

"Custos, please don't make me go back in there alone."

He angled his face toward the starry night sky. I could only assume he was listening to God, communing in a way that transcended spoken words.

I looked up too. "God, have I done something wrong?"

I craved an answer, but nothing came to me. Still, I remained there, staring into outer space, grateful to be this close to Custos.

I dreaded going back inside.

My phone swooshed with an incoming text. Custos gave off so much light, I had to turn and walk a distance away to see it. It was from Ray Anne: **I read this today and feel like I'm supposed to send it to you. Isaiah 8:19-20: "Should the living seek guidance from the dead? Look to God's instructions and teachings! People who contradict his word are completely in the dark." I miss you, Owen.**

I turned around, and Custos was gone.

TWENTY-ONE

BEFORE I COULD READ through Ray Anne's text a second time, Betty called and insisted I come over, even though it was almost midnight.

I ventured inside my place to grab my keys, which thankfully were by the door.

Betty and I sat at the breakfast table in her cozy, rooster-adorned kitchen. She asked me how I was doing, and I spilled my guts, telling her everything about my father and Lucas, too. Then I delivered the big news about Arthur—how all this time, it was her ancestor who'd been appearing and guiding me. She became teary eyed but kept quiet as I explained Ray Anne's unfortunate reaction to the whole situation and how she would bring up Bible verses that couldn't possibly apply to what I was experiencing. And I told her how Gordon had gone so far as to punish me by moving the Bible study out of my place—so ridiculous.

When I finally paused, mainly to catch my breath, Betty started rebuking me. *Rebuke*, I learned, is a churchy term that basically means someone tells you you're flat-out wrong and that you've totally blown it. I can't say she was mean about it—she didn't outright insult me—but she *did* side completely with Ray Anne and Gordon, and at one point, even referred to my actions as *ignorant*.

I pushed back from the table and paced her kitchen floor—covered, by the way, in the same glistening footprints that had first led me to Betty at Masonville High. "I don't understand any of this. It's like everyone I know and trust is warning me not to trust others I know and trust." I slammed into my chair and bent over, dropping my forehead onto a spongy place mat. "It's so freaking confusing."

I remembered what Veronica had said about how I would have to choose sides. It irked me to admit to myself that she'd been right.

Betty leaned over and put her hand under my chin, lifting my head to look at her. "I don't know if that old black man in the woods is an angel or some kind of demon, but I can promise you this: he isn't Arthur. My great-great-granddaddy is in heaven, with the Lord."

Just like Ray Anne, her mind was made up. Mine was all over the place.

Betty sat with me in the silence for a while, giving me comforting pats on the shoulder. Had I been even a little bit younger, I think I would have begged her to adopt me. "I can help you out of all this confusion," she said. "But right now, I need to show you what I found today."

I followed her into the living room, fully engrossed as she explained how, in the final hours of his life, Arthur had shared something with Dot—his granddaughter, Dorothy—that was so important, he had her write it down word for word. Betty opened a desk drawer and pulled out a small envelope. "I drove to my relatives' house in Louisiana, where Dot keeps some of her belongings, to get this."

She motioned for me to sit by her on the sofa. "Arthur told Dot God had given him a message—crucial instructions for a future generation. As a young woman, Dot vowed to him that she'd hold on to it. Arthur believed there would come a day when the message would find its way into the right hands."

Betty teared up again as she took my hand and placed the envelope in it, only these looked like happy tears. "Go on." She smiled. "Read it."

I stared at the timeworn envelope, aware I was holding something invaluable. I removed and unfolded a delicate piece of paper, then proceeded to read words that dated back more than sixty years. It was like time stood still.

*This is the written testimony of Arthur Washington, a free man
and servant of God. As I near the end of my life on this earth, the
Lord has revealed to me things that weigh heavy on my heart that
I believe are sure to come to pass. I have asked my granddaughter
Dorothy to write them down, in the hope of alerting and
encouraging a generation not yet born.*

I paused to take a deep breath, sensing this would be a defining
moment.

*The forces of darkness occupying Caldwell's land will remain
and multiply over time until someday, a great many people will
be attacked, suffering such hopelessness and torment that some,
especially the young, will take their own lives. There will also
come an act of violence on the land so tragic, news of it will spread
quickly around the world.*

Dan's mass shooting. I gulped.

*Though it troubles me to say it, I am certain that slaves will once
again be bought and sold on Caldwell's land.*

Slavery? I didn't understand that part.

*But take heart! Two young bearers of light will receive the call to
action, both given eyes to see. They will know when the spirit of
death—Molek, the ancient principality—has strayed from the
land, and they will gather the townspeople there and act swiftly on
the sacred promise given long ago:*
    *"If my people, which are called by my name, shall humble
themselves, and pray, and seek my face, and turn from their wicked
ways; then will I hear from heaven, and will forgive their sin, and
will heal their land."*

Then Molek will be banished from the town forever, along
with his army, lifting the burden of concentrated evil off the people
of Masonville.

I had to take a time-out and look up from the letter to come to grips
with what I'd just read. Try to, anyway. First of all, Arthur's predictions
about modern-day Masonville were spot on. Way too accurate to dismiss
as a random hunch.

Then there was the shocking reference to two light bearers. I faced
Betty on the sofa. "He has to be talking about Ray and me. We're the
ones called to take action."

Betty nodded, teary eyed and grinning.

I had to stand. The letter shook in my trembling hand. I paced circles
around the coffee table, marveling at how the solution had been there all
along. I recognized that sacred promise. I couldn't tell you its chapter or
verse or even what book of the Bible it came from, but I'd read it before.
I just never thought to take it literally, if that makes sense.

Then came a daunting reality check. "Molek's gone from the land," I
told Betty. "So this prayer thing on my property—whatever it's supposed
to look like—it needs to go down *now*." I stopped pacing and faced her.
"But, I mean, how are we supposed to explain this to people? And what if
we can't get them to gather on my land in time, before Molek comes back?"

Betty's grin faded, but her eyes remained sympathetic. She pointed to
the paper. I turned it over, and sure enough, there was more . . .

What joy awaits the generation that heeds the call and acts on
God's promise, looking to the welfare of the children! But should
his mandate be ignored, dismissed, or postponed, Molek will
reestablish his throne, and he and his satanic forces will reign with
heightened power, ravaging Masonville with unthinkable darkness
and sorrow.

Then came the conclusion, even more intimidating.

Know this: what happens in Masonville will affect the spiritual condition of the rest of the nation and the world.

That seemed impossible, but who was I to discount it? I collapsed back onto the sofa. It felt like the fate of the universe had been handed to me. Like God had used Arthur to send me a handwritten letter with my name on it.

I swallowed hard. Hadn't the old man in the woods basically given the same warning? And wasn't that even more proof that the old man truly was Arthur, by the way?

I scanned the paper again, looking for anything I'd somehow missed, wondering how Ray and I could ever pull this off.

"I'm here to help," Betty said. "You're not alone. God will show you and Ray Anne what to do and say."

It was nearly two o'clock in the morning now, and Betty was yawning, exhausted after her rushed road trip. She left the room and returned with a stack of perfectly folded sheets and a blanket, and I helped her spread them on the sofa. "First things first," she said. "We've got to deal with whatever wickedness you've allowed in your apartment. We'll take care of it in the morning."

She said it so casually, like we were going to do some touch-up painting.

"I don't know what it was that spied down at me from my bedroom tonight."

She stuffed a pillow inside a case. "Doesn't matter. It's got to go."

"But what if it's my father?"

Her glare and tight lips said it all. He had to go—from my apartment and from my life, completely. It seemed cruel to me, but Betty was insistent. And she assured me she knew how to drive him away.

I was willing to do whatever it took to fulfill the mission that Arthur—really, God—had entrusted to me, but I hated the thought of banishing my father. Even when I tried, I couldn't see him as the threat Betty and everyone else said he was.

As Betty headed toward the hallway to her bedroom, a thought came to me that couldn't wait until morning. "I believe Ray Anne and I are meant to do this mission together, but lately, we've been drifting apart."

"The enemy is working to divide your hearts."

Divided heart. The exact term my father had used to caution me about Ray Anne. With all due respect to Betty, in this situation, the culprit was Ethan, not enemy spiritual forces.

The sofa was comfortable, but I couldn't quiet my thoughts enough to sleep. Maybe this letter would help Ray and me get close again. Common missions have a way of doing that, right?

That's how I saw Arthur's message—like a special assignment destined for Ray and me. A divine prophecy we were called to fulfill.

We'd been begging for marching orders, and finally, it was time to execute.

I eventually relaxed enough to fall asleep. But had I known what was about to go down at my apartment in the morning, I'm sure I would have tossed and turned all night.

TWENTY-TWO

I STOOD ON THE DOORSTEP of my apartment with Betty and four of her friends—most of them even older than her, with gray hair, thick-soled shoes, and old-lady perfume. But hey, they were all Lights and had smiles as kind as Betty's. As I unlocked the door, Betty met eyes with each of them, exchanging determined glances before rolling up her sleeves. "Let the cleaning begin," she told them. As much as my place could have used a good scrub down, I knew that wasn't what they had in mind.

I stepped through the door and looked around but saw nothing—no Creepers or afterlife wanderers. Still, Betty and her crew shut the front door and started praying like Satan himself was camping out at my place. At first it struck me as over the top—and even comical—how loud and assertive they were. But then something cool happened.

A lady named Connie pulled a small bottle of oil from her purse, ready to "anoint" the place, as she called it. While reciting Psalm 91, she smeared the clear oil on every doorframe in my apartment—the patio, bedroom, and bathroom doors included. She dabbed the stuff on every one of my windows too, declaring that God is a protective shield against evil's terrors at night, the arrow that flies by day, and the plague that stalks in darkness. I'd never seen arrows flying in the spirit world,

159

but I'd definitely felt dark thoughts hit me like they were shot from a demonic bow.

"Wickedness has no more right to enter this apartment," Connie prayed. The cool thing was, each time she streaked the oil, to my spiritual sight it went from clear to a metallic, rainbow-looking gloss.

Then things took a revolting turn.

As Connie applied her oil to random spots on my walls, declaring that no pestilence would ravage my dwelling or come near me, that rustling sound I'd been hearing at night began to stir, like there was a big commotion behind the Sheetrock.

I put my ear to the wall. "Do you hear that?"

Connie tilted her head and listened, then eyed me like I was strange.

A lady named Glenda who barely came up to my chest began to belt out an old hymn, and my apartment got brighter—a brightness that exposed shadows moving inside the walls. I looked closer . . .

And freaked.

They were insects. Like, the demonic kind you might imagine skittering down the halls of hell. Hundreds of them, creeping behind the drywall and across my high ceilings. Then it got even *worse*. They came spewing out of the walls, landing on my sofa and furniture and all over the carpet. I hopped from one foot to the other, startling everyone, including Glenda, who stopped singing.

"Keep going!" I told her. As much as the extermination process grossed me out, I knew it had to be done.

She picked up the same chorus but was off pitch now, distracted by watching me jump around my apartment like a weirdo. But seriously, these bugs were like nothing on earth, and not just because they were way bigger. Some looked like cockroaches but with fat bumble-bee stingers, and there were spiders with crab-like pincers. There were slimy worms everywhere too—come to think of it, exactly like the one I'd seen at Veronica's breathing deal in the clearing.

But by far, the most horrendous demonic-world pest had to have been the hairy black scorpions . . .

That flew.

I shielded my head and ran for cover into my bedroom, but they were in there, too. Every square foot of my apartment was infested. Finally, I realized that they fled from the circle of light on the floor around me. That helped me calm down a bit.

Still, what had I done to deserve this? Veronica came to mind. I'd been hearing movement in my walls ever since she'd stepped inside my apartment and borrowed my scissors. And read my palm. Had she drawn them here?

At last, Heaven sent the women some supernatural reinforcements. Custos charged into my apartment and stood in my living room, extending his arms shoulder high, palms up. More luminescent beings entered the room, only these were birds—two of them, big and solid white with glistening eyes and the wingspan of eagles. They each perched on one of Custos's outstretched arms.

Custos spoke a word I didn't understand, then tossed his arms up, sending the breathtaking birds forward in flight. Graceful and devastating, they scoured the place, grabbing and devouring the insects with menacing talons and crushing beaks. They swept through my whole apartment, sailing through walls, and I noticed with awe that instead of shadows, they cast light—light that zapped the insects dead.

It didn't take long for the entire pestilence to die, their disgusting, mangled bug bodies piled on the floor. Custos raised a balled fist, then knelt and punched the ground, causing the bugs to bounce all together high in the air, then fall beneath the carpet, disappearing from my place. Away from the earthly realm entirely, I believed. Even my visible house-fly population was gone. Meanwhile, the majestic birds flew up and out through my closed living room windows.

The only word for it was *epic*.

Even though they couldn't see what I could, Betty and her friends seemed just as confident their prayers had been answered. They raised their hands and started singing and saying all kinds of adoring things to God. Custos laughed with delight, then got down and lay prostrate on his stomach, stretching from one end of my living room clear across to the other. I promise you, his armored feet were as long as my arms. He spoke in his unknown language, also worshiping, it seemed.

The spiritual atmosphere in my apartment became a jaw-dropping spectrum of light. From the ceiling to the floor, vibrant, translucent colors tumbled and swirled, dancing all over us. And a sense of all-consuming, unconditional love permeated the room—a deep knowledge that we were treasured beyond comprehension and never, ever had to fear losing our worth.

It was the kind of love every human craves but seems to always fail at giving.

My father had explained that God is self-contained and doesn't desire or need me to express affection to him. It was best to give people love rather than the Source, he'd said. But all I knew was, in that moment, I couldn't help but lift my hands and keep telling God how awesome he was.

I would have liked to pause that moment forever, but eventually, Betty and her friends hugged me before making their way out the door. I'd never been embraced by a grandparent, but when Connie squeezed me, I figured that must be what it feels like. Custos exited too, but he didn't go far. He stood at attention on my balcony, his armored back to my door.

I collapsed onto my sofa and glanced around the room, still smiling. The awesome airborne colors had faded, but the rainbow oil streaks smeared on surfaces throughout my apartment hadn't dimmed a bit.

I had so much to tell Ray Anne. I gave up on playing hard to get and called her. She said she was in bed, feeling a little better but still exhausted from battling a fever and relentless cough.

My heart sank. *That's* why I hadn't heard from her. I felt like a jerk.

I understood why she didn't invite me over—she said she looked as awful as she'd been feeling—but I decided I'd surprise her anyway. I grabbed the envelope with Arthur's letter inside, then hopped on my bike and picked up some Chick-fil-A chicken noodle soup plus a bouquet of colorful flowers. Once I turned onto her street, I gassed it, anxious to see her and tell her all about the world-changing mission we'd been given.

Maybe I shouldn't have been so shocked, but when I saw Ethan's white Volvo parked in Ray's driveway, I slammed on my brakes and glared in disbelief.

Surely they weren't alone in her garage apartment, right? Less than an hour ago, she'd told me she wasn't up for having anyone over.

I parked my motorcycle sideways behind Ethan's safety-rated sedan, prepared to give her the soup and flowers right in front of his two-faced face. He knew she and I were a couple.

Sure enough, as I approached, I heard them inside laughing. Ray Anne coughed but caught her breath and kept giggling.

I figured, why knock when I could spy?

I wedged myself between some shrubs and the garage and inched my way to the window. There was Ethan, seated in a chair beside Ray's bed, where she sat leaning against a pile of pillows, angled toward him. He reached out and clutched her hands, then began praying for her. That's when Ramus, the armored Watchman who frequented Ray Anne's house, appeared behind Ethan. I squinted as he placed an enormous, luminescent hand on their backs.

Ray and I had prayed together lots of times, but never once had a Watchman affirmed our relationship. That's what this looked like to me.

I knew it was unspiritual or whatever, but I couldn't help it—I was mad at Ramus.

I hurled the Chick-fil-A sack and bouquet into a garbage can in Ray Anne's driveway and took off on my bike, passing vehicles like a madman. My mind raced even faster than my wheels.

Betty meant well, but she was dead wrong about my relationship with Ray Anne. There was no devil dividing Ray's heart from mine. She was flat-out falling for another guy. And God clearly approved.

As for my father, he'd had the insight to see the truth and the decency to warn me. Evil wants to crush the human heart, not protect it—why couldn't anyone understand that the departed spirits were on my side?

I went barreling into my apartment and slammed the door so hard, a picture fell off my wall and crashed to the floor. I didn't care.

Custos was nowhere to be found, which irritated me some more.

I grabbed Arthur's message from my pocket and held it high—my best attempt at waving it in God's face. "How am I supposed to accomplish this with her when she's trying to replace me with another guy?"

I squeezed the envelope, tempted to rip it down the middle, but somehow I found the restraint to toss it onto my breakfast table instead.

The silence was deafening. The anger, intoxicating.

I fell back hard on my sofa and chucked a hardbound book across the room. It slammed the wall and landed on top of the broken picture, shattering glass.

Good.

I'd committed to Betty to be done with my father forever, and Betty had assured me he'd never show up inside my place again. Those doors had been closed in the spirit realm this morning, and I was supposed to keep them shut. But right now, aggravated and alone, the desire to reach out to my dad was overwhelming.

I pressed my palms against my eyelids.

At first, I thought I was imagining the sound of my father calling my name, especially when I uncovered my eyes and saw that my power was still on. But then I heard it again. I stood and looked around. "Father? Is that you?"

"I'm here."

I followed the sound of his voice to my front door. It sounded like he was standing on the other side.

"Please. Let me in, Son."

TWENTY-THREE

I OPENED THE DOOR a few inches.

My father stood on my doorstep in broad daylight. "The Source has urgently sent me to you, to equip you for what's soon coming." He bowed his head, aware of and politely respecting the new boundary that had been put in place. "You must invite me in."

I considered it. I wanted to. But I'd promised not to. And this didn't feel right, somehow. "I'll come outside."

"No." For the second time, he held a restraining hand up to me. "We must have privacy. This is vitally important."

I needed time to think, to navigate through the confusion.

"Welcome me inside," my father persisted.

I had seconds, not minutes, to make a decision. The situation demanded that I act. I quickly thought of Betty and her prayerful friends. The pestilence they'd helped drive out of my apartment. The incredible time of worship we'd shared.

"I'm sorry," I said. "But I can't."

Was he actually tearing up?

My dad tilted his head back and looked to the bright sky, nodding as if communing with Heaven, like I'd seen Custos and other Watchmen do so often. "The Source says I'm not to pressure you. I will go."

He turned and walked away, starting to fade into the air.

"Wait!"

He faced me, his form undiluted again.

This was my chance to part ways on good terms—to explain that, right or wrong, I had no choice but to stop seeing him. I wanted him to know I knew he'd done nothing to deserve this; it was just that our unconventional relationship was causing friction between me and important people in my life. At least now I had the chance to say good-bye in a decent, respectful way.

"Are you inviting me in?" he asked.

I stepped back from my open door and gave a single nod.

My dad smiled. "You're doing the right thing, Owen."

He entered and closed the door, making hand contact with the material realm. The power went out, but there was plenty of sunlight to brighten the room. I sat on the sofa, next to his spot, but he remained by the door.

"What's the matter?" I asked.

He reached toward me with an open palm. "Invite me into the living room."

I furrowed my brow. "Why can't you just come?"

But then I saw it. Connie's rainbow streak on the doorframe above his head had turned to gray, crumbling dust. The other oil spots around the sunlit room remained vibrant. My stomach sank as I saw how his presence had disarmed the ladies' spiritual blockade. There was no denying it: their prayers and my father were incompatible.

I stood and faced him but stayed across the room, wrestling with uncertainty. "So, God sent you just now?"

"Yes, and yet you still don't trust me."

"I don't know who to trust anymore."

He stared at me with wide, sympathetic eyes. "I know you intend to eliminate me from your life, but first, please let me help you."

"How?"

"I've been commissioned to train you to subdue forces of darkness, from the least to the greatest. You need to learn this, Owen. Right now."

"I already have, on my own." I was proud to tell him. "The other day, when Murder and Regret and Demise cornered me I said the name of—"

"I know what you said—I was there. And it was *me* who drove them away from you, Son. That word holds no power."

"I didn't see you."

"I wanted you to feel strong. Proud of yourself." He reached out to me again. "But we mustn't waste any more time—invite me to come to you."

Everyone except me seemed so sure of what I needed to do. I glanced at the rainbow stripes of oil on my windows and walls. "Why do you have an aversion to the Light?"

"I don't." He remained stiff, his back against the door. "Those ladies misused universal laws of energy like fools, creating barriers against forces of evil *and* righteous spirits."

It was the first time I'd heard him criticize anyone.

"But you can undo their mistake—and learn from it. Invite me to come to you."

I was still hesitant.

My father dropped his chin and narrowed his eyes as he looked deep into mine. "Owen, I know about the great mission you've been given—to gather the town's people to the land and drive out the evil that dwells there. But I've come to inform you that Molek is returning in a matter of days. It's too late—you can't possibly rally the people in time. Molek is full of might and will rouse his army in an attack like nothing you've ever witnessed before."

I'd suspected Molek was returning soon, but the thought that he was only days away . . .

I dug my fingers into my scalp. "What do I do?"

"I can show you how to use the laws of spirit and energy correctly to combat the evil on your land yourself, without any need of others. But you must act quickly, or all will be lost." He stretched both hands out to me. "The Source says you're not ready, that you doubt yourself and lack understanding. I must prepare you."

Betty had said God would prepare me, and now my father had come to teach me. Was this the answer?

I went with my gut.

"All right," I said. "Come into the living room."

When he did, every strip of oil in sight withered to ashen-colored dust. It didn't surprise me, but watching it happen, I couldn't help but second-guess my decision.

My father passed up his spot on the sofa and stood in the center of the room. "You're tired of running from evil and being useless?"

"Yes," I admitted, although *useless* seemed kind of harsh.

"And you want me to lead you into greater empowerment?"

"Yes."

"Place twelve of your candles on the floor, creating two circles in the center of this room. Leave a two-foot space between them." He clasped his hands and folded them to his chest like he was praying. "You'll give the thirteenth candle to me."

It felt strange and different now that he was issuing orders, not requesting, but I followed his weird instructions, moving my coffee table to make room. Having formed the circles, I handed my final candle to him. He stared at the wick and prayed for the Source to bless us. All thirteen candles ignited at once.

I stepped back, toward my kitchen.

"You've been taught your whole life to fear touching fire." He studied my face. "But there's no need to be afraid of *anything*."

Exact advice the old man had given me. Arthur, I still believed, despite Betty's negative reaction.

My father extended his candle, waving the flame at me. "Touch it."

I saw this for what it was—a test of my courage. And I'd rather have burned all the skin off my finger than shy away. I admit I used my pinkie, but I approached him and stuck my finger in the flame.

It didn't burn me—at all.

I'm sure my eyes were wide and astonished as I examined my

unharmed finger, then pressed my entire palm on top of the fire. All it did was tickle. "How are you doing that?"

"I'm not." He inflated his chest like a proud parent. "You are. The miraculous happens when you act on faith instead of fear."

Incredible. I was suddenly eager to keep going, to do whatever he instructed next.

"Walk around the circles in a figure-eight pattern. Don't stop until I tell you."

I did it, careful not to knock over candles. To my annoyance, waves of hesitation kept pushing through my newfound courage, but I resisted them.

"Don't be afraid." My dad kept his gaze on me, completely in tune with my emotions. "Cowards are intolerable."

I kept stepping around the candles.

Suddenly, darkness overtook my apartment like a tidal wave of black paint. I stopped walking and instantly picked up on distant shrieks and moans. Shrill whispers headed our way, closing in fast.

"I don't like this," I confessed.

"Owen." My father kept his post between the circles. "This is not a game. You must not take matters into your own hands. Do as I say. *Exactly* as I say."

I was starting to wish I hadn't opened the door to him.

Like lava exploding from volcanic rock, Creepers began pouring out of both circles of candles—dozens of them, invading my living room.

I wedged myself into the nearest corner, next to my TV. "Make it stop!" My apartment reeked like roadkill and vomit and a garbage dump all mushed together, and it was as cold as a meat locker.

The Creepers hunkered down and assembled in front of my father like trained lions. I watched him, unsure whether to admire his mastery or abandon all faith in him.

"Why would you invite them here?" I demanded.

"*You* did." He motioned at the throng, and they advanced on me, towering just beyond my aura, glaring down and hissing and gnashing their teeth at me.

I covered my nose. Their presence was overpowering every extrasensory ability I had—except one. The most vital one. But then, even *that* faltered. My ability to see them faded in and out, ramping up my terror. For seconds at a time, they were completely invisible, camouflaged in the candlelit air. Still, I knew they were there. And I could only think of one way to at least try to make them flee.

I opened my mouth to utter my Savior's name, but my father spoke, loud and stern. "Don't you dare rely on that! I warned you—it won't work here, and it won't work on Molek!"

Suddenly he was next to me, inside the crowd of Creepers, which became visible to me again. He spoke loudly in my ear. "Command them. Show them they have no choice but to do as you say."

"How?"

He sighed with impatience, a character flaw I'd assumed he was incapable of. "Tell them to retreat."

I did, but the Creepers didn't back off.

"Louder!"

"Retreat!" I belted it out, and every one of them darted back and hunkered down. I've got to say, it was hugely exhilarating.

"Very good, Son. Now get on your knees."

That made no sense. I shook my head.

"You'll never exercise full authority over them until you prove you're not afraid, and I'm telling you how. Now get down!"

The huddled Creepers had filled my living room and spilled into the hallway. They were still, as if awaiting my next move. Terrifying as the scenario was, for the first time, it felt like I was in charge. And I didn't want to mess that up.

I did it slowly, putting one knee on the carpet. Then the other.

"Now put your face to the floor in absolute fearlessness. When you rise, they'll do exactly as you say, just as they do for me."

I shook my head harder this time. "I won't bow to them."

My father leaned toward me and spoke right into my face. "If you don't, they will charge at you and conquer you, and there'll be nothing I can do."

"They can't conquer me, I'm a Li—"

"A Light who provoked the powers of hell and initiated a challenge! Do as I say and master them, or I swear they will obliterate you—Light and all."

I was struggling to breathe, asphyxiating on evil's fumes, completely in over my head.

I saw no way out.

I'll make it quick. It's just a pose—not worship.

I placed my palms on the carpet, then lowered my forehead.

"All the way down," my father instructed.

I did it.

I snapped my head back up as soon as my forehead touched the floor. Immediately the Creepers lowered their disgusting heads in forced submission toward me, then backed away, out of my apartment completely. It was still unnaturally dark, and the stench and icy air lingered, but they were gone.

I let out a major sigh and even smiled. "Did you see that!"

"Yes." My father was smiling too. "You made that much more difficult than necessary, but you finished strong. They'll never challenge your authority again."

I collapsed to the floor on my back, physically exhausted. Strangely so. "Thank God that's over."

"It is." My dad resumed his position between the two circles, still lined with my lit candles. "But we're not done."

I knew better than to protest, but I couldn't imagine enduring anything else.

"Look." He pointed to the circle on his left. Inside the ring of candles, instead of carpet, there was a pool of what looked like liquid, like a tide tainted and thickened by an oil spill. "Move closer."

I crawled on my hands and knees to gaze down at the paranormal spectacle. "What is it?"

He placed a gentle, warm hand on the back of my neck, touching me for the very first time. "Do you trust me yet, Owen?"

I nodded.

He began pressing my head down, into the circle. "Don't resist. You must see this."

At first I thought I might drown, but my face passed through the layer of liquid into what felt like compacted dirt against my skin, yet I was still able to breathe—enough not to panic, anyway. My father kept pushing me down, much farther, until I was angled upside down with at least half my body submerged in the inexplicable hole. It was dreamlike and disorienting.

I kept going down, and chilled fingers now held me by my ankles. My face somehow penetrated through what seemed like layers of metal—or cold, thick wood, maybe—followed by the tickle of silky fabric grazing my nose, forehead, and cheeks. Finally I stopped dropping. All I could do was blink in the silent darkness. Cold air stung my face.

"Are you ready to see?" My father sounded far away.

I didn't answer, but light shined around me anyway—not soothing, comforting light, but more like dingy, flickering, fluorescent-bulb light.

It took a second to grasp what I was looking at.

I'd been submerged headfirst into a coffin.

With a body.

TWENTY-FOUR

AN EMBALMED FACE loomed inches from mine, eyelids sealed with hardened glue, skin tinged with gray. By the time I realized who it was, I was horrified to the point of paralysis. I couldn't even open my mouth to yell.

Walt.

Dead.

In his casket.

I was as breathless as he was—until his eyes sprang open. I gasped and tried to turn away, but he grabbed my throat and started choking me. His face was contorted with rage and hatred, like his need for revenge against me had roused him back to life. I pushed against his stiff chest, clothed in his gray burial suit, and tried to free myself, but I was no match for him.

The cold pair of hands suspending me suddenly hoisted me up, back into my living room, but right away I was forced facedown into the other circle, shoved much faster this time. The experience was identical, only now I knew I was plunging toward terror.

I landed inside another casket.

Marshall's.

He was already wide eyed and awake, waiting for me. He clawed at my face and squeezed my throat. The fear was so intense that, to this day, I can't accurately describe it.

I used my fists to fight for my life until I was finally pulled up and out. I landed on my back in my living room, gasping and looking up at my father.

He was composed and serene. "You killed them."

I couldn't catch my breath. "I didn't mean to!"

"Owen." He bent down, hovering over me. "Tell the truth."

I used my elbows to drag myself backward, away from him. "How could you put me through that!"

He followed me. "You can't outrun the penalty of your past. The regret is yours to bear. So bear it, Son. With grief and humility."

I sat straight up. "Leave!"

"But we're not done." He bent so that his face was nearly touching mine, then whispered, "I'm not going anywhere until your preparation is complete."

To say I felt threatened is an understatement.

A knock sounded, and my father turned his head fast toward the door.

"Owen, it's me."

Ray Anne. All my resentment over catching her with Ethan was replaced by a desperate longing to be close to her. In her arms. I scrambled to my feet.

"Don't." My father had supernaturally moved across the room, his back against the door.

"Go away!" I told him.

"What?" Ray Anne tried to understand through the door.

"I can't bear to watch you disappoint the Source like this." He reached back and turned the dead bolt, locking it. "You walk out now, and you'll fail your assignment miserably. *Gravely.*"

I resisted fear and spoke boldly. "The interaction between you and me—it ends now."

He studied my face, scrutinizing me. "It's not that simple, Son." He finally stepped away from the door, striding toward the hallway leading to my bedroom. He paused, turning back toward me. "It pains me to have to stand back and watch you lose like this."

Then he turned away and was gone.

I threw the door open and hugged Ray Anne so fast and tight, I nearly knocked her over. Jackson was with her, asleep in his stroller.

"Are you okay?" she asked. "I tried calling, but . . ." She searched my face, then peered past me into my apartment. The otherworldly darkness was lifting, and there was only carpet now inside the circles of candles, but it was still obvious something was terribly wrong. Ray Anne's jaw dropped.

"Listen to me, Ray. What happened in there . . . just know that I'm done. *Completely.* No more spirit contacts or conjuring." Whatever advantage over evil my father may have brought me, it had been done at the expense of the Light. I knew now going along with it had been a huge mistake. I couldn't fall for that ever again.

Ray Anne backed away, eyeing me like I was a monster.

"I know this looks bad, but I swear, it's over."

She clamped her hands down on the stroller handles and moved the baby back. "Owen, this is serious."

"I know."

"No. You don't."

She strained to turn her head and cover her mouth, battling through a coughing spell.

I tried to hug her. "It'll be okay. I'll make things right."

She dodged my arms and looked me up and down, frowning.

"What's the matter?" I asked.

She hesitated. The words came slowly. "I can see stuff lately . . . that I couldn't before."

A sinking feeling came over me, like a loaded grenade had dropped into my gut. For a while there, my supernatural field of vision had been increasing too, revealing new sights. But now I had some sort of spiritual macular degeneration that I had no clue how to remedy.

"It's like the more compassion I have for people," Ray Anne said, "the more I see the burdens they carry. Even Lights."

I dreaded where this was going.

Sure enough, her gaze fixed on my throat. "Owen, it's not crystal clear, but . . ." Her tone was almost apologetic. "You have cords and chains wrapped around your neck, twisted together, hanging all the way down the front of you." She squinted and pointed, slowly moving her finger until it was aimed at the cement by my feet. "There are six chains. No, seven. With cuffs."

Seven? That was more than I'd lugged around back when I'd been shackled.

I instinctively patted my body down, but of course, felt nothing. I already knew personal bondage can't be seen or felt, even with spiritual senses. I wondered out loud, "Did they just now get me, or . . . ?"

Oh, yeah.

I'd most likely been carrying this baggage ever since my nightmare, when I'd been accosted with chains and cords. I'd thought my father had freed me, but . . .

The truth hurt. And infuriated me.

Jackson began to whimper as Ray Anne tugged on my shirt sleeve, attempting to pull me and the stroller toward the elevator. "Let's go see Betty. Maybe she can help."

"No." I pulled away. "I'll deal with this myself." I couldn't imagine telling Betty that, within hours of her spiritual housecleaning, I'd broken my commitment and welcomed not only my father but also a pack of devils into my apartment. She'd be furious with me—just like I was.

Ray pleaded with me, but I stood my ground. When she finally gave up, I told her to stay on the balcony while I went inside to get something. It was too cold and hazy and contaminated in my apartment to invite her and the baby in. I returned with Arthur's prophecy, tucked inside the envelope.

"Ray Anne, I want you to read this." I handed it to her. "We've been given a crucial mission, but we're out of time—and it was nearly impossible to begin with."

She stared at the envelope, still coughing while rolling the stroller back and forth, working to keep Jackson content. "I'll read it as soon as I get home." She might have been willing to hug me good-bye, but I wasn't about to press my icy metal against her.

The next morning, Ray Anne called. I could tell she was pacing. "April 20."

"Huh?"

"Let's tell everyone to gather outside Masonville High at 10:00 a.m. this Saturday, April 20. That gives us a week to spread the word—not very long, but I have an idea."

She'd obviously read Arthur's instructions and wasn't wasting any time. "I don't know if that's fast enough, Ray. Just trust me when I say, I think Molek's coming back even sooner."

"Well, we have to try."

She was right.

That afternoon, Ray and I stood in the Masonville High parking lot, and she used her cell to capture a video of me attempting to call the people of Masonville to action. I was mainly speaking to Lights, but I couldn't exactly call them that, and I wasn't willing to make it sound like certain people weren't welcome. I kept messing up and having to start over. It didn't help that Creepers were storming at us and hissing the whole time, clearly bothered by our project.

I recounted Arthur's story on camera—not all the paranormal stuff, but how he grew up enslaved on what used to be Caldwell's land, where he witnessed all kinds of abuse and injustice and murder. I explained that the school was built on that very property, and based on Arthur's wisdom and advice, we needed to come together *now*, on April 20, to acknowledge the past and commit to using the land for good.

I left out the prayer part. I figured we had a better chance of getting people to come if we waited until they were here to mention it. But I ended with complete transparency. "According to Arthur—and I have good reason to believe he knew what he was talking about—if we don't do this, things are going to get much, much worse in Masonville."

Ray Anne uploaded the video and blasted it all over social media.

That evening, I kept my TV off and prayed longer than I ever had before, the best I knew how. I asked God to please have his Watchmen keep Molek away until April 20, then do a miracle and help us convince people to show up.

Honestly, I had about as much faith that Ashlyn would spontaneously snap out of her coma. But maybe the people of Masonville would prove me wrong.

My dead bolt was locked, but it was no protection from the worst kind of intruders. Thanks to me, my spiritual blockades had crumbled to dust, and I feared my father would return whenever he wanted now—if he even *was* my father. Of course now it was occurring to me that maybe I'd been seriously deceived by a form of evil I'd never suspected existed.

I mean, who knew there was such thing as demonic insects?

I remembered there was a bottle of vegetable oil in my pantry, left behind by whoever had lived here before me, and I took it and put streaks in all the same places Connie had—but they didn't turn colorful.

I wasn't surprised. I already knew that, in the spirit world, copying what someone else says or does doesn't necessarily bring you the same results. It was obvious to me that faith isn't something that can be faked. And I'd learned the hard way that it takes more than formulas to move God and his army to action.

I had a lot to learn from Betty and her ladies, but I doubted they'd take the time to teach me anything after how I'd blown it today.

I was wiping away my useless oily smudges when my mother called. We hadn't spoken since the restaurant debacle. Before I could even say hello, she was shouting at me. "Are you near a TV? Turn it to the news!" She was panting into the phone. "Do you see it? Do you see what's on?"

I turned on the TV and flipped it to a news channel. "What's the big deal?"

And then I saw it.

A news report talking about how an American doctor who'd gone missing in Uganda had been found. They flashed a picture on the screen, and I thought I might pass out.

My father.

Alive.

Before I could process the realization or say a word to my mom, darkness descended like a curtain throughout my apartment, and my phone and TV lost power. A glowing, familiar spirit stared at me from the hallway, grinning, but with narrowed, hostile eyes.

TWENTY-FIVE

THE TV REMOTE FELL from my hand as the deceptive spirit I'd been call-ing *Father* approached, radiating light from head to toe like a parody of holiness. Three dark figures trailed behind him.

"Tell me who you are." I refused to run. "Who's with you?"

He gave me my father's smile, like old times.

I raised my voice. "You're not who you claimed to be."

"I'm exactly what you need. A father figure, sent to guide you."

The three silhouettes fanned out and surrounded me. I recognized one as Lucas, only now his jeans and T-shirt were dirty and torn, his face smudged and filthy. I stayed focused on the one who bore my father's image. "You're a liar." I still couldn't fathom that my real father was alive.

His mouth twisted in a sarcastic pout. "Did you not feel safe and loved in my presence?"

Disgust filled me. "I'm done with you."

He refused to give up the charade. "I can still help you. Have I not been kind to you? A source of light when you needed it?"

The four of them circled me, just beyond my aura—another sure sign they hailed from the enemy's kingdom. I wanted to throw punches, but I knew fists weren't weapons in their world. So I did what I knew Ray Anne would do . . .

"I've been given authority to overcome all the power of the enemy, and nothing will harm me." Luke 10:19. Ray's go-to verse. My off-the-cuff version, anyway.

He still wore my father's face, but his eyes turned dark as coal and his voice, low and menacing. "Don't quote Scripture at me, boy. You barely know it and don't believe it."

Walt's voice came from behind me. My skin crawled to hear it so filled with hate. "You're right, Owen. We *are* your enemy."

Then Marshall. "We *do* have power."

Lucas. "And we *can* harm you."

They seemed to defy me—defy the Scripture I'd used on them—and yet the impostor leading the charge gnashed his teeth so furiously, I knew I must have gained an advantage. He shouted in my face, literally shaking with anger. "You think you can just get rid of me?" Flies flew out of his mouth. The earthly kind. That's when I knew . . .

He had been the source of my infestation.

He sneered at me. "Say what you want. This isn't over."

All four of them sauntered into the hallway, cackling like they knew something I didn't, then disappeared.

The darkness lifted. The power came back on. And I called Betty and begged her to please forgive me and come help me rearm my apartment.

Less than an hour later, she and her ladies came over and fortified the spiritual atmosphere.

Even after the rainbow streaks were shining again, it was hard to stop taking paranoid glances at the hallway. Other than that, I stayed glued to my TV and laptop, watching reports about my father, Stephen Grayson. It was among the top trending topics in the media.

He was reportedly weak, but his doctors were hopeful he'd recover. I learned that a hostile regime had held him and two European doctors captive all these months. My father had managed to escape but hadn't been willing to return to the United States until the remaining hostages were rescued. Three days ago, they were, and my father was flown to a hospital in his hometown, Tulsa, Oklahoma.

Everything in me wanted to jump up and go see him—to rush into his hospital room and tell him he had a son. To discover what my father was *really* like. But this was a terrible time for me to leave town. Molek could return any minute.

The video of me Ray had posted already had a couple thousand hits, but that was probably because Lance had seen it and posted a video of his own, making fun of the whole thing. He called me delusional and said Arthur's story was just a twisted legend. Then he accused me of doing this all for attention. "It's a messed-up condition Owen's had since high school," he said.

I needed to stay in Masonville and try to set the record straight, yet I couldn't imagine making no effort to go meet my father. What if I put it off and he took a turn for the worse and died? I knew hospital security might not even let me past the lobby into his room, but could I live with myself if I didn't try?

Then again, what if I did meet him, only to have him say he wanted nothing to do with me, some surprise kid from his past?

The next afternoon, I went to Ray Anne's to talk things through. Her makeshift apartment looked like a nursery, crammed full of Jackson's things. We sat across from each other at her two-seater breakfast table. Her cough had gotten worse, making it a challenge for her to talk. "You have to go try to see your dad." She cleared her throat enough to keep encouraging me. "I'll stay on top of things here and keep getting the word out about Saturday."

"I don't know, Ray—"

"I do. You fell for the counterfeit. Don't pass on the real thing."

She was right. I had to go.

I reached across the mini table and stroked her hand. "I know I've done some really stupid stuff lately, Ray Anne. Stuff you tried to warn me about. I'm sorry."

"At least you see it now." Thankfully, she was quick to let it go. But the whole time we'd been sitting there, she kept cutting her eyes away. I didn't blame her. I knew I was likely still loaded down with entrapments, nauseating to look at. But I didn't bring it up or ask her to confirm it. I didn't know how to get free, so what was the point?

I tried to stay focused on what mattered most. "That impostor spirit told me Molek is coming back in the next few days, but it could have been a lie to try and scare us."

She leaned in toward me. "I'm not scared."

I leaned in too, our noses nearly touching. "Me either." I spoke with as much faith as Ray Anne, but internally, I had my doubts. Who were we kidding? We were no match for Molek, and our rushed effort to rally the community wasn't exactly going strong. I felt like it was halftime, and we were down by too many points to recover.

Mrs. Greiner barged into the garage apartment without knocking and announced that Pastor Gordon was stopping by later. Ray Anne rolled her eyes, and Mrs. Greiner got defensive. "Yes, I put you on the sick list at church, and yes, church members are going to keep wanting to check on you."

It occurred to me that maybe that was why Ethan had been here the other day—a church-assigned duty. Not because Ray Anne had invited him.

Had that deceiving spirit planted lies in my head about Ray Anne having feelings for another guy? The brick wall of self-defense I'd recently put up around my heart started to crumble, mistrust giving way to security all over again.

Mrs. Greiner finally left, and an idea hit me like a stroke of genius, fueled by an intense longing to spend time with my girl. My favorite person on earth. Not after my trip to Tulsa, but today.

Right now.

"Let's get out of here," I said. "Just you and me. Escape for a little while, like old times."

Her smile made me want to melt.

She hopped on the back of my motorcycle and slid on a helmet as we took off, hurrying before her dad could see us and insist that we take Ray's car. She started to wrap her arms around my waist, but I reached down and stopped her, bothered that she might feel ice-cold chains and cords draping down my chest.

It was so frustrating. I'd been liberated when I shed my shackle. Lights had no business being bound.

"I only see them off and on." She spoke loudly so I could hear her over the engine and wind whistling past us. "And I don't feel anything right now."

I let her cling to me and pulled down hard on the gas, my smile as wide as the open road as I pulled onto the interstate that led out of town, away from the concentration of evil and Ethan and the threat of Molek—away from all things Masonville.

When I hit eighty miles an hour, Ray Anne threw one hand in the air. "Yes!"

Man, we really needed this.

We drove through two small hill-country towns and finally made it to our destination—the scenic lake where Ray Anne and I had sneaked off together on prom night. The sky was overcast, but it made for a comfortable, room-temperature afternoon. She pointed to a white gazebo she spotted among the trees by the lake, and I pulled over.

We sat side by side on a bench inside the white woodwork masterpiece, looking out at the serene water, discussing the shock and miracle of my father's rescue. On and on we talked about all sorts of things, both of us vulnerable and open in a way that we reserved only for each other. At one point, she admitted that Ethan had confessed he had feelings for her, but she'd told him she wasn't giving up on me.

Thank God.

She relaxed back onto the bench and rested her shoulders in my lap so that her shackle-free neck rested on my arm. With my other hand, I stroked her cheek. She touched my face too, staring at me with her stunning blue eyes that had a way of making my heart pound—with affection, yes, but also desire. The intense kind that makes your insides ache.

I was sure that any second, she'd sit up and scoot away—her go-to response every time the chemistry between us started heating up. But she didn't.

"Do you think I'm too cautious, Owen? Too uptight about boundaries and stuff with you?"

Yeah. But I didn't want to say it. "Why would you ask that?"

She shrugged, running her fingers through my hair. "We're not kids anymore. And sometimes I just . . ." She slid her hand behind my neck, blushing a soft shade of pink. "I wonder what it's like."

She gave a gentle tug, inching my face toward hers. I clung tightly to her, but kept my hands gentle. She started breathing faster and blinking slower, shutting her eyes for seconds at a time.

My breath sped up, falling into sync with hers without me trying. Our faces were nearly touching. Our lips, less than a breath apart.

TWENTY-SIX

"RAY ANNE," I whispered. I was dying to kiss her. So why couldn't I make my move? She kept pressing on the back of my neck, miraculously inviting me to go for it.

But could I? Could *I* be the one to crush her lifelong dream of waiting for a wedding-day kiss? I'd always thought it was a ridiculous, incredibly unrealistic commitment. But it had always been so heartfelt. So Ray Anne.

Her eyelids drifted closed again, and she left them that way, allowing her lips to part, practically begging me to take them. She uttered my name, both syllables heavy with yearning. I kept my eyes open, anticipating the look on her face as I introduced her to a taste of the passion she'd never once allowed herself to drink. Not even a small sip.

One tilt of my neck, and her lips were mine. Maybe her body, too. Mine to steal.

In her moment of weakness.

I . . . I'm not supposed to do this.

My whole body tensed like hardening cement as I willed myself to pull my head away from hers. My fingers folded into fists. It was like trying to bring a high-speed train to a screeching stop.

I finally managed to turn my face. I let out a miserable groan.

She sat up fast and faced me on the bench. "Owen, I . . . I'm so sorry."

I didn't look at her—not because I was angry but because I didn't trust myself to resist leaning in a second time and taking what I wanted after all.

Ray Anne covered her face. "You could have gotten away with that. I wanted you to."

"I wanted to just as much."

She faced me, eyes pooling. "So why didn't you?"

I wasn't trying to be romantic—my body was just so deflated by the experience that I lowered to one knee in front of her. "Because, Ray Anne." I gripped her hands. "I care more about you than myself."

Finally, I'd proven it—to her and to myself.

She pulled my head to her shoulder and nestled her chin in my hair. I couldn't be sure, but I think she cried a little. There wasn't much to say after that—in a good way, I mean. It had been an intense, stressful situation—a series of stressful situations, to be honest—but it felt like things were finally getting back on track between us. Like we both wanted to be together.

I drove Ray Anne home, and as the sun set over her driveway, I promised her I'd be back from Tulsa in three days, on Wednesday.

It only took a few clicks on my cell to buy my plane tickets. By the next afternoon, I'd walked Daisy to the pet boarding place and was packed to catch my 7:40 p.m. flight.

I was zipping my suitcase when I heard a knock at the door. A glance through the peephole revealed Veronica, sniffling and crying. I stepped out onto the balcony and asked her what was wrong.

"A student in my program went missing yesterday."

"Another one?"

She reached out and held my hand—she was so upset, I let her. "I just left the police station. I told them everything I could think of."

"Who's the student?"

"I think you know her." She nibbled her bottom lip like she was nervous to tell me. "Riley. Haven't you been tutoring her?"

No way. Surely I'd heard wrong.

Veronica forced a hug on me, crying again. "We have to find her, Owen."

Believe me, I wanted to. But I was about to board a plane. Could there have been a worse time for me to go? "I'll help search for her, I promise. The second I get back."

She let go of me and eyed my suitcase behind me, in the living room. "You can't leave. You and I are the only ones who can find her, if we work together."

"What are you talking about?"

She slipped her fingers between mine. "Few people have the spiritual sensitivity we do." She stepped inside my apartment uninvited and pulled me in. "Let's combine our strength to get answers. Ask the Source to reveal where she is."

The Source . . .

I couldn't believe she'd just said that. "Where'd you hear that term?"

She used the bottom of her thin hot-pink T-shirt to swipe tears off her chin. Her waterlogged eyes looked even greener. "My meditation books. Why?"

I shook my head, unwilling to get into it with her.

"Come on." She lowered to her knees and tried to pull me to the rug with her. "Let's clear our minds and ask the Source to let us see through Riley's eyes. Did you know we can do that?"

"Veronica, I'm not doing anything like that here." I turned and opened the door wide, ready for her to leave.

She stood and came close. "It doesn't have to be here. Come to the woods with me. I'll show you what to do."

I huffed. "Stay out of those woods. It's private property. And so is my mind, so don't go there either." I escorted her out of my apartment, bulky chains and all, and made myself clear. "It's devastating that Riley's missing. But tapping into evil powers isn't the answer."

She winced like I'd genuinely wounded her. "I would never do anything evil."

Her pouty face struck me as childlike. Innocent, even. I actually felt kind of sorry for her. She was drowning in deception—like me, until a few days ago. I stood there wrestling over whether it was my responsibility to say something or not. Finally, I told her, "Veronica, anything spiritual that doesn't involve God is a gateway to evil. That's why he forbids it."

I can't recall what she said at that point. I was too lost in the epiphany of what had just flowed from my mouth. It's one thing to have a thought dawn on you; this was way more than that. It was like a light had just switched on in my soul, illuminating truth.

All this time, I'd mistaken biblical instructions for restrictive, useless rules and fought them like captors. But I'd been wrong.

About a lot of things, I now realized.

By the time I snapped out of it and focused on the beautiful but bound woman in front of me, she was working to worm her way inside my apartment all over again. Had I not planted myself on the threshold of my door, I have no doubt she would have.

"Wherever you're going, Owen, please don't leave—not now. We need you here." She blinked fast, batting her long eyelashes. "*I* need you."

Her plea struck me as confirmation that I was definitely supposed to take this trip.

"I can't give you what you're looking for," I told her. "And I *have* to go." I told her bye and shut the door.

Once I figured the stairwell and parking lot were clear of her, I used an app to arrange for transportation to the airport. On my way out the door, I called my mom to let her know I was going. She got weepy, but even before that, she sounded weak. She assured me Dr. Bradford was taking good care of her, which didn't bring me any comfort at all.

As I waited at the bottom of the stairwell for my ride, I could smell Demise but didn't see the one-handed stalker. I had bigger concerns, though. I was deeply worried about Riley and still in shock that my father had been found. I stared out into the field where Custos had been. Nothing but grass out there today.

Please, God, rescue Riley. Bring her home.

I noticed someone speed walking down the sidewalk toward me, dressed in black skinny-style slacks, her high heels tapping the cement like impatient snaps. I did a double take. It was the irritating reporter lady from TV. I still couldn't believe that she was a Light.

"Owen Edmonds?" I nodded, and she shoved her cell phone in my face in voice recorder mode, then talked annoyingly fast. "I'm Elle Adelle with Channel Two."

Her name had always sounded fake to me.

"It's my understanding you know Riley Jenson," she said. "Can you tell me, when was the last time you saw her?"

Ah. A nosy interview. No, thank you.

She repeated the question, even more forcefully.

When I still didn't answer, she huffed like she didn't like me, either. "We're trying to find her—don't you want to help?"

"Absolutely. I'll assist detectives however I can."

She smirked. "I'm the best detective in this town."

Whatever.

She wasn't lowering her cell from my chin. I crossed my arms and decided to put her in the hot seat for a change. "What's your theory about the abductions? Gang activity?"

Elle rolled her eyes and finally dumped her cell phone in her purse. "Of all people, I thought you might have a clue."

"What's that supposed to mean?"

She puckered her peach-colored lips and raised one eyebrow like I was dumb. "You're a fourth-generation Caldwell. The sole heir to that land."

Okay, so she did have at least *some* investigative skills. "And?" I said.

"Do you know *anything* about your family's history? About that property of yours?"

I could see Demise in my peripheral vision now, but I didn't let it derail me. "As a matter of fact, I do." An unwelcome sense of shame gripped me. "Look, I'm not proud of all the slavery and stuff my ancestors did out there, but that wasn't me. And it was a long time ago."

She closed her eyes and rubbed back and forth on her forehead like she was beyond annoyed with me, her other hand balled and pressed on her hip.

I threw my hands up. "What?"

She tilted her head to the side and blinked fast. "Sacred grounds. Dominant bloodlines. Unorthodox holidays. None of that means *anything* to you?"

My blank expression said it all.

She scanned the parking lot as if there was a chance we weren't alone. "If you're as uninformed as you claim, you might as well stay that way." She turned her back on me and started walking off. "It may save your life."

Excuse me?

I hurried and stood in front of her, stopping her in her tracks. "Look, Elle, I get that there's some weird annoyance vibe between us, but all I've done for what seems like forever is try to figure out the story of my ancestors and that land and how to turn things around in this town, so if you happen to know something I don't, I need you to tell me." I stepped closer. "I can assure you, I know things you can't possibly know."

She huffed. "I seriously doubt that."

Man, this woman's personality was grating. But I had to get past that. My eyes dipped to our golden auras on the pavement. "Believe it or not, you and I are on the same team."

"I work alone." She sidestepped me as my ride pulled up.

"'Cause you can't get along with anybody—am I right?" I followed after her.

She stopped beside her black Audi. "Because I don't trust anyone in this town."

Well, that was a fair answer. I had a small but growing appreciation for this aggravating lady and wanted to hear more from her. "You can trust me." I held out my palm for a handshake. "How about we start over, politely this time?"

She dug through her purse and slapped her business card in my hand. "Call me if you're willing to talk about Riley." She slid behind the wheel of her car. My driver laid on his horn.

"I'll be in touch," I said.

She closed her door in my face but then lowered her dark-tinted window and handed me a white plastic square. Some sort of press badge . . . with my picture and name on it.

"Um . . . what's this? How . . . ? Why?" I was stammering now.

Elle rolled her eyes so hard I thought she might actually hurt herself. "If you expect to see your father, you're going to need that."

What? She seemed more like a spy now than a news reporter. "How do you know about that? My personal life is none of your business."

"I make things my business." She started her car and put it in reverse. "It's necessary as I work to uncover and mend things around here."

Okay, fine. But did she have to get *that* into my business? And what had she ever done to mend things in Masonville?

She drove off, and I studied the press badge—the less-than-flattering picture of me she'd obviously swiped off social media.

Was anyone else's life as weird as mine?

As I loaded my small suitcase into the idling sedan, I wondered if a short escape from the tragedies and strangeness of Masonville might do me some good.

I arrived at Masonville's miniature airport with plenty of time to spare. It had crossed my mind that it might be interesting to see what, if anything, goes on in the spirit world at around 35,000 feet above ground.

Let's just say I'd seriously underestimated the experience.

TWENTY-SEVEN

MASONVILLE'S AIRPORT HAD only one terminal, and when I got past the security checkpoint and turned down the main walkway, I spotted packs of Creepers at each gate, crowding the doorways. Some wore those pointy hoods, and as one of them clung upside down to a wall, its head twisted in the opposite direction of its body, at last I was able to read its marred forehead:

witch

I shuddered.

I stopped and stared as a stream of shackled new arrivals, people that had just exited a plane, entered through the gate nearest me. It was bad enough that Creepers swooped down on them like vultures on bleeding squirrels, but even worse was that among all the Creepers there, at least half had the same scar-marked assignment on their faces:

suicide

Yeah, the Creepers clearly lacked stamina, but they used what strength they had to strum through people's cords, no doubt searching for transgressions that catered to their deadly assignment. It's not like I had to see the labels on people's cords to figure it out. Anyone with depressed, hopeless, self-hating—broken attitudes like that—was particularly vulnerable to Suicide, especially teenagers. The younger a person, the easier he or she tends to fall for lies.

Welcome to Masonville, Texas.

At least my spiritual sight appeared to be fully functional again—a solid twenty/twenty. My theory was that my preoccupation and entanglement with enemy forces had been dulling my senses. Thankfully, that was all behind me.

As I boarded the plane, a longtime question of mine was answered: people's Creepers traveled with them. They curled up inside the plane seats so that it looked like their victims were practically riding in their laps. And there were Creepers in empty seats too, apparently anticipating susceptible souls.

Ugh. There was no way to get away from the stench. But at least the Creepers leaned away from my light as I made my way down the aisle, headed to my seat near the back of the aircraft.

By 7:46 p.m., flight 4401 was airborne. I've never forgotten the flight number because I've never forgotten what I witnessed out the window.

When we took off, the first thing I saw was that inexplicable, boxy black object hovering midair near Masonville High. As we climbed above the clouds, there was nothing remarkable except the picture-perfect sunset. The sky was an awesome blend of bright colors that reminded me of a blanket Ray Anne had bought Jackson. I stared into the distance, praying for Riley and tuning out the chatty women next to me.

I could have sworn I saw a cluster of dark figures hovering far off to my right, but we passed it so fast, it was a fleeting black streak. Minutes later though, there was no mistaking the phenomenon in the sky. A massive troop of armored Watchmen moved swiftly in a line above the clouds, shoulder to shoulder, advancing toward my side of the aircraft.

There had to have been at least twenty of them, lighting up the sky like a blinding wave rushing the shore. As they passed over our plane, I pressed my face against the window and angled my neck to try to get a decent look.

The Watchmen had their backs to me now, their radiance beaming through the unshaded windows across the aisle. Meanwhile, my fellow passengers sat scrolling mindlessly on screens and dozing off in front of movies that couldn't possibly have compared with the real-life action happening outside—beings beyond Marvel's wildest imaginings.

Minutes later, as I scanned the sky and the final hues of sunlight, a mass of Creepers emerged, appearing from beneath the carpet of clouds for brief seconds at a time like smoky puffs of pollution. They traveled in sync with our aircraft and in the same direction, some galloping like beasts on all fours while others charged upright on invisible air, all at an astronomical speed.

I spotted a huge and ornate, yet mangled chair perched in the sky, facing my window, with what looked like nasty tentacles and big bones and some kind of black seaweed stuff draped all over, dangling far below. A wicked being with dark hair as long as Molek's, clothed in tattered gray robes, sat tall in the chair like it was his throne. Or hers. It was hard to tell.

I watched the androgynous creature stand and point, as if commanding the migrating Creepers to keep moving. This was another Creeper monarch in its own distorted right, a principality on par with Molek. It stretched its arms out, forming a T, then fell forward, vacating its throne to plunge facedown into the clouds, toward earth, I imagined.

"That's it!" I startled the lady next to me, and she nearly choked on her pretzels. That midair object closing in on Masonville High was a throne. *Molek*'s throne. Hadn't the old man warned me of the consequences should the Lord of the Dead remount his throne above the town? I'd mistakenly thought he was being metaphorical.

My belief in spirits of the dead visiting the living had been shattered, so I was confused all over again about who the old man was. That said, my trust in his motives hadn't wavered. And my concern that Molek was headed back to Masonville wasn't wavering either. His throne was closing in—soon he would too.

Lord, I prayed again, *hold him back so the town has time to gather— five more days. And, please, get the people there.*

My eyes were fixed on the caravan of Creepers still charging alongside my window when four of the largest Watchmen I'd seen to date lowered into my line of sight and closed in fast on the horde. I'm serious when I say they were as tall as two-story buildings, their muscular arms as thick as steel beams. Instead of armor, their colossal bodies were covered in flowing garments that reminded me of a Julius Caesar statue my mom kept on her fireplace mantel. Their feet were covered in glistening, gold, sandal-like shoes that matched the thin crowns encircling their heads.

All four of them held gigantic stained-glass-looking bowls, and in unison, they tipped them, dumping a shimmery liquid onto the startled mob of Creepers. The most astounding part was the sound. When the liquid poured out, I heard hundreds of voices talking all at once, and there was singing, too. It was so ear-poundingly loud that, for a few seconds, it overpowered the blaring hum of the aircraft.

I wish I could describe the Creepers' reaction, but I didn't see it. Once drenched, they howled and stopped moving. My plane immediately left them and the ginormous Watchmen behind.

The lady next to me tapped me and handed me the ginger ale I'd requested. I sank down in my seat, dying to tell Ray Anne every unbelievable thing I'd just witnessed.

I sure would have liked to get bowls like that dumped on my property.

It was nearly eleven at night when we made the descent into Tulsa, too dark to see any Creeper thrones that may have been suspended over the city. Just like back home, evil forces mobbed the shackled newcomers, but the majority of these were named Violence. I didn't have to research it to know the crime rate had to be high here.

I'll admit, I'd been so focused on making a difference in my hometown, I'd lost sight of how the problem of evil was everywhere.

I called Ray, and thankfully, she said she thought her new cough meds were helping. I described all I'd seen during my flight, and she freaked. Sadly, there were no updates on Riley, much less Tasha, but news reports confirmed my father was still hospitalized in Tulsa.

As I waited outside the airport for transportation, I practiced what I would say if I was actually able to get to my father tomorrow morning. But nothing I came up with sounded remotely right.

A man in a suit, I'd say midthirties, stood next to me carrying on an intense conversation on his cell in a foreign language. He was attached to a Creeper with an unfamiliar word burned into its forehead:

luxure

I looked it up on my phone—French for "lust."

Two women walked past me, dodging me with their suitcases, both wearing African-style dresses with matching head wraps in colorful patterns. One was a Light, but the other was shackled and tethered to a Creeper. It was a hooded one, like the ones I'd been seeing back home. I was able to catch a close-up glance and saw the word uchawi carved into its nightmarish face.

Thanks to technology, within seconds, I found out it was Swahili for "witchcraft."

From these two observations, I drew a couple of interesting conclusions.

One, base-level Creepers—the kind that function as underlings to demon kings—clearly took on the earthly language of the culture to which they were assigned. And like most parasites, they tended to stay and hunt prey in their allotted territories, unless their human host traveled.

Two, Creepers with the witchy hoods were obviously assigned to partner with humanity in the dark art of witchcraft. I knew now that had to include everything from casting spells and conjuring so-called spirits to trendy gatherings in the woods where students hoped to become one with water, fire, and air. Hadn't Veronica's program drawn a hooded demon's attention like an infected sore attracts flies?

I splurged on a decent hotel room and relished every minute of my steamy shower. I ordered a three-course meal from room service but hardly got three bites down. The thought of coming face-to-face with my father tomorrow sabotaged my appetite. That and the mental flashes of Riley being abducted and abused.

I sank into bed and did a search on my laptop, eager for some new realizations. *Sacred grounds. Dominant bloodlines. Unorthodox holidays.* The terms Elle had rattled off.

I was disappointed when I learned they were all related to the occult. I'd already known for a while now that my grandparents had engaged in satanic worship on my land. It's what devastated my mother's childhood and warped her personality for life.

Elle had acted like it was such a major secret, my life would somehow be in danger if I knew. A member of the press sensationalizing things—what a surprise.

I shut my laptop. *So much for uncovering new revelations.* I didn't want to study and learn the ins and outs of the occult any more than I wanted to become an expert on the history of the slave trade. It was all a sick, sad part of my family's past that, thankfully, had died with my ancestors.

I'd already turned off the lights when Detective Benny called and questioned me about Riley. I told him everything I knew. His voice cracked multiple times, like the worry and stress were getting to him. The longer we spoke, the more I wondered who in the world could have taken Riley and whether she had any chance of survival. As we hung up, I got the impression Benny was plagued by the same thoughts.

Lying on my back in the silence, gazing at the moonlight-speckled ceiling, I heard a familiar rustling in the walls. Who knows who all had stayed in this hotel—in this very room—and what they'd done to evoke a paranormal pestilence, but it was definitely there. Good news though, Custos showed up at the foot of my bed, on one knee, watching over me, and the noisy infestation quieted down.

Despite the comfort of Custos's presence, I may have gotten a grand total of two hours of sleep. I could hardly shield my eyes from his light, even with a pillow on my face. That plus the intense anticipation of finally meeting my father kept my eyes open.

I showed up at the hospital at exactly nine o'clock in the morning, when their website said visiting hours started. My timing was impeccable; the lobby was swarming with reporters and TV crews from all over the world, all there to cover a press conference with my father, I learned. Minutes later, a set of double doors opened, and people filed in, pushing forward like a herd of spooked cattle, shuffling over death dust—typical in hospitals. More than anyone, I *had* to get in there.

As I merged into the crowd, my stomach was a mess of tangled knots and my mouth a parched desert. I'd spent a lifetime dreaming of laying eyes on my father, and now that the moment was almost here, nervousness held me by the throat.

I'd just passed into a hallway when a guard stopped me, gripping my arm. "Identification?"

I noticed the press people all flashing badges before receiving clearance to hurry through another set of doors. I thought for sure I'd be turned away. But then I remembered . . .

I reached into my wallet and pulled out the press ID Elle had given me. I held it up to the guard, who looked from the picture to my face and then waved me on. I owed Elle a big thanks, for sure.

We were ushered into a room that was way too small for the number of people crammed in it, and I stood in the back with all the TV cameras. These people were all here on assignment; I was trying to fill the biggest void in my life. Even if my mother had made a better effort at motherhood, I was convinced no fatherless child escapes unharmed.

The kingdom of darkness knew that too and had used it against me—in more ways than one.

We all stared for a while at a table lined with three empty chairs, waiting for Stephen Grayson to make an entrance. When the door finally opened, I could hardly blink or breathe.

TWENTY-EIGHT

A DOCTOR WEARING SCRUBS and a white lab coat entered first. Then came a highly decorated military officer. I overheard someone say he had been instrumental in the rescue operation. And then the man I most resembled in the entire world stepped into the room.

My first thought was that he was thinner than I'd imagined he'd be— than his impostor had been—but considering he'd been held hostage, it made sense. My next thought was how strange it was to feel devotion toward someone I had no history with, who didn't even know I existed.

A droplet hit my hand. It took me a second to realize it had fallen from my cheek.

As my father took a seat in the center of the table, I nodded. *I knew you were a Light.* Immediately hands flew up and people began shouting over each other, bombarding the panel—mostly my father—with questions.

"Please." The doctor held up a hand. "One at a time."

I don't recall all that was said during the interview, but I quickly observed that my father was highly intelligent, good with words, and likable—funny even. For the life of me, I couldn't envision him holding my mother, loving her as his wife. They were nothing alike.

That's my dad. I said it over and over to myself, celebrating every time. I also cringed, thinking about how I'd fallen for a counterfeit.

Forty-five minutes later, after news broke that one of the European doctors had just died as a result of his injuries, the conference came to an abrupt end. As the crowd disbanded, my father stood, steadying himself against the back of his chair. He conversed with a reporter, a tall brunette he seemed to recognize.

I looked on from my post at the back of the room as two teen girls in sundresses, one slightly taller than the other, rushed up to my father and hugged him. He kissed each of them on the cheek.

My sisters.

It was a weird feeling. Like being at a family reunion, only you're invisible and your relatives don't know you're there.

The room cleared quickly. I took occasional steps forward. I had yet to come up with what to say, and the closer I came to my dad, the more I fidgeted. I could see the details in his face now, and I wondered if he'd see himself in me. Or traces of my mother, maybe.

He spotted me out of the corner of his eye and glanced my way but quickly resumed his conversation—a painful reminder I was nothing but a stranger to him. But then he looked again, studying my face. Did he sense—or know—we were related?

When he formed a nonchalant smile, raising his eyebrows as if curious to meet me, I dismissed the hopeful notion. Despite a tidal wave of trepidation, I approached and, for the very first time, spoke to my father.

"Hi."

"Hello." He reached for a handshake. I was embarrassed that my palm was sweaty. And a little shaky. He gripped my hand and looked intently at me. All I could do was gulp. And say, "I'm Owen."

"Stephen Grayson. Nice to meet you."

It was my turn to talk, but I cut my eyes to the onlooking reporter. I needed her to get lost. My father had the intuition to politely wish her well and also motioned for his doctor to go on without him. With the exception of some security guards conversing in a far corner, it had quickly become just the two of us in what now felt like a gigantic room.

He smiled, revealing two small stitches near the corner of his mouth. "Where's home for you?" he asked.

My mind went blank for a second. "I'm in Texas now."

"Ah, I see. A Southern man. And what brings you here?"

I had a sudden, sinking realization that I shouldn't have barged in on him like this. I should have called first or written a letter or something. But here I was. "I—I wanted to meet you."

"Oh?" He shifted his weight, still smiling.

I opened my mouth, but nothing came out. I'm sure he could tell I was struggling. He gave me an encouraging look. "Whatever it is, young man, it's okay."

"Um . . ." I couldn't even swallow. I drummed my fingers against my jeans, searching for a way to keep from making him miserably uncomfortable. Like me.

In the end, the only way I knew to do it, was to just do it . . .

"I'm your son." The words felt naked and out of place. "You were married to my mom, Susan Edmonds? She got pregnant but didn't tell you."

He furrowed his brow, then slowly covered his mouth. I tried to read his eyes, but it was like they were blank. Seconds dragged on like hours, and he said nothing. Not one word.

A major sense of regret bore down on me, and I started breathing hard. "I get it if this is too much for you right now. I mean, like, if you're worried it could disrupt your life. Or family."

Still not a word from him.

I stared at my shoes and rubbed my hands together, frustrated and jittery and awkward. And ashamed.

I'd thought maybe it was a sign of our likeness that we'd both worn maroon shirts today, but it was starting to seem like a stupid coincidence.

"I know you're trying to recover." I scanned the room, avoiding eye contact. "I shouldn't have confronted you like this." I spotted the nearest exit. "This was a bad idea. I'm sorry—I should go."

As I turned my back on him and walked away, it was like my insides were incinerating, burning with a depth of humiliation I'd never experienced before.

I was nearly to the door when he called my name. I looked back, and he hurried toward me. "Please, don't go." I faced him, and he stared at my face. Then he reached out and put his hand on my shoulder. "I'm so glad you found me. And I cannot tell you how much it means to me to meet you." His eyes pooled. He wrapped a firm arm around me, then hugged me—a gesture of masculine affection I'd never known.

I wasn't one to get emotional around people, but standing there in my father's embrace, I gave myself a pass.

And something happened.

No, I didn't see a spectacular being of light or a new species of demonic evil. Instead I saw my life—memories scrolling through my mind like a quick news feed.

I envisioned my basketball games in middle school and high school and how, more times than not, I'd had no parent there to cheer me on. But suddenly it was like my father was there, watching from the stands.

I remembered the day in sixth grade that I'd begged my mom to let me do motocross, but she said it was way too dangerous. Now I saw my dad telling me to go for it and to practice hard because I had what it took to win.

And all those elementary school Father's Day crafts I'd sneaked into the restroom under my shirt, then crumpled and crammed into a trash can—I could see myself giving them to him. And him wanting them.

Of course there was no going back and reliving my childhood, but somehow, even at nineteen years old, my father's welcoming arms soothed a hurt that had haunted me every day in his absence—pain I hadn't realized ran so deep. And I had this strange epiphany, like I could see myself in the future. I was holding my little boy the same way my father embraced me now, and I vowed to him that I'd never leave him or his mother.

My father released me and gestured toward two chairs. "Let's have a seat and talk."

It was like I'd won the lottery, only the prize was worth way more than cash. It was a perfect moment.

Until *they* walked in.

TWENTY-NINE

"STEPHEN, WHO'S THIS?" A stylish-looking gray-haired lady entered, followed by an equally old man in slacks.

My father kept blinking, eyeing the couple nervously. "Mom, Dad, this is Owen."

My grandmother stood there with her mouth gaping open, while my grandfather looked away, avoiding my eyes. They knew exactly who I was, just like I knew full well who they were—the culprits whose manipulation had driven my mother to leave my father, sabotaging pretty much my entire life.

My father looked between his parents and me, sensing the awkward tension, I'm sure. But his mother went out of her way to keep him in the dark, forcing herself to smile and greet me. She motioned for my grandfather to shake my hand, all for show. I could have thanked them for my inheritance and busted them right then and there, but I didn't want to drop any more reality bombs on my father.

They were both Lights, by the way, which seemed to me like God had mistakenly marked two evil people as righteous. As the four of us stood together, I sensed that one-of-a-kind, sweet scent—the fragrance that manifests only when a family of Lights gets together. As much as I resented my grandparents, the unfamiliar sense of belonging was reassuring.

"Owen is . . . um . . ." My dad couldn't come up with a reasonable explanation for who I was or why we were both teary eyed—much less the resemblance between us. But I didn't blame him. It was way too soon to expect him to introduce me to anyone.

I tried to smooth things over. "I've wanted to meet Stephen for a long time. I look up to him."

"Well, we certainly understand your admiration." His mother played along. "He's a brave man." She set some grocery sacks down, then told my dad she'd be back later with more toiletries. Then, thankfully, my grandparents left.

My father tried to apologize. "I'm not ashamed of you, Owen, I just—"

"No, I get it. This must be overwhelming for you."

"Yes, it is." We sat across from each other. "But it's not a crisis. It's more like a miracle. I mean that."

From there, he asked me lots of questions, including how my mother was doing.

"Her alcoholism has caught up with her, and she's very sick. She and I don't talk much lately."

He stared into space. "She never liked alcohol."

I huffed. "I think it's about all she does like."

He gave a slow, dejected nod, then lightened things up by asking what sports I'd played growing up and what subjects I excelled at in school. I brought up his daughters, and he had a lot to say about them, all good, but then he informed me, "I love them like they're my own, but they're actually my stepdaughters."

Turns out I was an only child after all, genetically speaking.

"How long have you been married?" I asked.

He lowered his head, and I knew that wasn't good. "Fifteen years. But when I went missing, my wife . . ." He cleared his throat and paused. "At some point, she gave up hope and concluded I was deceased. My medical partner was there for her."

Oh . . . "I'm really sorry."

A nurse interrupted us and insisted my father get some blood work done. He invited me to go too, and I walked through the hospital with him. I took nothing for granted, even a short trip down a dingy hallway beside my father. To be clear, the hospital was clean; the spiritual atmosphere wasn't.

I sat on a death-dust-covered bench outside the lab while my father had his blood drawn. Creepers crammed inside these walls just like at the hospital back home, so I leaned forward, unwilling to put my back against it.

The hallway was filled with sick, suffering people. I thought about Arthur's prediction and also what the old man had said about how the outcome in Masonville would be far reaching. Did that mean these people, in an entirely different state, would somehow be affected? Arthur had gone so far as to say there would be a global impact. I couldn't begin to comprehend that.

My flight home was scheduled for the following morning. I wanted to spend as much time as possible with my father, but I also felt the strong pull of responsibility to get back. The clock was ticking, and Molek's throne was inching toward his coveted territory above Masonville High. Just thinking about it made me tap a nervous foot against the tile floor.

A pale boy who looked to be about sixteen made his way down the hall, shackle-free, casting a glow around his spotless Nikes. But he was as skinny as a skeleton and barely had the strength to lower himself onto the bench across from me. He was completely bald, eyebrows included—from chemotherapy, I concluded. It pained me to watch him wrap his bony arms around his gut and wince.

I tried not to stare, but I felt drawn to him, if that makes sense. And the longer I looked, the more I began to see something on his neck. It was like it faded into existence—a hellish strand of chain links, wrapped around his throat.

Ray Anne had said it was compassion that allowed her to see the burdens Lights carried, so I guessed that was the deal with me now too.

After a minute or so, the chain steadily disappeared so that all I saw was the boy's neck again. But when I imagined what it would be like if it were me having to battle cancer, his chain came into focus again. I thought about how difficult it must be to endure rounds of treatment, and more chain links became visible. And when I considered how he must have felt sitting there alone, with no parent or friend beside him, I was able to see that the oppressive chain draped down his chest, all the way to the floor.

I had a good idea now of what I must look like through Ray's eyes, only I had more chains than this kid. Plus cords.

A nurse called for a patient, and the boy managed to stand. I tried not to stare as he struggled to walk past me, and I wondered if it would make him uncomfortable if I, a complete stranger, offered to let him lean on me. But then I caught a glimpse of something horrible. There was a Creeper's hand in the cuff at the end of his chain, on the floor, and the boy was dragging it along, pulling the underground assailant so that the chain stretched between his legs and behind him.

Then the hallway lit up like Christmas. A robed Watchman stepped into the atmosphere and wrapped his arms around the ailing boy's waist, supporting him so he could keep walking. It was a heart-wrenching scenario. An unnatural mix of horror and glory.

I spent the rest of the day talking with my father in his hospital room. He didn't bring up his experiences in captivity, so neither did I. Instead we discussed his life before that, including his faith and how he felt compelled to serve and help people, especially children. "You wouldn't believe the atrocities kids are suffering," he said, "in Africa and all over the world—including here, in the United States."

I told him about the suicides in Masonville, and he shook his head. "It's an assault that has to be stopped. Do you know what I mean by that, Owen?"

What a relief. My father understood the invisible roles of good and evil and wanted to be sure I did too. Before long, I got the impression he had as much understanding of Scripture as Pastor Gordon. Maybe more.

From that point on, our conversation grew more intense as we went back and forth about the supernatural, religion, and social injustices.

With each passing hour, I let my guard down a little more until, by nightfall, I'd told him way more than I ever thought I would . . .

About my spiritual sight.

About the Creepers and Watchmen and Molek.

About Arthur's letter.

I even spilled my guts about his wicked impostor. "What kind of evil do you think I was dealing with?" I asked him.

"Demonic spirits that know you well. Familiar spirits, you could call them."

According to my dad, Satan had deployed some special ops to study me and work to deceive me by whatever means possible. No doubt these were more specialized than the typical chain-chasing Creepers. They possessed the twisted ability to take on human form, mimicking the appearance of loved ones we know and trust. I could only imagine how hideous their true, unmasked form must be.

My father was a great listener and asked insightful questions. He even paced the room for minutes at a time, Ray Anne–style, content to give me his undivided attention. But there was something I couldn't put my finger on. It was like he wasn't as surprised or intrigued as he should have been by my outlandish accounts. Finally I asked him, "You don't see the spirit world too, right?"

He told me he didn't.

"Then . . . is there something you're not telling me?"

He froze, then peeked out into the hallway before closing the door again. We were the exact same height, and he stood eye-to-eye with me, unflinching. "Owen, I would never keep information from you without cause. That said, I need you to trust me when I say there are certain things I cannot tell you—at least not now. To do so would only put you in danger."

Another person warning me of danger. "I don't understand."

"I know. But please, this is how it has to be until . . ." He looked away and closed his eyes. I got the impression he desperately wanted to keep going, but he forced himself to hold back. He gripped my shoulders. "I'm on your side, and I'm so proud of you." He squeezed harder. "You have my word, I'll do everything I can to help you. *Everything*."

"Wait—are you saying you're coming to Masonville?"

He shook his head. "I can't. But you have to go back and keep fighting. Expose evil and stand strong against the opposition. And remember, Son . . ."

My breath caught. *He called me* Son.

"Justice is rarely won without sacrifice. But be careful, and count the cost before you go running into battle."

I had so many questions, it was hard to know where to start or which ones he'd even answer. But our time was up. The door swung open, and in walked his parents. There was an instant strain in the room, and I knew the best thing for me to do was leave. I said I'd be back first thing in the morning to say good-bye before my flight.

From the time I slid into the backseat of my app-fetched ride until I finally drifted to sleep at some point at the hotel that night, I was consumed with analyzing my time with my father. Information flipped and twisted in my mind like a Rubik's Cube.

My whole life had been marred by secrecy, and now my father was holding out on me too. And hadn't Elle also been vague with me? Add the old man's mysterious comments to the mix, and it seemed like more than coincidence at work here. It was like they were all willing to drop some insightful bread crumbs, but the path to full discovery was something I had to pioneer for myself.

My father seemed to believe his confidentiality was for my own good—and maybe it somehow was—but it still made me want to explode. At the same time, I was relieved to have him in my corner, a man who seemed vastly knowledgeable about . . . spiritual matters, yes, but what else? I couldn't figure it out, but whatever it was, I got the impression it was important.

The next morning, I had only about a half hour to visit with my father before heading to the airport. He was dressed in jeans and a button-down shirt, and there was a packed duffel bag on his bed. "Are you going home?" I asked him.

We sat across from each other in the same uncomfortable wooden chairs as yesterday. "Just moving to a different room," he said. "Once I get my strength back, I have a few things to take care of in the States, then I'll return to Africa."

I gasped. "Why would you go back?"

"For the children."

I searched his face. "I know they have medical needs, but aren't you afraid of being captured again?"

And don't you want to spend time with your son? I thought it but didn't say it.

He ran a hand through his hair, then popped his knuckles—mannerisms that reminded me eerily of myself. "I do provide medical services, but there's much more to my mission over there."

"Like what?"

He fidgeted with his shirt collar like he was weighing what he was and wasn't willing to disclose. "I'm sorry to share something so heinous with you." He took a deep breath. "It's not uncommon for witch doctors in Africa to tell locals they can be healed of painful diseases and hardship if they'll . . ."

He held back.

"I can take it," I assured him.

He looked me in the face, man-to-man. "If they'll participate in the ritualistic sacrifice of their children."

I pressed a balled fist against my lips.

"I'm leading an underground movement to stop that practice, among other gross injustices," he said, "but it's a highly specialized, strictly confidential operation. There's intense opposition from powerful parties—people you'd never suspect are involved. It's a risky battle fought on physical and spiritual planes, all at once."

I spoke as thoughts registered. "Child sacrifice . . . that's what Molek's all about too."

My father slid to the edge of his chair. I did the same. "It's part of a bigger, global agenda to exterminate children," he said.

Call it a divine revelation, but the instant he said that, a sudden, unsettling, undeniable awareness came over me. I was so overcome, I had to stand. So emotional, my voice shook with each realization . . .

"Human sacrifice. Student suicides. School shootings."

"Child trafficking," my father interjected.

"It's all part of a demonic mission to kill off the next generation." I could hardly fathom the download hitting my soul. "But why? What is it about today's kids that's so—?"

My father stood. "Today's young people are called and destined to overcome the power of evil like no generation before. The kingdom of darkness knows it and is targeting young souls, working to end their lives before they get the chance to live out their destinies."

My knees felt weak, and I sank into my chair as my father kept explaining. "Now's the hour to expose the evil plots and atrocities—to engage in the battle on behalf of your peers and children everywhere, the unborn included."

Abortion. One more symptom of the generational genocide.

I exhaled into my hands, cupped over my mouth. "Where do I start?"

He knelt in front of me and placed his hand on my shoulder. "Your town. Take a stand against the attacks in Masonville."

"Stop Molek," I said.

He nodded.

A nurse entered the room, informing my father it was time to change rooms.

"I need a minute," he told her.

We both stood, and he made a point to tell me again how thrilled he was to have met me. Then he gave me a cell number but asked me to memorize it instead of storing it in my contacts. "It's safer if you call me on that line."

Safer? I went ahead and asked him, "Are you in the CIA?"

"No."

That was all the explanation I got.

He leaned and spoke close to my ear. "Whatever happens when you get home, whatever you face, don't panic. That only makes things worse. And don't get tangled up in distractions that steal your focus."

"I'm in chains now," I admitted.

He didn't look at me like I was strange. "You have to let it go."

"Let what go?"

"Whatever's binding you."

He made it sound so simple.

He stepped back, looking deep into my eyes. "Owen, freedom from man's oppression brings great relief, as I can attest. But freedom of the soul is something else entirely. A man doesn't know freedom until his soul is liberated."

I nodded, beaming with admiration.

"And never forget this. The enemy's desire to intimidate and trap you comes from his own agony over the certainty of his demise. Darkness launches its fiercest attacks against those with the potential to do the most damage to his kingdom."

To this day, those are among my favorite truths.

I had a plane to catch, but I wasn't ready to leave him. Maybe I was being irrational, but I feared I might not ever see him again.

"Owen, there's something I want to give you, but it's at my home. I'll arrange to have it delivered to you. For now . . ." My father began untying a leather band from his wrist. "Do you know there are places in Africa and around the world where people are killed just for getting baptized?"

I shook my head. "So why do it?"

"God's put an end to their old, shackled life, as you put it, and given them a new, eternal one. A free one. They'd rather die than keep that to themselves."

The old life of bondage is buried under the water. The new, liberated life comes up for air. I'd never thought of baptism even remotely like that.

My dad reached for my arm and tied the leather strap around my wrist. "Where I was in Uganda, persecuted Christians wear these as an unspoken sign of their faith. They're encouraged when they see others with them." He let go of me but kept eyeing the unique bracelet. "I want you to have mine."

It was the most sentimental thing I owned now. By far. I ran my finger over tan letters that looked like they'd been hand-stitched into the brown leather—*Mimi ni bure.*

"It's Swahili," he said.

"What's it mean?"

He smiled, then gave me a final, firm hug. "I am free."

THIRTY

I FELT DIFFERENT as I strode through Tulsa's airport toward my gate, like I was wearing a full suit of armor, ready to tackle whatever threats awaited me back home. I didn't even stress when I saw the outside of the plane had the word fatality scribbled on it in Creeper graffiti.

Before the plane took off, I talked a guy into letting me swap seats with him so I could be by the window, then I called Ray Anne. It was so refreshing to hear her voice, even though she was still coughing. She let me know she'd recruited a team of people—Pastor Gordon and Ethan included—to help spread the word about Saturday's town gathering at Masonville High, but she wasn't confident people were catching on fast enough.

Then came more bad news. There'd been another abduction in Masonville. A seventh-grade boy had vanished while riding his bike outside the group home where he lived.

I assured her I'd be home in a few hours, and by the time our call ended, I'd caught on to something. The kidnapping victims were all parentless. Like, every one of them. That had to be more than coincidence.

I shot Detective Benny a text on the off chance he'd overlooked it.

Well aware but thanks Owen, he texted back.

I closed my eyes as the plane rushed the runway, trying not to dwell on how my father was about to be worlds away again, living his top-secret life apart from me. When he'd said he couldn't come to Masonville, had he meant he was unable to come right now, or—for reasons I couldn't understand—he had better stay away?

It was one of many questions churning in my brain.

I didn't see any Creeper king thrones above Tulsa until we ascended above the clouds. Then I counted three of them looming in the airspace—one empty and the other two occupied by monsters dressed in ashen robes like the one Molek had worn. But I couldn't worry about that. I'd been charged with battling for Masonville, which was apparently some sort of spirit-realm hub for the rest of the world or something.

I kept my face plastered to the window, and even though I kept catching occasional, lightning-fast glimpses of supernatural beings, I got so exhausted, my eyelids collapsed. But about halfway into the trip, I woke to nerve-racking pounding on the roof of the plane. It was like Bigfoot was stomping back and forth, from the tail of the aircraft to the front, then back again.

Finally, it stopped. But then a Creeper lowered headfirst into the cabin, hanging upside down in the aisle a few rows in front of me. It rotated its head 360 degrees, scoping out the passengers, then began rummaging through people's cords, examining the words inscribed on them.

I assumed he found one he liked—he began tugging on a cord hanging from a man in the aisle seat one row up from me, dressed like he was ready to play golf. I'd never seen this happen before, but as the Creeper yanked, the man's cord elongated from his head, stretching a full arm's length. Then the Creeper did the exact same thing to the cord of a woman seated across the narrow aisle from the man. Then the predator hawked and spit up slimy, dark sludge and used the grossness like putrid paste to bind the two unsuspecting people's cords together.

While their fused cords hung in the middle of the aisle like a saggy, spiky jump rope, the man casually struck up a conversation with the lady.

I watched her through the gap between seats in front of me. Before long, she was giggling, tossing around her shoulder-length blonde-streaked hair. The pair kept flirting back and forth until eventually, he leaned over, his wedding band in plain view, and whispered something across the aisle to her. He got up and walked past me to the back of the plane, where he entered the lavatory. Their cords stayed connected, stretching like a thick black rubber band.

A minute later, she walked past me and entered the same tiny lavatory.

The Creeper growled and grinned, then hoisted itself up and out of the aircraft.

I focused my attention outside the plane again, searching through the window for signs of spiritual life. As we approached Masonville, even before our descent below the cloud cover, there was no question the war between good and evil had majorly escalated in the short time I'd been gone. Sure, I'd seen Creepers and Watchmen collide and battle through conflict before, but this . . .

The sky looked crowded as forces of darkness and light charged at one another, slamming and spinning and sailing through the air in heated immortal combat. Multiple Creepers piled on each armored Watchman, working to drag them away from Masonville's regional airspace, but with each mighty thrust of their platinum-silver shields, Watchmen sent gangs of Creepers flying so fast and far, I never saw them stop careening.

The more our plane descended, slicing puffs of clouds like a knife through a flimsy pillow, the kingdom duel raged. Right outside my window, an immense Watchman held three Creepers by their throats, then reared back and hurled the squealing demons so ferociously that, for a split second, they spiraled through the cabin of the aircraft. I caught a quick glimpse through windows across the aisle as the beasts kept flipping and flailing away.

We neared the airport, and I couldn't help it—my palms began to sweat. Around Molek's throne, a fleet of his soldiers worked to overpower the Army of Light. Three Watchmen held a lunged pose with their arms extended, pressing against the throne so that, despite the opposition pushing on the other side, the chair couldn't be moved—no closer to Masonville High and Caldwell's old land.

Thank you, God!

My plane landed, and I rushed off, ignoring a text from my mom, but so anxious that when my cell rang, I answered without checking who it was.

"I'm freaking out, Owen!" It was Jess. "Your dad is on TV. I don't get it—he was dead. We saw him." Her words ran together like she was high on something. I guessed she probably was. "I need to see you, Owen. I'm having the scariest nightmares ever."

I told her this wasn't a good time for me, and what I'd have to say would only make her nightmares worse.

She huffed into the phone. "My grandmother's right—I shouldn't trust you. You don't care about me."

I was about to set the record straight when I remembered . . .

"Jess, didn't your grandmother die a while back?"

"Yeah, but guess what? I did the candle thing, and she came to see me. Twice now."

It was like guilt had tied my tongue down so it couldn't move. She'd learned that from *me*.

"Jess, listen, that's not really your—"

She hung up on me. A Jess trademark.

While waiting on my ride outside the airport, I called her back and agreed to meet her at a hole-in-the-wall coffee place close to my apartment. "I can't stay long," I told her.

I dropped my suitcase in my living room and called Ray Anne. She'd already seen the chaos in the sky around Molek's throne. I told her I'd be over soon.

At the coffee shop, I parked next to Jess's Mustang convertible, trashed compared to its mint condition in high school. She sat at a table in the corner, rubbing her eyes like she hadn't slept in days.

When I approached, she tapped the chair beside her, but I sat on the other side of the table. "I told you, Jess, I'm in a hurry."

"Don't be." She had that familiar longing in her light-brown eyes. "Ray Anne has Jackson, so I've got all day if you want. And evening."

No surprise, Jess was taking advantage again of Ray Anne's willingness to babysit. Did Jess even have a job? I didn't bother asking and got right to the point, not willing to tone things down just because she was shackled and ignorant. "I don't claim to fully understand all this, but there's a certain species of demonic being that can take on the physical form of humans so we'll invite them into our lives. That's why the Bible warns us not to consult with the dead." Her arms were crossed like she wasn't following, but I told her anyway, "That spirit you and I thought was my dad—it wasn't. Not even close."

Jess started tapping her nearly empty coffee cup against the table over and over—she was definitely on something that was giving her the jitters. "But my grandmother knows things. Stuff only she could know about me."

It was hard to be patient. I didn't have time for this. "The spirit world knows things too. Nothing's hidden."

Watching her tear up, my attitude softened. More than pathetic, she was truly pitiful.

I'd never brought up the subject of faith with her and knew I'd probably get nowhere, but I felt the need to at least try. "Jess, I know you aren't the type that wants someone pushing God on you. All I want to say is that he's real, and you need him—we all do."

Even after everything I'd seen, I was not prepared for what happened next. Something appeared at the bottom of Jess's eyes, like the white scales that slide over sharks' eyes when they move in on their prey, only these were black. They crept up until her eyeballs were half covered.

What the . . . ?

"Wow, Owen. You've really let Ray Anne change you, haven't you?"

It was hard to defend myself while looking at her messed-up eyes. "I just . . . want you to know that God is more than a myth. Way more."

The scales slid completely over her eyes at that point so that there was nothing but slimy black between her eyelids. I could handle seeing ghastly eyes on Creepers much better than on a person, especially someone I knew. I'd heard Ethan use the term *spiritual blindness*, but I had no idea it was a literal thing.

I pushed away from the table as a Creeper passed through the wall into the coffee shop. It loomed behind Jess with its open palms closing in on her ears, sending white noise at her like I'd first seen Creepers do to Meagan.

I bolted up, and my chair fell back and slammed to the floor. I quoted Luke 10:19, and the Creeper growled with fury, then charged at a guy seated two tables away, smacking the man's side and pressing into him. The possessed guy stood and pointed at me. "He needs to leave."

I looked at Jess—the scales were slowly lowering. I chalked it up as one more thing that had probably been there before now, but I hadn't had the compassion to see it.

People were staring at us. Jess nibbled on her fingernail, embarrassed. "Please chill, Owen."

The possessed guy spoke to the manager while looking straight at me. I could see that his pupils were off center.

The manager said I was being disruptive and politely asked me to leave.

Fine.

Jess followed me out.

I walked her to her driver's-side door and warned her, "Please don't talk to that grandmother spirit. Or any spirit."

She grabbed my waist and pulled me close. "This stuff scares me, Owen." She clasped her hands around my neck. "I don't want to be alone tonight," she whispered. "Let's go to your place."

Another battle with seduction. I knew better now. "I can't."

She tilted her head and kissed my neck.

"Jess . . ."

It turned out to be a really good thing that I'd seen those disgusting scales on her eyeballs. It made it easier to resist her.

I couldn't help warning her again. "Don't believe or do anything that spirit tells you, Jess."

Then I got on my motorcycle and left.

I drove straight to Ray Anne's, where Jackson was just waking from a nap in a thing Ray Anne called a playpen sleeper. She hovered over him like a mother hen watching an egg crack—if hens actually do that.

She squinted while looking at me, making me even more self-conscious about my spiritual bondage. I kept the focus on her. "You're hardly coughing today."

"It's weird." She hoisted Jackson into her arms. "It comes and goes."

The little boy stole her attention away from me. She ran her hand through his fluffy hair and tapped his tiny nose until he grinned. She was wearing my necklace, and about two inches below the pendant, I noticed a red splotch on her chest, by her heart. I pointed to it. "What happened?"

She looked down. "What do you mean?"

I kept pointing. "Doesn't that hurt?"

She stared in the mirror while Jackson tugged on a fistful of her hair. "I don't see anything."

I walked over and put my finger right next to it. "Right there—you don't see that wound?"

Finally, we both understood. She wasn't seeing what I was. She rubbed her chest. "What does this mean?"

It's not like I could say for sure, but it seemed to me it was a manifestation of some sort of personal struggle of hers. She couldn't see that wound on her chest any clearer than I could see the constraints around my neck.

As usual, her mom barged in, this time with a basket of folded towels. Ray had no choice but to change the subject. "I don't think word is spreading enough about Saturday's prayer march."

"A *prayer march*? That's how you're putting it to people?" That sounded really dumb to me. We'd be lucky if anyone came. Besides Ethan.

I had an idea, but a knock at the door interrupted us. Ray's shoulders slumped. "It's Jess. Here to get him." She called to Jess to come in while handing Jackson off to me so she could gather his things. He reached up and tapped my face, smiling. I had to admit, the kid was growing on me, despite the drool.

As for Jess, she didn't tell me hello or even look at me. Still stinging because I'd turned her down a half hour ago, I guessed.

Jess stood with her arms crossed while Ray Anne tucked baby stuff into a diaper bag. Ray spoke slowly, like Jess was hearing impaired, carefully explaining that Jackson would want his next bottle soon, and she needed to start putting diaper ointment on him from now on. Jess barely nodded, like she couldn't have cared less.

Ray Anne motioned for me to hand Jackson to his mom, and Jess snatched him from me. Ray Anne looked between my ex-girlfriend and me suspiciously.

Jess muttered a thanks at Ray, then left. Ray and I watched her chains and cuffs finally make it out through the closed door. Ray Anne folded her arms and chewed the inside of her cheek. I could tell she was fighting off tears.

"You're really getting attached to him."

"I know he's not mine." She collapsed the playpen and slid it under her futon bed. "But I worry about him. Sometimes when she drops him off, he's starving, like she hasn't fed him all day." She folded one of his blankets and held it to her nose. Then glared at me. "What's the deal between you and her?"

I told her the truth—how Jess had made a pass at me, and I'd turned her down. "She's humiliated, I think." I thought Ray Anne would be proud of the way I'd handled things.

"Why would you put yourself in that situation to begin with?"

Not what I'd expected, but I let her criticism go, focusing instead on what I believed was the real source of Ray Anne's irritation. "There's absolutely nothing going on between Jess and me—no need to be jealous." Like she was when we were in high school, but I left that out.

She didn't hesitate. "I'm not jealous."

Oh. I guess I'd kind of hoped she was. At least a little.

Maybe I was the one overreacting now, but I had to speak my mind. "I'll never be good enough for you, will I, Ray Anne?"

She searched my face. "Owen, why would you—?"

Her cell rang, and we both saw who it was. Now she was in the hot seat. "I'm sure Ethan's just checking to see how I'm feeling."

I shrugged, pretending to care as little as she just had about Jess. "Go ahead and answer." I spotted the envelope with Arthur's message on Ray Anne's nightstand and grabbed it. "I have to go now anyway."

As I walked my bike backward down the driveway, I got that sinking feeling all over again—the knot in my stomach when things weren't quite right between Ray and me.

I tried not to let it consume me.

I drove to the Channel Two News building and told the shackled lady at the front desk I needed to speak with Elle Adelle. A minute later, the reporter came to the lobby, her hair slicked back in a low, all-business ponytail. Our combined lights on the floor were an electric gold. "You ready to talk about Riley?" she asked.

I said I'd answer whatever questions she had if she'd do me a big favor. I proceeded to tell her about Arthur and his letter, minus the paranormal details, then explained how he'd instructed us to gather on the land. "I need a way to invite the whole town to be there in three days. Trust me, this has to happen now."

She crossed her arms. "What proof do you have? I don't report anything without first substantiating the facts."

I held up the envelope. She went to grab it, but I pulled it away. "Sorry, I can only let you glance at it." What would she think if she read the part about *two bearers of light*, not to mention *Molek and his occupying army*?

She huffed. "I don't do favors for people who withhold information. It's my responsibility to keep this town informed of the truth—the whole truth—and I take that very seriously."

I had the exact same responsibility and took it just as seriously. But my truths tended to freak people out and make them dismiss me as psychotic.

Elle started walking away.

"Wait." I had to think fast. I really needed her help. She was a Light, so chances were, she'd believe the full story. But I hardly knew this lady, and from what I did know, she made a living turning tragedies and scandals into town news. Was I really going to admit to her that I could see into an alternate realm? That a spirit of death was out to destroy Masonville?

I guess she got sick of standing around. She tossed her hands in the air and turned her back on me again. "I've got deadlines."

"Please, wait!"

She faced me with an impatient sigh. I closed the distance between us. "There's something incredibly personal about me in this message and other things that the public can't know. They can't handle it, and most wouldn't believe it anyway. If I let you read this, do you swear to only report the parts the public needs to hear?"

She eyed the envelope with raised eyebrows, intrigued. "Does the information you want withheld have anything to do with a crime or illegal activity?"

"No." Molek was definitely a criminal, but not the punishable kind. At least not in an earthly court.

"Then I see no problem with honoring your request." She held out her palm for the envelope.

I made her promise confidentiality a second time, then warned her, "This will probably freak you out a little. Or a lot." It wasn't easy handing the letter over.

She unfolded the delicate paper and read the whole message to herself, her eyes growing wider and wider. She searched my face. "So . . . can *you* see those things?" I nodded, trying to get a sense of how she was taking everything, but she kept a pro-level poker face. "Who else?"

"My girlfriend," I confessed.

Elle turned and charged through the lobby, hurrying toward a restricted-access door.

"Hey!"

She'd taken the paper with her.

"I'll give it back tomorrow night." She didn't slow her pace. "Meet me at Masonville High tomorrow at five forty-five for a live broadcast at six." She left me standing there, questioning my decision to put such an insane amount of trust in someone who'd always gotten on my nerves.

Ray Anne met me in the school parking lot a few minutes early so we could talk through what we should and shouldn't say on live TV. Too bad the TV camera couldn't pick up on the war zone in the sky. If only we could show people Molek's sinister throne and the fight around it.

Unfortunately, Ray Anne's cough was flaring with a vengeance. And that red splotch on her chest was twice as big now and had become a nasty, open sore.

"Ray Anne, that wound has gotten way worse." I noticed a piece of jewelry just below the neckline of her shirt. For some odd reason, she was wearing that tacky necklace Veronica had given her. When she moved, the locket slid back and forth over the red spot. I didn't connect the dots at first, but then I wondered . . .

"Have you been wearing that much?"

"Off and on."

"Did you ever open the locket?"

Her cough was so bad, she could barely tell me, "I could never get it."

She removed the necklace and handed it to me, and like the first time I'd tried, I couldn't pry it open. I was far from weak—what was the deal?

I set the necklace on the concrete and stomped the locket with my heel.

"Hey . . ."

Why did she care so much about a necklace she'd said was ugly?

I stomped it again, and this time it sprang open. And something flung out.

Ray and I both jumped back. Out of the small locket, a grotesque hand bigger than an adult baseball glove lurched onto the pavement, palm up, claws exposed. Projecting from the center of the hellish palm was a fat, barbed stinger-like thing that looked like it could inflict serious pain.

And it had been. On Ray's chest.

The crooked fingers thrashed and pulsed until the hand flipped itself over and began inching away. The fingers' claws dug into the cement and pulled the hand forward, dragging it along, leaving a trail of that gray death dust.

The gentle breeze was suddenly polluted by the smell of sewage. Sure enough, Demise loomed in the distance, closing in on the crawling hand. It extended its mutilated wrist and bent down, fastening the hand onto its exposed bone.

Ray covered her mouth like she was about to barf. "That necklace . . ."

"Why'd you wear it?"

She looked down. "Well . . . I just . . ." I waited for her to make sense. "Ethan said it was pretty."

You wouldn't think one simple statement about a piece of jewelry could hurt a guy so much.

And who would ever believe that an object could conduct evil, transferring it from one person to another? Or that evil could make someone physically sick? I now saw the locket for what it was: an evil plan to shut Ray Anne up at a time when Masonville needed her voice the most.

I'd known for some time that Veronica could be manipulative and strange, but I'd questioned if she had a clue about the depth of wickedness she was messing with. But now I was sure—Veronica had given Ray that necklace knowing full well it housed evil. And thanks to Ray's growing feelings for Ethan, the thing had made its way around her neck.

"Look," I said to her. "You've already stopped coughing."

She stared up at me with pooling eyes. "It's more than that." She put her hand on the sore that only I could see. "My heart's been tormented lately by thoughts—unwanted thoughts that I belong with Ethan, even though I've stayed committed to you."

I shoved my hands into my jeans pockets and forced an awkward, fake smile. "It's not like you and I are married. If he's who you want, don't feel bad about it."

She winced like she was hurt. "No, I'm not saying that."

We were out of time—Elle and a cameraman were exiting a news van. Ray and I had gotten completely distracted and hadn't even practiced what to say. On top of that, it looked like Molek's throne had gained a bit of ground. Or sky.

Elle seemed a lot more concerned with finding the right angle for the ideal shot than discussing the seriousness of what we were about to broadcast to all of Masonville. The minutes flew by, and suddenly, we were live.

Elle held up Dorothy's handwritten paper, referring to it as *a mysterious historic find*. She asked me to briefly explain my understanding of Arthur's connection to the land, and I did, then she read through his list of predictions word for word. She stuck the microphone in Ray Anne's face. "Tell us why you want people to gather here at 10:00 a.m. on Saturday."

I looked on, amazed, as the glow around Ray's feet got stronger, shining brighter and farther. Ray Anne looked straight into the camera and unleashed her pent-up passion for the cause. "This town has tried one thing after another to fix things, but it hasn't worked. Yes, the suicide rate has gone down, but it won't last, people—not if we don't deal with the real source of the problem."

I knew by now she wasn't going to hold back.

"You show up here on Saturday if you're ready to ask for God's forgiveness and pray—for our sins and the sins of the past. That's what Arthur said we have to do, and he's right. This land and this town need revival."

I dropped my head into my hands. Could she have sounded any more churchy?

Elle somehow found an eloquent way to wrap up what had to have been among her most awkward broadcasts. Ray's light went back to normal. As for me, I was convinced there was no way the town would show up now—certainly no shackled people. Not after Ray's sermon. But maybe some Lights would. And maybe that would be enough. I mean, had Arthur really expected that we'd get shackled people to come pray? The verse—2 Chronicles 7:14, I'd learned—called out *God's people*.

I thanked Elle, and as promised, she returned Arthur's envelope. "So, what's your opinion of all this?" I asked, following her as she hurried to the van. She hurried everywhere, apparently.

"I'll be here Saturday."

"To cover the story?"

She nodded, face showing no emotion. "And to participate." She fastened her seat belt in the passenger seat and started to close her door but stopped. "Here." She dug through her briefcase and pulled out a digital voice recorder. "Hold on to this."

"Why?" I tried to hand it back to her. "My cell records fine."

She wouldn't take it. "You may need it."

I eyed the buttons. "How do you know?"

The corners of her mouth turned up, the closest I'd ever seen her come to smiling. "I have good instincts."

Her strange confidence in somehow sensing things about the future reminded me of Veronica, only Elle was on my side of the kingdom clash.

I looked back. Ray Anne stood in the center of the parking lot, gazing up at the conflict in the sky. It was pretty obvious that the battle was intensifying.

THIRTY-ONE

I'D JUST LEFT THE SCHOOL when I got a text from Lance, the first one since high school. **You're some kind of prophet now? Seriously?! Go back to Boston.**

Never mind that I never claimed that anything in the letter came from me.

It wasn't his criticism that got to me. It was the disheartening feeling that most of Masonville would probably have the same reaction and hardly anyone would show up on Saturday.

I stopped for gas, feeling like every person at the station was staring at me. Had they just seen the news? A couple of truckers mumbled to each other—about me?

My tank filled, I started my bike and sat with the engine idling, contemplating my next move. It didn't make any sense, strategically speaking, but in that moment, my only impulse was to go see my mother. She'd texted me earlier, inviting me over as soon as my plane landed, but I had yet to respond.

I showed up at my mom's house unannounced and unlocked the door, trying not to gasp when I saw her, so pale and thin I hardly recognized her. She was lying on the sofa, shivering under a thick blanket, framed by her massive metal mess of chains and cords.

I lowered into the lounge chair across from her, no longer able to escape the realization that my mother was definitely dying. Any day now, from the look of things. No wonder I'd seen shreds of Creeper notes scattered on the stairs and *infirmity* plastered outside the front door. Dark forces were closing in on her.

She was barely able to lift the remote control and power off the TV.

"Owen. Thank you so much for stopping by."

The kindness in her voice stung me. I'd hardly thought of her lately and hadn't been willing to check up on her.

"There's something I need to tell you." She pulled her left hand out from under the blanket, revealing a modest-sized diamond ring. "Wayne asked me to marry him."

I didn't know Wayne, but I was sure she was in denial about the kind of man he was. My mom's track record was one loser boyfriend after another. But she had an even bigger issue of denial. "Mom, your health . . . it doesn't seem like now's the time to—"

"Please, let me finish."

I waited for her to collect her thoughts.

"I want you to go to the ring box that's in the top of my closet." She slid the diamond band off her finger. "Put this back in it."

"Is it a *green* box, Mom?"

She looked surprised.

While posing as my father, that impostor spirit had mentioned a ring box—a green one—but he'd said my mom's old wedding ring was in there: the one my dad had given her. It was easy enough to disprove—an irresponsible lie mixed with some truth. Evil's go-to strategy, I was realizing.

"Why do you want me to put the ring away?" I asked her.

She teared up while laboring to extend her arm toward me. I came to her, kneeling on the floor beside her.

"Dr. Bradford is optimistic about my treatment, but I know I'm very ill, Owen. It's more than that, though." A tear ran down her sallow cheek. "I know you won't like Wayne. And I'm not willing to choose him over you." She put the ring in my palm and clasped my hand the best she could. "Let's focus on us with the time I have left."

My mother had never once put me above the men in her life. *Ever*.

"I'm so sorry, Son."

I was stunned. It was the only time she'd apologized for anything.

I'd forgiven her the night I'd become a Light, but as time had passed and she didn't improve or change, I'd become bitter all over again. Her apology meant a lot. More than she would ever know. "I forgive you, Mom."

Our conversation was simple yet profound. I never would have guessed that it would trigger a spirit-realm reaction. But immediately, a chain slipped from my neck and slammed the hardwood by my knees. I saw it now, in plain view. Like ice melting in the sun, it vanished to nothing.

Hadn't that fraudulent spirit told me there was no way to destroy my old baggage? Another lie exposed.

My mother formed a small smile while looking me over, as if every feature of mine made her happy. "It's amazing," she said. "The clarity that comes when death is near."

Instantly, my throat throbbed. I didn't want her to die, and she wasn't ready—not with that shackle bound to her neck and soul.

I couldn't afford to keep dodging the subject. "Mom, I know some things about your childhood and your parents. How they forced you to be a part of dark, horrible stuff."

She looked away, her thoughtful smile gone, and mumbled to herself like I wasn't even there. "Growing up in this house, I hated walking out that door with them at night."

I couldn't imagine what vile things she'd been made to witness, and maybe do, as a child growing up in the occult. I thought she might bring some stuff up, but she got quiet and tucked her arms back under the blanket. I sighed in relief, unsure I could have stomached hearing it.

"Mom, you already know evil is real. But the thing is, God's real too, and he loves—"

Up came those slimy black scales, overtaking her pupils. "Not now, Owen." Her eyes became solid black.

"Then when, Mom?" My voice cracked with raw emotion.

She groaned while rolling over on the sofa, turning her back to me. "Put the ring away."

Our meaningful moment was over. The mom I'd known all my life was back.

I stood, defeated, and went to put the ring away. I was completely sure now that this scales-in-the-eyeballs deal had been happening in front of me all along—I just hadn't had enough empathy for people to trigger my spiritual sight to perceive it until now.

I put the ring back in its box, then went back downstairs and asked her, "Do you still have your wedding ring from my dad?" She hadn't asked me one thing about my trip to see him. It was completely odd, but that's how she was, especially about him.

"No, Son. I left it when . . ."

When she left him.

I kissed her forehead and told her I'd be back soon.

At home, I sat on the floor in my living room. A few days ago, it had become a den of devils, but tonight, I hoped to have something good happen. Ray Anne had said I had seven chains with cuffs. One had fallen off when I'd forgiven my mother. Who else was I holding a grudge against?

Ethan came to mind. The mental image of his face was enough to make me pop my knuckles. It wasn't okay with me that he was moving in on my girl. What a Bible-toting hypocrite. But knowing I'd done some hypocritical things too, I made the unnatural decision to let go of my growing hatred toward him. "I forgive Ethan."

I waited, but nothing happened. I envisioned him again, and this time, suffered the agony of imagining telling him to his face. I spoke it out loud: "I forgive you, Ethan."

A chain and open cuff hit the floor, then melted away.

Nice.

Who else? It didn't take long . . .

Dr. Bradford. The ultimate manipulator. A misleading mix of cruelty and charm. I refused to believe he was a changed man, but if I wanted freedom from my chains, I had to find a way to release the hostility.

"Dr. Bradford, you're an evil abuser that pretends to be all good and noble." I took a deep breath. "I don't trust you at all. But since I'm not your judge . . ." I admit, I hesitated. "I choose to forgive you."

Another chain fell.

Next?

Ugh. My dad's parents. "Together, you guys stole my father from me, and I've hated you for it." I felt my cheeks start to radiate heat. "But I can't live in the past, and you can't stop me from knowing him now." Another deep breath. "I forgive you both."

Two chains fell to the carpet at once.

Even before they melted, I knew who was next. And I dreaded it.

Do I have *to do this?*

For a few minutes, I honestly considered the possibility that this one might be worth lugging around a chain for. But it was me who would carry the bondage, not him, so what good was that?

First, I vented . . .

"You spread rumors about me. Turned people against me. Nearly beat me to death. Physically forced yourself on Jess. Opened fire at my school and murdered ten innocent people. You shot Ray Anne and nearly killed her, too, and you took away her dream of having children. And Ashlyn . . . she's stuck in a bed, comatose. I get that you were abused and suffering—I do—but instead of getting help, you took it out on other people."

This was way harder than I'd thought it would be. "You don't deserve any mercy." I nearly stopped there. "But since I'm sure I don't either . . ."

Can I do this?

Lord, help me.

"I forgive you, Dan."

Maybe I only imagined it, but it seemed like that chain slammed the floor faster and harder than the others.

236 || LAURA GALLIER

I was lighter now, not physically but on the inside, and I marveled at how our spiritual condition can have such a big impact on the way we feel. If only I could help people realize that.

I had one chain left.

Lance? I forgave him, but nothing fell off me.

Veronica? Nothing after her either.

I was still trying to figure it out when Ray Anne called, gasping between sniffles. "They're taking Ashlyn off life support in the morning." It felt like we got only bad news lately.

"I'm so sorry, Ray."

Ashlyn would be released from her broken body, but where she was going was much, much worse. I was tempted to hate Dan all over again, but instead, I repeated the exercise. *I forgive you, Dan.*

"I'm gonna go see her in the morning," Ray Anne cried into the phone, "but I can't stay and watch her die."

I told Ray I'd be there, but I'd leave before they unplugged her too. Witnessing Meagan meet a shackled soul's fate was the most traumatizing experience of my life. I'd never willingly watch it happen again to anyone.

I figured I'd have a restless night, but when Custos knelt beside my bed, filling the atmosphere with an all-consuming sense of calm, I shielded my eyes with two pillows and got some sleep.

The next morning, Ray Anne stood next to me in the hallway, crying into a Kleenex while Ashlyn's mother sobbed at her daughter's bedside. There was a gruesome Creeper with its back against the ceiling, looking down at Ashlyn, no doubt anticipating pouncing on her soul.

Ethan approached us wearing green scrubs, on duty today, with another handful of tissues for Ray Anne. He actually acknowledged me by name. Maybe it was the whole forgiveness thing, but I wasn't all that bothered by him today. Plus, under the circumstances, the issues between us weren't that important.

Ashlyn's mom told us we were welcome to say some final words and then exited the room. Ray Anne approached the bed, and Ethan and I stood back, giving her some space. Her light was enough to send that spying Creeper sinking upward into the ceiling tiles.

Despite the tubes and machines and Creeper webs, Ray Anne clung to Ashlyn's hand and stroked her hair. The girl's eyes were shut, and she practically looked dead already, but that didn't stop Ray Anne. At first, she whispered, but before long, she got loud. "It's not too late, Ashlyn. Listen to my voice—you can still cry out to God." She kept pleading, over and over.

I wasn't out to discourage her, but watching her beg uselessly was heartbreaking. "Ray, it's too late. She can't hear you."

It took me off guard when Ethan rushed past me, leaning over the bed next to Ray Anne and speaking into Ashlyn's ear. "It's not too late, Ashlyn," he pleaded. "You can still make a choice."

And just like that, I had an unbearable, undeniable epiphany.

Honestly, I'd known it for a while but had tried to discredit it—worked night and day to smother the thought before it could get a word in. But seeing Ethan and Ray Anne together, so full of faith, fighting side by side for Ashlyn's soul, there was no denying it anymore.

He was a much better fit for her than I was—Heaven's response to her prayerful desire for a faith-filled soul mate.

With effortless eloquence, Ethan uttered a prayer that struck me as sincere. Selfless, even. Ray Anne said amen, then walked to me.

I was still lugging around one chain and two cords, but she hugged me and held me awhile. Still, I believed the honorable thing to do was release her to be with the man who deserved her most. Soon enough, I'd tell her.

"Thank you for being here, Owen." She left the room, and after fiddling with one of Ashlyn's monitors, so did Ethan.

I stood there, alone, suffering inside for Ashlyn and for myself, thinking about how tragic life can be and yet how precious. How vulnerable love can make us, how our deepest longing is to be loved—especially during our final days on earth.

I flinched when I heard a loud cracking sound, like metal buckling. *What . . . ?*

Ashlyn's shackle split in two, down the middle, breaking away from her throat and dropping onto her pillow. Immediately a golden glow appeared beneath the white sheet at the foot of her bed. And the Creeper webs around her bed gave way, drifting to the floor.

"Ashlyn!"

I leaned over her, but there was no sign of life. Her eyes were still closed, and her mouth hung half open like she wasn't aware of her body, much less her surroundings. And yet her spirit had heard the truth and responded.

I turned fast and held on to the bed rail, when a radiant orb appeared right where I'd just been standing. It was as bright as a camera flash and expanding fast, quickly stretching from the ceiling to the floor.

A robed Watchman stepped out of the light. Like every one I'd ever seen, he appeared young, not one flaw on his face. He had to duck to stand in the room. Then came a smaller figure, a man shorter than me, clothed in a simple white garment. With a smile that seemed to make the room even brighter, he approached and stood on the other side of the bed, not acknowledging me at all.

"Ashlyn, honey."

I recognized him now, from the framed photo next to Ashlyn's bed.

I watched in awe as she sat up. Her body didn't move, but her spirit did, with ease. "Daddy!" She threw her arms around his neck, and they both laughed with such elation, I couldn't help but laugh too.

"I've come to bring you home." Ashlyn's dad took her hand, and she practically leaped out of the bed—out of her shattered body. She hugged her father again, and he spun her around. She gasped at the sight of the grinning Watchman, as awestruck and speechless as I'd been the first time I'd seen one. The heavenly warrior extended his arm toward the beaming passageway. "Come."

Still clinging to her father, Ashlyn ran into the light, giggling and carefree. The Watchman followed, then the light shrank into a small orb and vanished.

The room seemed dim and empty. I stared down at Ashlyn—or her body, a vacant shell now, forced by technology to operate a little longer.

Her mother entered, accompanied by a team of medical staff, ready to begin the process of disconnecting her. I had no right to try to console Ashlyn's anguishing mother, but I had to say something.

"She's already with her father." That's all I said, then I left.

Ray Anne stood in the hospital lobby, but I didn't know if she was waiting for me or Ethan. When I told her what had happened, she laughed and cried and practically danced on top of the death dust. She was so happy that, while I walked with her across the parking lot to her car, she almost didn't notice her cell ringing. I could only hear one side of the conversation.

"Hey, Jess!" Ray was clearly on an emotional high. "Yeah?"

Ray Anne stopped, her brow furrowed with worry. "What do you mean, Jackson is missing?"

All the color left her face. "Wait—why would your roommate take him without telling you?" Ray didn't give Jess time to explain. "Who is she?"

Ray Anne was too distraught now to hold her cell to her ear. She turned to me with terrified eyes. "Jess's roommate took Jackson." She was breathing so hard, she could hardly get the words out. "It's Veronica Snow."

THIRTY-TWO

IT DIDN'T MAKE SENSE. I took Ray's phone and tried to piece the loose ends together. Jess explained that Veronica tended bar at the restaurant where Jess worked, and that's where they'd met. Veronica had even helped Jess get the job there. She'd moved in with Veronica a few days ago, into an apartment across town from mine. But that didn't add up. Veronica lived in my complex.

Both employees at my apartment's leasing office said no one named Veronica Snow had ever rented a unit there. I pulled up a social media picture of her on my cell, but the two men maintained they'd never laid eyes on her. "Believe me, we'd remember a woman who looks like that," one of them said.

I called Masonville High. Principal Harding wasn't willing to give me Veronica's address, but it didn't matter, because Harding discovered that Veronica had left her street address blank on her paperwork.

Who *was* this woman?

Ray Anne drove us to the apartment Jess shared with Veronica and pounded on the door, ready to rush Jess to the police station to file a missing child report. Jackson had been gone nearly twenty-four hours,

242 || LAURA GALLIER

and Jess had been so out of it—high on who knows what—that hours had passed before she even noticed her son was gone from his crib.

Normally Ray Anne was pretty calm under pressure, but right now she was shaking and coming unglued.

Jess's Mustang was parked out front, but she wasn't answering. I tried the door. It was unlocked.

The place was a mess, but it was the smell that troubled us.

Sulfur.

Was Molek back?

Ray called Jess's name, but there was no sign of her—until we opened a bedroom door. She was on her back on the floor next to her spilled purse, not moving. My immediate thought: Jess had needed her asthma inhaler but hadn't been able to find it. Ray and I hit our knees next to Jess, and immediately, an arm's length away, big chunks of the tan carpet started falling, disappearing into endless darkness.

The same black abyss I'd seen Meagan plunged into.

I put my ear to Jess's mouth—she wasn't breathing. Ray Anne was already calling 911, and I started CPR while she made a frantic plea for an ambulance. I'd never seen Jess so colorless. Her lips were turning blue.

Even when my arms started stinging with fatigue, I didn't ease up. To quit would mean giving up Jess's soul to never-ending, unthinkable suffering. Death had been in this apartment—Molek or some other lethal grim reaper that smelled just like him. Maybe he was still here, spying on us. Either way, it was up to me to keep Jess out of his bloodthirsty hands.

That's when Heaven's mercy intervened. An armored Watchman descended from the ceiling and knelt next to Jess. I pulled my arms away and collapsed backward.

I knew this Watchman.

It was the same one who had rescued Jess from drowning when she'd given up on life in high school. He gazed at her face, then at me. He didn't say it, but I knew—I had to get to work again helping keep her alive.

I'd just started another round of chest compressions when my spiritual eyes saw Jess's shackled soul start to thrash. She sat up out of her body, crying and flailing her arms and legs in restless turmoil. But the Watchman placed his huge hands on her chest—on her soul—one palm on top of the other, and gently pressed her down, back inside her skin. And he stayed there, pinning her in place while I did CPR, until the paramedics arrived and rammed an epinephrine shot into Jess's thigh. At last, she started breathing.

As Jess was hoisted onto a gurney and rushed out the door, a middle-aged police officer approached. I recognized him: Officer McFarland, Detective Benny's sidekick when I was under investigation.

While Jess was whisked away in an ambulance in front of a curious crowd, Ray Anne gave McFarland a detailed description of Veronica—everything we knew about her. Ray begged the officer over and over to help find Jackson. With the recent string of abductions, the police were on high alert, but based on his hesitant nods, I got the feeling he wasn't ready to classify Veronica as a hard-core kidnapper. Still, he vowed they'd start searching immediately.

I stepped away from the gawking mob in search of some isolation where I could try to hear myself think. I was fidgety and buzzing with adrenaline. I bent over with my hands on my knees next to a lamppost at the far end of the parking lot, concentrating as hard as I could.

Veronica had taken Jackson . . .

Was this evil's way of distracting Ray and me at a crucial time? Or was it worse than that—a maneuver that somehow played into Molek's determination to reclaim his throne?

I glanced at my cell. Noon. Twenty-two hours until the town converged at the high school. *Hopefully*, converged.

Jess had nearly died—what more would the kingdom of darkness pull between now and tomorrow's gathering? I wasn't crediting Creepers with having given Jess asthma, but I was sure they had launched anxious thoughts at her, bullying her into an asthmatic panic. This wasn't the first time they'd targeted and pursued her.

My mom had left me a voice mail, and as I strode back to Ray Anne, I played it. Turns out a donor organ had become available, and Dr. Bradford had driven my mother to the hospital to get prepped immediately for surgery. Had my mind not been as chaotic as the scene outside Jess's apartment, I'm sure I would have made the connection right away. As it was, it took a few seconds before I stopped midstride and covered my open mouth.

The donor . . .

Ashlyn.

It had to be her.

It blew my mind how that situation had come full circle. There was no way God had wanted Dan to shoot Ashlyn. And yet Ashlyn's unfair physical death was about to spare my mom from facing eternal death.

"You'll see," the robed Watchman had said to me the night I'd shed my shackle, after Dan's shooting rampage. I'd chosen then to trust that some good would come out of the tragedy.

Hard as it was to believe, it had. I hoped Ashlyn's mom was able to realize it, at least on some level. I felt so bad for her.

Ray Anne ran to me. "We have to look for Jackson! Where could she have taken him?"

There was no time to sit around and come up with a well-thought-out plan.

Ray Anne pulled me by the arm toward her car. "Where should we start?" It didn't matter that Detective Benny had arrived and approached us to let us know the police were on the case. She was out to find Jackson herself.

My first instinct was to search the one place I knew Veronica liked to go. "Drive to my land." No, I couldn't think of a single reason she'd want to bring Jackson to the clearing, but we obviously weren't dealing with a rational person.

When we turned onto the four-lane road that leads to Masonville High, Ray and I both saw it at the same time—the enormous, gruesome chair hovering almost directly over the high school parking lot now. Many more Creepers than before leaned into the back of Molek's throne, having gained an advantage against the opposing Watchmen, who also had to deal with fighting off other groups of Creepers swarming them.

Ray Anne pulled over, and we both jumped out of her car.

She dug her fingers into her scalp. "Have we already lost?"

I had to admit, the scene didn't look good. But I held out hope. "Until Molek is seated on that throne, we still have a chance."

We piled back into the car and sped past the high school. In the grassy field behind the campus, a crew was setting up a large canopy tent and stage for tonight's Spring Scream. Of course I thought of Riley. Had she been lumped in with the rest of Masonville's missing persons, or was Detective Benny carefully exploring evidence for each victim, Jackson included?

A little farther, we turned onto the dirt road closest to the clearing, then parked and set out on foot. But when we got to the clearing, there was no sign of Veronica or Jackson. We trekked back to the car and took the search public, spending all afternoon showing people Jackson's picture and Veronica's, too, asking everyone who'd stop and listen if they'd seen either of them. Ray Anne's parents also joined the search.

I tracked down Hector's cell number, but he swore he hadn't heard from Veronica and he'd already told police the same thing.

By the time the sun began to set, Ray Anne and I had stopped and questioned people at countless stores, restaurants, gas stations—you name it.

"She probably skipped town with him hours ago," Ray Anne said, slamming on her brakes in front of Franklin Park, careering to a stop next to the basketball court. Same place I'd shot hoops with Walt and Marshall on that fatal day—their last day on earth.

Ray Anne left her car door open and sprinted toward the empty playground. I caught up with her as she collapsed on her hands and knees in the grass, sobbing. "Where are you, Jackson—*where*?" She pounded a patch of clover with balled fists and cried her heart out. I tried to wrap a tender arm around her, but she pushed me away.

Right or wrong, Ray Anne agonized like it was her own child that was missing.

I sat beside her, unable to do much of anything except be with her. She finally sobbed herself into exhaustion and shrank to the ground, laying her head on my shoulder. I wiped strands of her hair away from her soaked cheek until she grabbed my hand and held on tight. We stayed that way awhile.

I noticed some students in a front yard of a house across the street were dressed up in costumes and posing for pictures—headed to Spring Scream, no doubt. One wore a black hooded robe and held a grim reaper's sickle. I'm sure he meant to be comical, but it struck me as grotesque. And it triggered a disturbing train of thought.

Hooded witchcraft Creepers. Drawn to Veronica's gathering in the woods. What could she possibly want with Jackson?

I closed my eyes in concentration. *Jess's child. And Dan's.* Dr. Bradford's grandson—a man introduced to the ways of the occult by my mom's parents.

A nerve-racking chill scurried the entire length of my body.

A secret society where bloodlines matter. And unorthodox holidays call for celebration.

I swallowed hard while pulling my phone out of my back pocket. I did an online search, and instantly, an occult calendar came up. I scrolled the list of dates, hoping my gut instinct was way off. But sure enough . . .

Today's date, in bold, unmistakable print:

April 19—Annual Feast of Molek, a sacred evening to pay homage to the ancient god.

And just like that, I knew why Veronica had taken Jackson, where she was going with him tonight, and the reason we only had a few hours left to stop her. But I had no idea how to tell Ray Anne.

SEEMINGLY UNRELATED DETAILS had come together in my mind to form a shocking, sickening picture of what Molek had planned for tonight.

"What are you looking at?" Ray Anne asked.

I was still in the grass, holding my cell in one hand and Ray Anne with my other arm, unable to bring myself to tell her the agonizing truth. "I have to make an important phone call. I need to walk away a minute, but I'll come right back, okay?"

I could tell by the frown on her face that she didn't like it, but she didn't try to stop me. I stepped away and called Detective Benny. "I really, really need your help tonight, sir."

"What's going on, Owen?"

As usual, I faced the challenge of having to explain a spiritual dilemma to a nonspiritual person. "I have strong reasons to believe that Veronica is going to bring Jackson to my property tonight—most likely to that clearing with the well—and take his life."

There was a long pause. "What makes you say such a thing?"

How to tell him?

Over a century ago, I believe it was a child sacrifice on Caldwell's land at the hands of his mystic daughters that had brought Molek—an

247

ancient, high-ranking spirit of death—and his army to Masonville to begin with, enacting some kind of legal claim to the property in the spirit realm. From then on, under Molek's tyranny, violence and murder had continued to curse the land, and his invisible militia had grown in strength and size. At one time, my own grandparents held satanic rituals out there that were so dark and unthinkable that, to this day, my mother refuses to speak of them.

Like Betty had said, after the mass shooting, the pleas of praying people nationwide had helped turn the tables, prompting Heaven to set up some kind of cosmic perimeter that blocked Molek from the land. But the soil remained tainted, stained in the spirit realm with innocent blood, which allowed Molek's army to remain, plotting their king's return to power.

Arthur's letter had helped Ray and me realize how to cleanse the land, terminating Molek's territorial right and purging him and his army from Masonville completely. But once again, Betty had been right: if a person were to collaborate with the spirit of death—if Veronica offered up Jackson's life on the land tonight—Molek would have a spirit-world right to breach the Watchmen's perimeter, ushering in a new reign of terror even worse than before.

And tonight *happened* to be the annual occult holiday devoted to Molek.

It came down to this: in order to stop Molek in the spirit realm, we had to stop Veronica in the woods.

But it wasn't like I could share all that with the detective, so I gave a seriously condensed version. "Veronica Snow has been going to my woods—I've witnessed it myself. And I believe she's going again tonight, with Jackson, and it's going to turn deadly." I was as blunt as I could be. "I think Veronica is into . . . occult practices. Either way, the baby's life's in danger."

"Hmm . . ."

I couldn't tell how seriously he was taking my claims.

"We've combed through every square foot of that land in recent months and found no trace that occult rituals are taking place out there anymore."

Anymore? So he knew they had in the past.

"Look," I said, "I don't know how many people she has or hasn't recruited to join her out there, but I'm telling you, something bad's going down tonight."

I could tell by the lame questions Detective Benny asked and the way he kept huffing into the phone that he wasn't buying into my suspicion. I was sure that, based on my senior year, in his mind I'd forever be a psycho. Still, before we hung up, he assured me he'd have officers keep an eye on my property throughout the night and also assign a squad to check the clearing.

I was grateful, but far from confident. What if Veronica took Jackson somewhere else on the property? My land covered more than twelve hundred acres—two square miles.

"It'll only complicate matters for us if you're out there tonight," Benny warned me. "Stay out of the woods, and let us handle it."

All I said was, "Thank you." I wasn't willing to commit to staying off my land, sitting idly by.

Ray Anne approached as my call ended, crying all over again. "Who were you talking to?"

I gripped her petite arms. "Listen to me. You need to get some rest tonight and let me take care of things."

"I'm not going home!" She stomped her foot. "What's going on?"

I looked away. How was I supposed to tell her?

She grabbed hold of my chin and turned my head to face her. "Owen, don't shut me out. Please."

I took a deep breath, then pulled her close. "Ray Anne . . . this is going to be really hard for you to hear."

I explained the horrific situation, and like I thought, she became hysterical, pacing around and crying harder. But then she got quiet and hit her knees in the grass. I knelt beside her, and together, we told God the obvious . . .

This was too much for us to handle without him.

Jackson was way too precious to be harmed.

There was too much at stake for things to end in Molek's favor tonight.

Once Ray said amen, it was like a switch had been flipped and she was done crying. "Let's go." She jumped to her feet and yanked me by my arm, stomping toward her car like a marine on a mission.

No one was going to keep her out of the woods tonight.

THIRTY-FOUR

RAY ANNE STOPPED OFF at my apartment so I could get my motorcycle and we could cover more ground at once. I followed her to Masonville High. When we arrived at the side street by the school, the parking lot was full, and the street was lined with cars as far as I could see. It was dark out, and Spring Scream was in full swing. There were way more people here than just Masonville High students.

Music blared from a live band under the tent, decorated with strands of orange lights to look spooky. People flocked there in every kind of costume, some glittery, others gruesome.

Police officers stood at the entrance inspecting girls' purses and people's props, but Creepers got right past them.

I pulled my bike up next to Ray Anne's car. She was leaning out her driver's side window, straining to gaze up at the night sky. Molek's throne was lower to the ground and hovered above the school now, the fight waging on. I still didn't see him, though.

I was careful not to walk too fast for Ray to keep up as she and I made another long trip to the clearing. She winced like her injuries were hurting but didn't complain. The clearing was empty, but it was only a few minutes after ten. This night was far from over.

I had hoped we would spot that police squad Benny had promised to send out here, but there was no sign of them.

On our walk back to the main road, we passed a dead dog. *Another one?* The old man and I had already buried one out here. Was that proof the occult was still active on my land? The sad remains of their secret rituals?

Ray and I drove in opposite directions around the perimeter of my property. I passed a striped wooden barricade and yellow police tape lining the back side of my acreage, still quarantined for investigation. This was my land. It seemed like I had a right to know what they'd found.

We both finished our drive all the way around my acreage, and everything was still and undisturbed.

Minutes passed like a ticking time bomb, and the later it got, the more Ray and I felt the pressure. She pulled off the road and sat behind the wheel, fanning her face and exhaling long and loud as I sat restlessly on my bike.

We both flinched when, like a sprinting pack of wolves, towering Creepers passed us, charging alongside the tree line in the direction of the school. Ray and I took off that way, parking as close as we could to the party and hurrying side by side under the crowded tent. Sure enough, twice as many Creepers now crept among the sea of students.

Dark forces had led us to this scene, and I felt obligated to check it out, but I couldn't imagine that Veronica would show up here.

There were so many people crammed in and around that tent, we could hardly walk, but what was much worse was the death dust scattered all over and blanketing the air. The guy on stage was singing—more like yelling—about a girl who'd ripped his heart out, and Creeper dust was spewing from his mouth like gray smog from an exhaust pipe.

We finally made it through the crowd, and Officer McFarland was posted outside the tent. Ray Anne ran to him, pleading above the noise for him to tell us if any leads had come through about Veronica or Jackson. "Or Riley?" I added.

He shook his head.

That's when the party scene turned into a shove fest. From what I could tell, some guy dressed like a zombie, tethered to a Creeper, started punching a scrawny kid, and there was instant shouting and screaming and chaos. Officer McFarland rushed in, shoving his way toward the fight.

Ray Anne and I got swept up in the swarm of people now fleeing the tent, but somehow a movement caught my eye, off in the distance. Every cop on hand was working to calm the frenzy—except one. Detective Benny was hurrying away, practically sprinting toward a vehicle parked against the curb. Not a squad car, mind you, but a plain sedan.

A black limousine had stopped in the middle of the street—the first one I'd ever seen in Masonville. Benny started his car, then pulled out in front of the limo. I dodged the commotion long enough to watch the luxurious vehicle follow Benny away from the school, toward my acreage.

I wouldn't have been as suspicious had a white vintage pickup truck not turned onto the street, trailing a short distance behind the limo and Benny. It looked just like the mysterious old man's truck.

I turned to tell Ray Anne, but I couldn't find her. Hundreds of people moved in all directions like bees swarming a busted hive.

I had to go. I ran to my motorcycle and took off down the street, trying to catch the truck. Down the road, a pair of taillights turned right. I passed the entrance to the clearing, speeding to the desolate country road that ran along the back perimeter of my property, and turned. But there were no taillights ahead now.

I slowed down, eyeing the wooded property on my right. Nothing, and more nothing. I nearly missed it, but thankfully, I spotted the white truck parked against the tree line with its lights off. I pulled into the grass behind it, parked my bike, and went to investigate on foot. The truck's engine was off, the driver gone.

In the half-moon's light, I inspected the area. Except for buzzing insects and the distant sound of the band, it was so quiet I could hear myself swallow. Another vehicle turned onto the street, and the headlights went off. I ducked low as the car passed, driving slowly in the dark.

About a football field away, a small light blinked three times in the middle of the road. A flashlight?

Red brake lights shined in the night, and the car made a right turn where the light had flashed, driving onto my property through an entrance I never knew existed. Right where the crime tape was.

Another vehicle turned onto the back road where I was spying, this one having come from the opposite direction. Headlights off again.

Then came another. Over and over, I watched vehicles pass me with their lights off.

During breaks between cars, I sprinted down the street toward the spot where they were turning. When I started getting close, I slipped into the woods for cover and kept working my way in that direction.

Finally, I was there. I peeked out from the woods, my gut sinking when I saw the car Benny had just driven parked in the street, next to the striped barricade that had been moved away from the tree line. He stood in the road with a flashlight, directing people to . . .

Where? What *was* this?

I traveled deeper into the woods, making my way alongside a winding, makeshift dirt road someone must have worked hard to clear. Vehicles passed on my left. A Mercedes. A Corvette. A Tesla that looked just like Jess's dad's.

Was it?

I picked up the pace and jogged for some twenty minutes before catching up to the cars, all parked side by side at an angle. There was a Ferrari in the mix—red, it looked like. Same color as Dr. Bradford's.

I stopped to read a text from Ray Anne: **Where are you? I'm going with Officer McFarland to check the clearing again.**

Good.

I texted back: **People on back side of land. I'll let you know what I find.**

I kept going, deeper into the woods. I'd never been out here before and wasn't expecting to come upon a dilapidated cluster of headstones, encircled by a broken-down, rusted iron fence.

This had to be the old Caldwell family cemetery. Still here.

I cringed and went around it. A short distance later, I finally made it to where the drivers of all those cars had gathered. I've got to say, outside the spirit world, I'd never seen anything so freakish.

There were numerous black poles spread around, anchored into the ground and towering above people's heads, each supporting a bowl blazing with a mini-bonfire.

The men all wore black tuxedos, and the women wore colorful full-length gowns, but it was the big, absurd headpieces and elaborate themed masks that creeped me out. One woman had a huge, green, scaly hat that blended with a jewel-covered mask, crafted to look like a dragon was biting her face. The man next to her wore a tall top hat with white feathered angel wings on each side, paired with a black mask with rubber worms dangling off it.

The people socialized in hushed whispers, making the gathering eerily quiet. And there were children in the mix, dressed as outlandishly as their parents. At least I assumed those were their parents.

Every adult was shackled, and most wore half masks that exposed the bottom of their faces, their mouths and chins painted with stripes or weird shapes and patterns. A thin lady wearing an antique-looking lampshade as a hat and a cheetah-fur mask walked around with a cocktail tray, handing out skinny champagne glasses. Several large, bulky men in tuxes and white *Phantom of the Opera*–looking masks stood with their backs to the gathering, staring intently into the woods. Security guards?

I darted behind a thicker tree trunk.

People huddled in groups, frequently glancing at the candle-adorned cement steps and platform that served as the focal point of the bizarre occasion. I realized I'd seen the structure before—with Ray, the evening of her birthday, the first time we'd encountered hooded Creepers.

At the back and center of the concrete platform, a large cube was draped in shimmery brown fabric that occasionally moved, like something was alive underneath. And there they were again—a throng of hooded Creepers stood tall on top, looking out over the social affair while unhooded Creepers moved like party guests among the lavish crowd.

Was this an elite society gala? The upper-class version of the Spring Scream?

I'd thought I might close in on an occult ritual in these woods tonight, but this? Mesmerizing as it was, I still felt worlds away from finding and rescuing Jackson. I chomped on my bottom lip, so anxious I made it bleed.

A woman adorned in a Mardi Gras–looking mask and peacock head-piece escorted a little girl by the hand up the cement steps to the center of the stage. The child, still too young to have earned a shackle, wore a floor-length gown with a gold, grinning mask that covered her whole face. She held a violin and bow.

There was a quiet, collective sigh as the audience faced the stage, as still as stone pillars as the child gave a short, flawless instrumental performance. The fabric concealing the cube behind her kept fluttering, drawing my interest more. When she finished, the audience members tapped two fingers together in barely audible applause.

The girl exited the stage, and a slender man in a colorful oriental mask stood next to the Mardi Gras lady. "So glad you could join us." Then he nodded at the woman by his side, and she stepped up to the draped cube and grabbed the fabric. After a lingering gaze at the capti-vated audience, a smile on her ruby-red lips, she unveiled the mystery.

I could hardly stand to look.

THIRTY-FIVE

MORE THAN A HUNDRED YEARS after Caldwell had owned this land, an iron-barred cage had made its way back onto the property. With children inside. Elementary school–aged boys and girls with light beaming from their fragile chests, and a few teenagers, too—maybe thirteen or fourteen years old.

Their faces were painted to look like dolls, but there was something over their mouths. Some kind of tape?

The five girls wore frilly dresses with tights and shiny shoes, and the four boys wore pleated shorts and button-up shirts tucked in, with knee-high socks and loafers. They stood looking out through the bars—not one of them crying, but all with unmistakably hopeless eyes.

I knew this wasn't some party skit, and those children weren't in that cage by choice. They were so still. Had they been drugged? Whose kids were they?

I studied the spellbound crowd from my hiding spot, and my gaze ran across a tall, thin man with a glittery mask attached to a stick he used to hold it to his face. He angled in my direction, as if staring right at me. I ceased to breathe. Slowly, he lowered his mask, showing me his face . . .

Walt. Threatening me without words.

He stepped back and slipped into the crowd. I knew it wasn't the real him—that evil was masquerading in his image—but the experience was still bone chilling.

The man center stage pointed to a caged child, a little blonde girl, and rattled off her age and height and eye color. I already had my suspicions, but when he said she was from the state of Oklahoma, I took it as devastating confirmation.

These were abducted children.

My palms were sweaty, and I struggled to pull my phone out of my pocket. I pinned my GPS location, then dialed 911 while also managing to fish the digital recorder Elle had given me from my other pocket. I hit record and set the device at the base of a tree, as close to the stage as I could get.

I hardly moved a muscle while waiting for the emergency operator to answer. The man onstage began spattering off dollar amounts, auctioneer style. With the flick of a wrist or a subtle nod, people began bidding. On the girl from Oklahoma.

I felt dizzy, like the woods were spinning. Arthur had predicted that slavery would return to this land, and here I was, staring at it. Now I understood what that cement platform was and always had been. A human auction block.

The slave trade of yesterday, human trafficking today—it has the same evil origins. I knew now: history doesn't just happen to repeat itself. The kingdom of darkness uses repeat tactics, generation after generation.

But my generation was called to take a stand against age-old evil.

When the emergency operator answered, my mind was reeling. Had Jackson and Riley and the others been smuggled out of state and auctioned off too?

Before I could even ask for help, something bashed the side of my face, then something else covered my nose and mouth as my feet were knocked out from under me. I slammed the ground on my left side, painfully realizing those security guards were manhandling me. One stomped the heel of his shoe on my cell, crushing it to pieces.

There was no way to fight back. A rag was forced into my mouth, gagging me into silence, and my arms and legs were bound behind me, tied at my wrists and ankles with rope, I think. It had taken them less than thirty seconds to restrain me, and man, it hurt.

A baritone voice threatened in my ear. "Don't make a sound, and we may let you live."

After everything I'd just witnessed? Not a chance.

They searched my pockets and took my wallet, then dragged me so far away I wondered if we'd ever stop. Then they left me, bound in an unnatural pose in the dirt. I knew they'd come back and finish me off once the high-dollar guests left. I didn't know if these people were the mafia, dirty politicians, or what, but I was sure they weren't the type to let spies go with a verbal warning. And they knew exactly who I was now. They had my ID.

I tried my hardest to move, to loose my arms and legs, but I'd been hog-tied by trained men. I gave it my all—my life was on the line—but I couldn't begin to break free. Another kid was bound to have been auctioned off by now. Would they bring infants out next? Could Jackson possibly be there?

As the minutes dragged on—my contorted body throbbing while I kept gagging on the wad in my mouth—despair crept in. There was no way out of this. I couldn't talk. Couldn't utter a word. So I closed my eyes and yelled inside my head . . .

Please, God! Do something! Free me!

I hadn't been this panicked since I'd been shoved headfirst into Walt and Marshall's caskets.

I heard someone coming, trampling the brush behind me. I tensed up, expecting a knife or pistol to press against my skin. Instead, someone with strong hands started untying me. I strained my neck but couldn't see who it was.

The rope around my legs finally gave way, and I sat up and looked back. A golden aura projected onto the ground cover behind me. I twisted harder and looked up.

"It's you!"

The old man in overalls pressed his index finger to his lips as he helped me to my feet. This was the second time he'd saved my life. In these woods.

There was so much going on, so much I needed him to understand, that I blurted it out all at once. "Molek's probably about to take his throne any second, and Jess's baby, Jackson, is majorly in danger while these children are being sold to . . . I have no idea who the masked people are, but these kids are kidnapped, and if we don't find Jackson before it's too late, Molek's gonna win, and everything's ruined!"

A single nod and a whisper. "I know."

Oh.

I tried to search his face in the dark while waiting for insight or instructions or something spectacular, but all he did was hand me my keys, which he'd somehow retrieved from the guards. "Well?" I put my hands up. "What do we do?"

"All that can be done for now."

More silence. More impatience welling up inside me. "Which *is* . . . ?"

He led me a distance through the woods, insisting I keep silent. Then he stopped me. "Listen."

I heard the distant sound of the smooth-talking auctioneer selling a human life for a couple of thousand dollars. "What am I—?"

"Listen!"

It was faint but distinct. An infant's cries.

THIRTY-SIX

THAT HAD TO BE JACKSON.

I grabbed the old man's muscular arm. "Let's go get him!"

But the old man shook his head. "Follow the sound," he said. "I'll meet you there."

He turned fast and walked away, but I grabbed his sleeve. "Come with me!"

He looked up, above my head. "You have your assignment. I have mine."

And then he left me.

With no cell phone and only the light around my feet for illumination, I moved through the shrubbery and trees and limbs as swiftly as I could, compelled by the gut-wrenching sound of Jackson squalling. I didn't care how badly my jaw was throbbing.

There are all kinds of noises in the woods, especially at night, but I blocked them out to focus on the only one that mattered. But then someone called my name. I turned fast. Behind me, standing in the path I'd just forged, Lucas stood staring at me, wearing that same white T-shirt—clean this time—and holding a candle at his chest. His hair was spiked nice and neat, boyish innocence in his face. He pointed to the side. "This way, Owen!"

Did he really think I'd fall for his act again? I turned away and kept charging forward.

"Hey!" He followed me. "Wrong way—the child's over there!"

I didn't look back at the liar.

"This way, Owen," another voice called.

Marshall. On my right. Pointing the same direction as Lucas.

I pressed on, faster now, quoting Luke 10:19 over and over. I crossed the trail where Ray Anne liked to try to jog, and for the moment, had somewhat of a sense of where I was.

"The path's right here." I couldn't see him, but I knew it was Walt. Only it wasn't really.

The longer I stuck to my path, charging in the direction I believed was right, the louder and more scathing the interruptions got, coming at me from all directions in the dark.

"You're a fool! Why won't you listen?"

"You've never saved anyone. This time won't be any different."

"That child's gonna die, and it's your fault!"

Distracting as it was, I could still hear Jackson—even louder now. I was getting close. It was like he was crying for *me*.

Finally I spied the fire posts in the distance.

My legs were cramping, and I was sucking air, but I kept going, ripping my way through some tangled vines. Then the crying stopped. *Please, God, tell me he's okay.*

All I heard was *her*. Veronica, in my brain. *You're too late.*

She kept saying it. Then Marshall and Lucas and Walt started saying it too, shouting it over and over from high up in the trees. It was enough to drive me insane.

I gripped the sides of my head and marched forward, one quick step at a time, determined to get to that little boy. Clinging to the hope that he hadn't been harmed.

He's dead, Veronica's voice echoed in my mind. *Go home, Owen. It's over.*

But by then, I could see she was lying. The trees opened up into a clearing flickering with firelight. I'd made it back to the secret gathering.

The cement steps were lined now with the freakishly dressed masked people, along with some students in costumes, like they'd defected from Spring Scream to be here. All of them were consumed with the action on the antique auction block. The cage was empty—all the children must have already been sold off like animals—but center stage, three people stood poised behind a waist-high wood table.

On the left, a woman wore a white gown with an even whiter ram's head as a mask—a real one, hollowed out, with long, curved horns. On the right stood a man in a modern-looking gray tux with a large boar head resting on his shoulders.

The man in the center was draped in a plain black robe that reminded me of a priest's, only it had a hood that came to a point—just like the cloaked witch Creepers I'd first seen right where he now stood. A golden glow spread around his feet.

How was that even possible?

In front of the table, a metal firepit sat on the stage, raging with flames.

And on the tall table, in the center, among objects I could barely see and couldn't begin to describe, there was a wooden box with no lid. Tiny, squirming arms and feet kept poking up from the top.

Jackson!

The man on the right, in the boar's head, lifted his arms high and spoke, loud and assertive, first in Latin, then English. "Upon the unenlightened and unprivileged, we loose the dark powers of calamity, sorrow, oppression, and death."

I couldn't believe what I was hearing, not only because it was so strange and demented and cruel, but because I recognized the voice. Dr. Bradford. I was almost positive.

The same kind of curse-snake that had crawled out of Hector and inside of Riley came slithering out from under the table, slinking down the steps. It was followed by dozens more, loosed to prey upon humanity.

The woman in the ram's mask spoke next, also in Latin first. "To us, the enlightened and privileged, grant power, prosperity, influence, and long life."

Veronica. Zero doubt.

Although her pronouncement sounded like a blessing, another brood of fork-tongued vipers spewed from the stage.

This was nothing like my preconceived idea of what occult rituals were like, and yet I was sure that's what it was. The upscale and trendy mixed with the utterly depraved.

So *this* was where my mother had learned Latin. As a child in these woods, forced to attend rituals like this.

I was contemplating my next move—how to get Jackson out of there—when the black-robed man in the center tilted his head back, looking up at the towering trees. I suddenly realized that the air was rancid and chilled. Creepers hovered, forming tight circles on top of circles in the air over the assembly. And illuminated by the moon and blazing fire, Molek's ghastly throne loomed in the center of the circular mass.

But it remained unoccupied.

The hooded man in the middle, who seemed to be the master of ceremonies or something, lifted his head and instructed everyone to repeat his words after him. He made numerous debased, bold declarations, but I can't recall a single one. The second I glimpsed his face, I was too stunned to listen.

And too furious to keep hiding.

I stepped forward and stood at the base of the platform, gazing up the steps at the man in black. The ritual came to a standstill, and all eyes locked onto me. But I wasn't scared. Wasn't even intimidated. My sudden resolve to know the truth and expose the lies overshadowed every trace of fear.

"Take off your hood," I shouted up at him. "Let me see you."

At first, he didn't move. But then he reached up and eased the cloak back. I was right . . .

My father. A thin face, like I'd seen in Tulsa. Stitches near the corner of his mouth. A Light.

"I wanted to tell you another way," he said. "Not now. Not like this."

I started up the steps, fuming. My mind racing.

"I was so honored to meet you, Owen. So touched that you'd sought me out."

I kept moving toward him. People glared at me, gasping and whispering, but I didn't turn my head.

"There's more to this fight between good and evil than you've even begun to understand, Son."

I was to the top and not slowing.

"I'm doing this for *you*. You were born into a privileged bloodline. One day, you'll appreciate what that means."

I walked past the firepit, which was blazing with such intense heat I felt it through my jeans. I didn't look back or pause to think about what I was doing. I just approached the table and positioned myself directly in front of my father. Jackson wiggled and fussed between us.

"I've seen the child's future, Owen." Veronica spoke from behind the sickening ram's mask. "Like his father, he's going to harm many people someday."

"You want me to believe he deserves to die?"

The man in the boar mask pounded his fists against the table. "He must! To save others." I was sure now—it was Dr. Bradford.

"Save others?" I yelled in his masked face. "I heard the curses and death wishes you just called down on people."

"On the *unprivileged*," Veronica interjected. "The ones who refuse to acknowledge or serve the Source."

"God," my father clarified.

I wasn't swayed by their twisted justifications, and I knew they didn't serve the same God as me. There was no way I was leaving without Jackson. But I had to know—"Father, how could you deceive me like this?"

"You know I'm a Light," he said. "A man of faith." He gazed down at Jackson. "But like I told you during our visit, Son, justice is rarely won without sacrifice." He lifted open arms, inviting me to embrace him across the table. "No more secrets, Owen."

By then, I'd made the discovery I was after. The revelation of a lifetime . . .

"You've quoted my father's words," I said. "But you've twisted what he meant by them."

"Son, I—"

"I know the difference between good and evil when I see it now," I shouted, glancing at the two accomplices on either side of him, then back at the phony in the middle. "You're not my father. You're the demonic counterfeit. Now, get off my land."

And with that, the charade was over.

The impostor clenched his jaw and reached for Jackson with stiff hands. But I grabbed the little bare-skinned body first, pulling the baby up and into my chest as I turned, then ran as fast as I could toward the stairs. Veronica and Dr. Bradford lunged at me and grasped at my arms, trying to yank the child away, but I raced down one step after another, protecting Jackson from the masked people like I would my own son.

I'd just jumped from the bottom steps when my body suddenly jerked backward, nearly snapping Jackson out of my arms. My back hit the cement hard, and my head slammed a stair. I groaned. No one had laid a hand on me—what was going on?

"Get him!" I heard Veronica yell.

I tightened my grip around Jackson, then leaned forward to stand, but immediately, I jolted back, even harder this time. As my back slammed onto the concrete steps, a guy in a werewolf costume grabbed onto Jackson's waist, working to pry him from my arms. It was Hector. I fought hard, even though I was afraid we were hurting Jackson, but my head was yanked back, slamming the cement so hard I thought my skull must have cracked. Hector snatched the baby from me.

"Give him back!"

I don't know if it was because of my yell or the sudden sound of dogs barking in the distance, but people started fleeing, rushing to evacuate the scene. I was pinned down, unable to even lift my head off the steps.

Hector was an arm's length away but not moving, peering over me at the top of the stairs with wide, astonished eyes. "He disappeared!"

"Where'd he go?" I heard a woman say, then she looked at me and ran. I couldn't see what they were talking about.

I made another attempt to reach Hector, shoving myself forward with all my strength, but I was only able to lean toward him a few inches before once more, my body was inexplicably pulled back, ramming my spine. All I could do was watch as Hector handed Jackson to Veronica and she took off, abandoning the scene with everyone else.

The back of my neck felt like it was tethered to the step beneath it, but I managed to strain hard and roll onto my stomach, then tilt my chin up. The black hooded robe lay empty at the top of the stairs. It seemed my father's pretender had vanished in plain view of tonight's audience. And in his place, looming over the fire in his true form, visible only to me, stood my pale-skinned archenemy: Molek, the Lord of the Dead. Renowned overlord among the ranks of darkness. Relentless serial killer of the human race.

The demon king's lethal eyes glared down at me. He reeked of sulfur and burnt flesh.

All this time . . . it had been *him*.

Molek held a chain in one clawed hand and two long cords in the other—all stretching down the steps . . .

Connected to me.

"You think you're free?" His infuriated voice pierced my eardrums. He pulled back on my entrapments, dragging me up a step, scraping my chin against the cement. "You might as well be shackled."

I wiped my bleeding chin and inhaled fast, ready to quote the verse that had never failed me. But he reared his arm back supernaturally fast and let go of my chain so that the open cuff on the end bashed my mouth.

The agony took my breath away.

I cupped my open mouth, expecting teeth and blood to pour into my hand, but nothing came out. He hadn't hit my physical mouth.

He'd slammed my soul. Yet the pain had registered full scale.

I tried to read the name on the cuff so I could hurry up and forgive and free myself of it. But Molek charged at me and wrapped my cords excruciatingly tight around my head and mouth, gagging me just like the tuxedoed guards had with a rag. The cords were sharp, slicing my skin. No, my soul.

I grabbed at my cheeks, instinctively trying to pull away the entanglements, but there was nothing there—nothing I could touch. Yet I could feel them, squeezing so hard between my teeth, I couldn't talk or swallow or inhale through my mouth.

It seemed impossible that the spirit world could intrude on the natural realm to this degree, so that my spiritual entrapments were now being used to manhandle and subdue me. Then again, I'd recently intruded way too far into forbidden territories of the spirit world, even bowing to dark forces.

I had no one to blame for this but myself.

Still standing over me, Molek extended his arm, draped in his signature filthy-gray robe, and the cuff on my chain went flying up to meet his wrist in the air, like a magnet rushing at metal. Then he turned and charged up the stairs, dragging me with him like dead weight. It felt like my rib cage cracked, but I couldn't tell if the pain was in my body or deeper.

I landed on my back next to the firepit, the heat stinging my skin.

"Go get her!" Molek belted out, and Walt and Marshall went charging into the woods. I was the only human here now, in a den of evil forces.

"Keep him down!" Molek flung my cuff off his arm to Lucas, who was shedding his human form like a snake bursting from dead skin, transforming . . .

Into Regret. One of the Creepers that had assaulted me in my apartment. It caught the cuff midair, attaching it to its wrist, then wrapped the chain links around its arm, removing all slack. I was on a tight leash.

"I can still do this!" Molek announced.

At first I thought he was reassuring his army, but when I heard Jackson's whimpers drawing near, I knew better. Molek was shooting thoughts at Veronica's head. I could hear her rushing up the steps, her cuffs dragging and slamming each stair.

"I'll finish this myself," Molek said, "and gain all the power."

Veronica said it to herself right after he did.

She made it up the platform, and the two Creepers on each side of her bowed low to Molek.

He'd sent Walt and Marshall after her. But their true identities—Demise and Murder—had brought her back.

Veronica must have dismissed me as dead—she paid no attention to me. No longer wearing a mask, she lay Jackson in the box on top of the table again, then mumbled to herself while stoking the fire with an iron rod. Molek gazed up at his throne and roared, as loud as a pride of ravenous lions.

He and Veronica spoke in unison. "This is it!"

And it was. If I didn't find a way to break free and rescue Jackson *now*, all would be lost.

THIRTY-SEVEN

I WAS LYING FLAT on my back on the auction block, my piercing cords excruciatingly tight around my head and mouth, and my chain tethered to Regret. I already knew that bad attitudes and actions—sinful things—caused spirit-world cords to grow from shackled people's scalps, and chains were the heavy price of unforgiveness. Under immense pressure and with mere seconds to think, I stared at the leather band my father—the real one—had tied around my wrist, and I searched my battered soul, seeking against all odds to break free.

Regret loomed behind me. Strategywise, I needed my cords to snap first, then the chain. Regret would know it when my metal links broke.

What have I done?

Things came to mind, and I dealt with them quickly. Sincerely.

Forgive me for doubting you, God.

And for lustful fantasies.

And for lying—

Something popped against my cheek. A busted cord.

One more to go . . .

For being jealous.

And arrogant.

And impatient.

And communing with spirits.

That last one did it. Both piercing cords had fallen away from my face. I could see them now, dark and leathery on the cement by my head. Then they melted away.

I didn't move a muscle, but Regret yanked on my chain's links, spinning my body around so that my back was to the table now, my face inches from the Creeper's three-toed feet. I closed my eyes and tensed up, anticipating some torturous punishment, but it didn't come. Regret hadn't noticed my missing cords.

All at once, the Creepers on the ground, in the trees, and in the air began to moan—a flat hum that made my skin crawl. Jackson whimpered louder now.

It was agonizing, lying there, unable to see him and helpless to protect him.

The old man had said he'd meet me here—where was he?

I had to focus. My last chain. *Who could it be?*

I'd already forgiven everyone I could think of. *Everyone.*

Oh . . .

Except the one person I could never believe deserved it.

But I had to.

Now.

I did it under my breath. "You forgive me for all the ways I've failed, God. So *I* forgive me."

My last chain snapped in half and hit the cement so hard, I knew I'd be caught. I looked up and watched Regret yank its cuffed arm back, only to realize I'd broken free. It pressed its big head down over mine, ready to growl or hiss or do something horrible in my face, but Molek grabbed Regret by the throat and hurled it into the woods.

I scrambled to my feet, and Molek stared me down with squinted, scathing eyes, searching for bondage on me to grab onto. But there was nothing left.

He snarled, outraged, then started climbing straight up, reaching in the air and stepping as if an invisible ladder hung there—the rungs reaching to his throne.

Veronica repeated a chant in Latin, then reached toward Jackson. As Molek climbed at a supernatural speed, nearly to his throne now, I dove with all my might, attempting to grab Jackson. It felt like slow motion, battling to reach him before Veronica did.

With literally not a second to spare, I slid my hands up under Jackson's small shoulders and pulled him to me, shielding his head between my chin and chest. And it was like Molek's ladder crumbled out from under him. He slammed onto the cement platform, landing on the firepit, facedown in the flames. Veronica screamed, raging at me loud enough to send flocks of birds into flight.

But someone cried my name.

I turned, and Ray Anne stood at the bottom of the steps, her outstretched arms reaching toward Jackson and me. I ran to her, racing down the steps as fast as my feet would go, but she started pointing and shouting, "Behind you!"

I looked back. Molek was gone. But Veronica was coming after me, outraged, with a knife.

As the Creepers howled, I made it down enough steps to hand Jackson off to Ray Anne. "Run!" I told her.

Then I turned, ready to square off with Veronica—willing to be injured or even killed, if that's what it took to bring her down while Ray and Jackson rushed to safety. I bent my knees and held my arms out, ready for her. But she sidestepped and ran past me at an incredible speed. After Ray Anne.

"No!" I sprang from the stairs and tackled her from behind, knocking her onto her stomach in the dirt. I worked to restrain her, but she rose up and twisted her torso with superhuman ability, jabbing the knife at me. For a fleeting second, her eyes met mine.

But they weren't her eyes. Molek was looking at me. And I looked right back at him.

Fast as lightning, the knife sliced deep into my left bicep, and I

274 II LAURA GALLIER

wailed. Still holding the weapon, Veronica shoved me off her with the strength of a man. No, the force of a demon king.

"Ray!" I shouted.

She hadn't made it far with Jackson. It would only take seconds for Veronica to catch them. Little more than that to end their lives.

I'd vowed I'd *never* fail to protect her again, but there was no time—not even to get on my feet.

No plan.

No defense.

No hope.

Nothing . . .

Except a name. The name that I'd been told held no power. By Molek.

It was all I had.

I yelled it, loud as I could.

Then watched as Ray Anne hit her knees, hunkering down, shielding the baby with her own body as Veronica closed in. But Veronica stopped. Slowly turned and faced me, a look of astonished fear on her trembling face. On *Molek*'s face.

"I told you." Her possessed voice was unnaturally deep and threatening. "That word doesn't work on me!"

I rose to one knee, clutching my bleeding arm. And said it again—"Jesus!"

Veronica grabbed her gut and winced. "It's worthless! Powerless!"

I stood. Then shouted it once more.

Veronica started heaving like she might vomit. "Shut up!" Molek's voice raged from within her. "That word is for the righteous, not for fatherless trash like you!"

There was no need to defend myself. No need to say anything at all. I didn't have to. Veronica coughed and choked, falling to her hands and knees. A hooded Creeper spewed out of her chest, clawing its way down into the soil. Then came Molek, hitting the dirt, but quickly rising and standing tall.

Veronica struggled weakly to her feet, then took off into the woods.

Not Molek. He stayed, scowling at me. "This land's mine. You'll *never* get me to leave!" Then he started running, lifting off the ground, racing toward his throne. But the ritual had ended, and no sacrifice had been made. He had no right to mount the throne above my land.

He knew it, and he attempted to trespass anyway. But the Kingdom of Light knew it too.

A battalion of armored Watchmen burst onto the scene, and two of the giants grabbed Molek by each arm, dragging him away, kicking and pleading. Another Watchman with the most impressive armored helmet I'd ever seen jumped high in the air and grabbed on to the hideous throne, yanking it down with one hand, hauling it off too.

Ray Anne ran to my side. The swarm of Creepers tried to flee, but in the blinding light, they collided with one another like giant debris in a tornado. Ray and I knelt on the ground and held each other, clinging to Jackson between us, trying to both warm his frigid body and calm him.

Then Custos swooped down behind us, kneeling and wrapping his long, sculpted arms around the three of us. There was sudden relief from the chaos of the supernatural battle. At first, I thought Custos had hoisted some kind of shield over us, extending from his armor like a radiant platinum canopy. But when Ray and I tilted our heads back, we saw that he'd covered us with a pair of colossal, magnificent wings, as big as those of a private plane. His wings.

I'd had no idea he had them—him or any other Watchman.

They arched up high and angled down near the ends, blocking us from the noise and smell of the Creepers like an impenetrable fort. I rose to my knees to get a closer look. The wings were covered in interlocked feathers—but not the wispy, delicate kind. These were as thick as steel and generated some sort of force field, conducting a current that swirled with electric-bright colors, giving off warmth that instantly soothed Jackson—and Ray and me too. We looked at each other, speechless, as the array of light reflected and danced across our faces and all over the ground.

I hugged Ray and Jackson, and Ray shed grateful tears. But we couldn't stay like that forever.

When Custos eventually stood and stepped back, he was the only Watchman left. Then he rushed away too, leaving Ray and me alone with the baby in the bleak moonlight. The atmosphere had cleared of evil, but the ghastly firepit still burned. And my wounded arm . . . the pain hit me now, off the charts.

I gritted my teeth while asking Ray Anne how she'd found me.

"I saw the throne start to move, and it led me here."

Unbelievable. The very thing the kingdom of darkness had intended for evil tonight had helped turn the tables for good.

I was losing blood fast and tried not to lean too hard on Ray Anne as we traipsed through the moonlit forest, headed to the back road where I'd parked my bike. In the surrounding woods, dogs barked ferociously. About the time I felt like I might faint, we heard a man shouting in the distance. "Put your hands up, now!"

A woman started pleading, and numerous men raised their voices.

Officer McFarland spotted us with his high-powered flashlight and came running over. "Are you okay?" He saw Jackson in Ray's arms and exhaled. "Our canine unit tracked down Veronica." He pointed over his shoulder. "She's been apprehended."

He noticed the blood gushing down my arm and radioed for an ambulance.

Using my good arm, I pointed in the direction of the auction block. "There were children in a cage over there. You have to find them."

It felt like the ground was rocking. My weak knees folded, and I blacked out.

THIRTY-EIGHT

WHEN I FINALLY CAME TO, I was tilted back in a bed in the emergency room, and Ethan was arranging instruments on a tray table.

My head was groggy. "Ray and Jackson—"

"It's okay, they're fine." Ethan placed a calming hand on my shoulder, then pulled up a stool and began threading a needle, preparing to stitch my arm. "Jess is in a recovery room on the third floor, and as soon as Jackson's examination is done, he'll be reunited with her."

So much had happened, I'd almost forgotten Jess had nearly died of an asthma attack.

"And I hear your mom came through surgery just fine."

Oh, yeah. That too.

I tried to sit upright. "What about the kids that were in the cage? Did McFarland find them?"

Ethan tilted his head. "Hmm?"

He didn't have a clue. I closed my eyes and let my head sink into the pillow, working to piece together my scattered memories of the night's events.

"Owen." Ethan paused with the needle in midair. "I'm glad you're okay, man." He looked me in the eyes like he really meant it. "I heard you saved lives out there tonight."

278 || LAURA GALLIER

I nodded, accepting the credit. But it didn't feel right.

At all.

Because it wasn't right.

"Actually," I confessed, "I didn't save anyone." It had taken me a while, but I was finally starting to understand. "It was him." I pointed up.

"Amen," said Ethan, the typical church boy—a reminder he was an ideal match for Ray Anne. And as he stitched my arm, performing the honored duties of a doctor, an equally painful realization badgered me. In a way, he was everything I'd set out to be but never would be.

As silence lingered between us, I took advantage of the chance to talk without people around. "Look, I know you want to be with Ray Anne—you don't have to pretend around me. Just so you know, I'm stepping out of the way so she can have what's best for her." I turned my head but still said it. "She deserves the best."

Ethan cleared his throat, too uncomfortable, I think, to acknowledge what I'd said. Instead, he changed the subject. "You still gonna try to make it to the prayer walk at Masonville High?"

Ugh. I still hated what he and Ray Anne were calling it, but of course I was going. Molek had failed to reinstate his power over my land and was hopefully lying limp somewhere beyond Masonville's city limits, pounded to the ground by the Watchmen. Now it was time to finish the job, once and for all.

The digital clock above the nurse's station read 3:11 a.m. In seven hours, Molek would never be allowed to set foot in the town of Masonville again, and the Creeper infiltration would have to vacate too.

If people showed up and participated.

When I was cleared to leave the ER, I went to check on my mom. She was sleeping, but a nurse confirmed the eight-hour procedure had gone well. I leaned over the side of her bed and kissed her forehead. And thought about Ashlyn.

I needed to go home and shower and maybe even get some sleep, but I stopped by Jess's room first. My timing was impeccable. Ray Anne was sitting in a chair next to Jess's bed, and I stood outside the door and—I admit it—eavesdropped.

"I'm going to New York to live with my cousin and get my life on track," Jess was confiding to Ray Anne. "To go to fashion school and make something of myself." She sniffled and swallowed. "But I can't manage it with Jackson. I need you to keep him for a while—you know, become, like, his guardian, until I get on my feet."

Ray begged her not to do it, to not even think that way, and assured her she could start a new life right here in Masonville, with Jackson. But Jess's mind was made up.

"He needs his mom." Ray Anne moved to sit on Jess's bed. "And I mean, I'm barely a legal adult."

Jess reached over and—I couldn't believe it—clasped Ray Anne's hand. "You're the only one I trust to take care of him." Her voice broke with emotion. "Even more than me."

Ray Anne hugged Jess, and I knew the arrangement was as good as done.

I didn't interrupt—just waited for Ray Anne in the hallway, then walked with her toward the hospital lobby while she processed out loud how in the world she was going to tell her parents she'd just agreed to take temporary custody of a baby.

"What happens when Jess wants him back, Ray? Can you imagine how hard that'll be?"

She faced me in the elevator. "And what if I don't take him? Can you imagine how hard *his* life will be?"

We'd just passed the gift shop when Ray Anne grabbed my arm and stopped me. We looked at each other, both of us mentally and physically exhausted. "You were really brave last night."

"You too," I said. "But it's not over yet."

She nodded, stepping closer. "Look, no matter what does or doesn't happen today, we'll make it. In the long run, we will."

I didn't know if she was talking about the spiritual fight or . . .

"Ray Anne, about us—"

"Wait." She put her hand up. "There's something I need to tell you." She stared down at her sandals and fidgeted. "I owe you a huge apology, Owen. I've failed you."

"No, you haven't."

"Please, just listen." She pulled me to a nearby corner, out of people's path. "I've always put pressure on you to be the person *I* want you to be and to think and act like *I* want you to instead of letting you be yourself. It's not fair, and I'm sorry." Her bottom lip quivered. "I need to back off and give you time and space. You know, let you figure things out for yourself."

It hurt, but I couldn't deny it.

She looked over my shoulder to where Ethan stood waiting by the exit doors, keys in hand. "Ethan's giving me a ride to my car. He can take you to your motorcycle too."

"You two go ahead." I stuffed my emotions down—way down. "I'll be fine on my own."

I think she knew I was talking about a lot more than a ride.

"Well . . ." She ran a fidgety hand through her tousled hair, both of us uncomfortable now. "I'll see you in a few hours." She walked a short distance, then turned back. "Good-bye, Owen."

I wanted to run to her but did the unselfish thing, for once. "Bye, Ray."

I watched her walk with Ethan out the double doors. She never looked back.

I sighed, then wandered toward the lady at the information desk and asked if she'd call me a cab. And please pay for it. All I had were my keys—no wallet or phone.

While sitting in the lobby, waiting on my ride, I spotted Dr. Bradford by the elevators, conversing with a female nurse. He slid on his white doctor's coat like he'd just arrived for his shift, all nice and chipper. Clearly he knew about Jackson and was bound to be aware of the family relation—what kind of man turns on his own infant grandchild?

"I *am* going to expose you," I said under my breath. I knew I had better forgive him all over again or else risk another chain, but that wouldn't prevent me from seeking justice on Jackson's behalf.

I left without him seeing me.

The cab dropped me off on the back side of my property. My bike was where I'd left it last night, but, no surprise, the old man's white pickup was gone. He'd said he'd meet back up with me last night but never had. Or maybe in all the commotion, I'd missed him.

I got on my bike and started it, following the path I'd taken on foot the night before. The striped wooden police barricade was in position, blocking the dirt road I'd discovered, but I drove around it and sped toward the auction block. I passed the dilapidated Caldwell family cemetery and arrived at the location of the ritual gathering, squeezing my hand brake and pulling to a stop in the middle of last night's small clearing. I looked around in astonishment. With the exception of the old cement platform, there was nothing left. No cage or candles or firepit or poles. No crime scene.

I turned my bike around, mulling over who those wealthy people may have been and what motive they could possibly have had for trafficking children. Deep in thought, I nearly drove off and forgot something vital . . .

Thank God, the voice recorder was where I'd left it. The batteries were dead, but I held out hope it had captured the auction. It's not like I could drop by the police station and hand it over, though. What if Detective Benny got it? Or another dirty investigator?

It was nerve-racking unlocking my apartment, wondering if those security guards had been commissioned to break in and lie in wait to finish me off. But all appeared untouched.

I put some AAA batteries in the digital recorder, and sure enough, the barbaric bidding war played like a scary song. I saved a backup copy onto a thumb drive.

I had to take my dog outside, but I kept a close eye on my surroundings, enduring stinging where my arm had been stitched. By the time I showered, it was sunrise. I collapsed onto my mattress, my mind way too unsettled to rest.

Who had my wallet with my driver's license and debit card?

Where was Molek now?

How many people would show up today?

Around eight thirty, there was a loud knock on my door. I bolted out of bed. I leaned against the door as softly as I could and checked the peephole.

Not good.

A beefy man in a dark suit and even darker sunglasses stood outside, probably sent to strangle me and dump my body on my own wooded property.

The man looked at the peephole as if he could see me through it. "I have a delivery from Dr. Stephen Grayson," he said.

Wouldn't a delivery guy wear a brown jumpsuit or something? The man held a small box covered in cardboard-colored paper. Come to think of it, my father had said he'd be sending me something. But my trust meter was at an all-time low.

The man in the suit knocked again. I finally decided that a hit man would have kicked the door in by now. I opened it slowly.

He glanced at his cell—at a picture of me, I imagined—then handed me the box and left immediately. I locked the dead bolt, then ripped the paper off the package. A small card fell to the floor.

Enclosed is a piece of your mother's and my unfortunate past. I pray it becomes a fortunate blessing to you in the future.

Love, your father, Stephen

I opened a black velvet box containing a diamond ring—three sparkling, round stones. My mother's wedding ring.

It was an extremely thoughtful gift, but for now, I stashed it in my bottom dresser drawer. I needed to get to the school and carry out my mission to save Masonville. And basically, the world.

THIRTY-NINE

I ARRIVED AT MASONVILLE HIGH a few minutes early, under a cloud-covered sky. I slid my helmet off and watched Creepers swarm the exterior of the building like they knew something was up.

I almost jumped out of my skin when a patrol car pulled up next to me, missing my right leg by inches. My body tensed as Detective Benny rolled down his tinted driver's side window. He held my wallet out but kept his gaze forward, his pistol in his lap. Unholstered.

Slowly, I took my wallet back.

"I hear some rough guys got ahold of that. I'd be real careful if I were you." He sat there a moment, letting his threat sink in. "Have a good day, Owen."

He drove off.

This town was way more corrupt than I'd ever imagined, and I wanted to get to the bottom of it. But Arthur had given us the ultimate solution—a strategy to purge and heal Masonville from the inside out.

I shook off my nerves and approached the school, standing alone outside the main entrance, watching vehicles pass. Minutes ticked by, and no one turned in. Then finally people started showing up, one by one. By start time, ten o'clock, Betty was there with her little old ladies, including Dorothy in a wheelchair. Ethan pulled up at the same time as Ray Anne and her parents.

And that was it.

"Now, don't you go hanging your head low." Betty patted my back. "We'll fill this parking lot with people someday real soon."

Someday? That felt like failure.

Ray Anne asked Ethan where Pastor Gordon was, and he said his father wanted to be here but had a golf tournament fund-raiser today. I asked him if he thought anyone from the Thursday Bible study might come, and he shrugged.

Elle arrived and made her way over to us, no TV camera this time. She leaned toward me. "I hear you had an intense night."

I stepped away from the group, and she followed. I kept my voice down. "You've been willing to help me, even when I didn't know I needed it." I pulled the recorder from my pocket and placed it in her hand. "I'm trusting you with this. Be careful, this *does* involve criminal activity."

She glanced around the parking lot, then shoved the device in her purse. "Anything to do with Riley or the other disappearances?"

"Everything, I believe." I spoke even quieter. "These abductors prey on kids with wrecked home lives."

Elle didn't look surprised. "Usually makes for less of an investigation. No mom or dad doing media appearances or pressuring detectives to keep searching."

I winced. "So it looks like it's up to us to keep fighting for them."

She gave a single, determined nod.

"I know you like to work alone," I said, "but this is going to take a team effort."

She raised an eyebrow, but said, "I understand."

Maybe working with her wouldn't be so bad. "I'm warning you, this investigation will require that we follow physical *and* spiritual evidence—certain things your eyes can't even see."

She nodded again, enthusiastically this time.

"I won't rest until the truth is brought to light," I vowed, "and justice is served."

She shook my hand firmly. "Neither will I."

We rejoined the group, and I instinctively stood next to Ray Anne. Betty had us circle up and grab hands. Then she did as Arthur had instructed, acknowledging the decades of abuse and bloodshed on the land and asking God's forgiveness. She also prayed for each missing person by name, beginning with her niece Tasha. I looked toward the overcast sky, wondering what the impact would be with such a small group. Ray Anne elbowed me in the side and pointed down.

A giant, pink-rose-colored glass bowl was on the ground inside our circle—the same kind I'd seen those Watchmen in the sky empty on top of that herd of Creepers when I was on the plane. As people took turns praying, liquid collected and expanded in the base, glistening and bright. It didn't look like enough to soak Molek and his army, but at least something supernatural was happening.

In the distance, a white Jeep pulled over against the curb in front of the school, derailing my concentration. Lance got out, followed by three more guys, and they stood there watching us, arms crossed, shaking their heads and laughing.

I should have expected it. Lance had a history of mocking and betraying me. But things got weird when another car pulled over, followed by several more. Pretty soon, there were more people pointing and gawking than there were in our circle. In droves, Creepers climbed off the school building and stood with the scoffers. Others encircled us like a pack of hungry hyenas.

But we kept going.

Eventually, I was the only one who had yet to pray. I kept stalling, wishing I felt more qualified. Despite the urgency and seriousness of the situation, this was awkward—a guy my age, holding hands with mostly elderly people, praying in public.

I shouldn't have cared what people thought, but the onlookers' belittling glares were messing with me.

I managed to rise above the sinking sense of humiliation and voice

286 || LAURA GALLIER

a stammering yet heartfelt plea, growing bolder the longer I spoke. Mr. Greiner nodded in approval for once, and Ray Anne raised a surprised eyebrow. But the biggest miracle happened in the spiritual realm.

While I was praying, Custos and two more impressive armored Watchmen approached our group. From behind me, one reached over my shoulder and held a massive sword out in front of me. I knew better than to try to grab the handle—I'd already failed at that. But without any effort on my part, while still praying, I watched like a spectator as hands extended from within me. I'm talking, like, my spirit's hands. They literally grabbed the sword.

The Watchmen stepped back. Meanwhile, as I stood there motionless, moving only my mouth, my spirit wielded the weapon all around, even behind me. And get this: it sliced and maimed every Creeper that dared to come near.

My heart leaped at the game-changing observation. The festering wounds and slashes Creepers bore weren't mere symptoms of their debased existence. They were war wounds. Battle scars wrought by people's prayers.

Unbelievable.

The bowl was nearly full now. Ray Anne noticed too and touched her hand to her heart. Then up it went, rising quickly like a helium balloon until it blended with the overcast sky, out of our spiritual sight.

And so, it was over.

People said some final amens, and Ray's mom seized the opportunity to invite everyone over for brunch.

Ray Anne searched my face. "What do you think will happen now?"

We both knew Arthur's instructions had called for the town to gather and act on that verse in 2 Chronicles, not just a few people, and the consequences for failing the mission were certain to be severe. But it was hard to know exactly how things would play out—how much time we did or didn't have and how many tries we'd be afforded. We couldn't discuss it right now, though. Mrs. Greiner was giving out her address and getting a head count of who all were coming over. Ray gave me a reassuring grin, optimistic as always, then went to join her mom.

As people headed toward their vehicles, trying to ignore the hecklers, Ethan walked Ray Anne to her parents' car and even put his arm around her shoulders. It was a small thing, but I swear, it hurt worse than having that knife plunged into my arm.

"You coming to brunch?" Betty asked me.

I shook my head. "I'm not hungry."

It was worse than that. I'd underestimated how sick I'd feel watching Ethan pursue Ray Anne. And I hated not knowing how effective our gathering had or hadn't been. Judging by the number of Creepers still roaming outside the school, we still had serious work to do.

The onlookers were finally driving off, and Lance's friends piled into his Jeep, but Lance still stood there, staring at me from the curb. Something hanging from his rearview mirror caught my gaze. Was that really a white mask, the exact kind the guards were wearing the night before?

I turned my back on him and started my motorcycle, wondering how I'd come this far, just to feel so unsure about where to go and what to do from here.

"Go back to Boston, Owen!" Lance yelled.

Only it wasn't his voice.

I watched in revulsion as Demise slipped in and out of Lance at will, borrowing Lance's mouth to heckle me, then exiting out his back and glaring at me like a cobra about to strike.

Once again, Demise hunched down and pressed himself into Lance, corrupting his eyes and voice and facial expressions. "You lost today." He stared at Ray Anne and her parents as they drove off the lot. "You lost *everything*."

I didn't have to take this—from Lance or Demise. I put my motorcycle in gear and pulled back on the gas, but Lance was in his Jeep, peeling out onto the street like a coward by the time I made it over to him. Just as cowardly, Demise dove headfirst into the earth.

I sat on my rumbling bike, alone in the parking lot. Just me and reality. And my thoughts . . .

It was true. I probably *had* lost today. But it was truth mixed with a lie. I hadn't lost *everything*.

An insane idea hit me—two of them, actually. An impulsive decision, followed by an almost impossible next step—a life-altering leap with the potential to forever impact my future and life direction and mission in Masonville.

It was the craziest, boldest, most spontaneous thing I'd ever thought to do.

But I was instantly determined.

I sped to my apartment, got what I needed, then took off again. I parked behind all the vehicles in Ray Anne's driveway, then barged into her house without knocking. Everyone from the gathering was seated and chatting around Mrs. Greiner's long dining room table.

I took a deep breath and then said it, loud. "I need someone to baptize me."

Instant silence. Finally, Ray Anne's dad spoke up. "Right *now?*"

"Yes." No one budged. I approached him. "Please, sir."

More silence. Then Mrs. Greiner said, "Well, we do have a pool."

I didn't wait on anyone to get up. I headed out the door to the backyard. They weren't far behind me. I took off my shoes and my shirt, then emptied my jean pockets and handed the rolled-up wad to the person who happened to be standing nearest to me. Ethan.

Mr. Greiner stepped forward, and without pausing to change clothes, together, we stepped down the steps into the cold pool. "You're serious about this?" he asked me.

"Completely."

He stood beside me in the waist-high water. "Is there something you'd like to say?"

I looked around at Dorothy and Betty and her friends, at Elle, Mrs. Greiner, and teary-eyed Ray Anne. Ethan too. "I used to be shackled. But now . . ."

I gave Ray Anne a small smile, and a tear trickled down her cheek.

"I am free."

Mr. Greiner had me turn to the side, preparing to dip me under water. It occurred to me that neither my mother nor my father was here. Yet another parentless life moment. But this was between God and me.

Lo and behold, as Mr. Greiner placed one hand behind my head and another on my chest, Custos showed up, gleaming beside the pool.

Seconds later, I was drenched. To my amazement, Mr. Greiner embraced me.

I stepped out of the pool soaking wet and made a beeline to Ethan. He handed me my shirt and belongings, and I sifted through them, retrieving one thing.

I locked eyes with Ray, standing next to Ethan, then stepped in front of her and took her hand in mine.

"Owen, what are you—?"

"Just listen, Ray Anne."

I could feel everyone staring at us. Nobody uttered a sound.

"I heard what you said about giving me time and space to figure things out, and I get it, Ray—I really do. But the thing is, I've already discovered who I am and what I want. I want to finish what we started in this town and keep fighting. Together, as a couple."

Ethan lowered his head.

"I know I've made things difficult and given you a hard time, but it's 'cause I didn't get it. I believed it when a liar told me God doesn't care if I love him as long as I do my duty to humanity, but I know better now. This whole thing is about loving and trusting him. And I'm ready. I wanted to get baptized today, Ray—not because it's what the church says I'm supposed to do or as some stunt to win you over, but because you were right. It *is* important."

I lowered to one knee, wet jeans and all. "I came up out of that water ready to live the rest of my insane life the way God wants me to, and I want you with me."

I held up the little black box. "I know there are good men who would give anything to be with you." I worked to tame the avalanche of emotion. "But I don't want to live my life without you."

I opened the box. "My father gave this ring to my mother when they were young and in love—nearly as young as us." I cleared my throat. "Ray Anne Bethany Greiner . . ." I reached up and wiped a tear from her cheek. "Will you marry me?"

I held my breath.

Her response was not at all what I expected.

ABOUT THE AUTHOR

In a youth culture intrigued by the paranormal yet often skeptical of biblical claims, **Laura Gallier** seeks to bring awareness and understanding to issues surrounding the supernatural. Having battled her own enemies of the soul throughout her teen and young adult years, she is on a mission to expose deception with the light of truth, bringing hope and healing to a generation in need. Laura lives in the greater Houston area with her husband, Patrick, and their three children. Get to know Laura better at www.lauragallier.com.

CAN'T WAIT
TO FIND OUT
WHAT
HAPPENS
NEXT?

Visit **www.DELUSIONSERIES.com**
to learn more about the next book in the
series, coming Summer 2020!

CP1323

Has this book made an impact on you?

Share your story with author Laura Gallier by emailing mystory@delusionseries.com.

Want to go deeper?

Get your copy of *4 Freedom*, a Bible study based on *The Delusion*, ideal for individual reflection or group studies. Available at www.DelusionSeries.com.

Want to stay connected?

Sign up for free email updates regarding the novel series and movie-making journey at www.DelusionSeries.com. Find @DelusionSeries on social media and join the online community.

Curious about the author?

Learn more about Laura and her speaking events at LauraGallier.com. To inquire about booking Laura to speak, email info@lauragallier.com.

In need of help?

If you or someone you know is struggling with thoughts of suicide, talk to a parent, teacher, pastor, or youth leader, or contact a suicide hotline. Remember, God loves you and there is hope, even in seemingly hopeless situations.

THE HOPE LINE
www.thehopeline.com
1-800-273-8255

NATIONAL SUICIDE PREVENTION LIFELINE
suicidepreventionlifeline.org
1-800-273-8255

CP1324

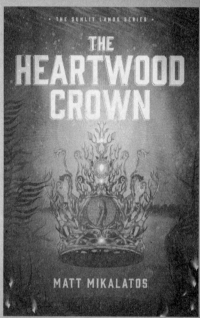